PURRFECT PRINCE

THE MYSTERIES OF MAX 74

NIC SAINT

PURRFECT PRINCE

The Mysteries of Max 74

Copyright © 2023 by Nic Saint

Edited by Chereese Graves

www.nicsaint.com

Give feedback on the book at: info@nicsaint.com

facebook.com/nicsaintauthor
@nicsaintauthor

First Edition

Printed in the U.S.A

PURRFECT PRINCE

For Skingle and Country

Christmas had come and the four of us were looking forward to a fun time spent warming up to the fire crackling in the hearth, enjoying plenty of delicious snacks and the company of our humans. Unfortunately this was not to be, for an urgent royal summons arrived that whisked us away to Liechtenburg, a small country located in the Swiss Alps. One of Europe's oldest royal houses found itself besieged by a pernicious thief eager to divest its residents of their most prized possessions. But of course this was before a string of murders rocked the nation and plunged us headlong into a Christmas mystery.

CHAPTER 1

The sun shone through the window of Vaasu Castle, eager as always to spread some sweetness and light amongst the inhabitants of that ancient pile, located in the heart of Vaasu, the capital of Liechtenburg, a pleasant little country wedged in between Liechtenstein and its bigger neighbor Switzerland. For centuries Liechtenburgers, as they were affectionately called, had been ruled by the noble House of Skingle, and even to this day, King Thad, the most recent spawn of his family's infamously fertile loins, inhabited the family's royal dwelling and reigned not with an iron fist but with a benevolent hand. Supported by his consort of thirty-five years, Queen Serena, King Thad was a much-beloved sovereign, and if some thought it anachronistic that a monarch would still be as invested in the day-to-day running of his country, at least his subjects didn't seem to mind. Then again, Liechtenburg was a prosperous country, and so no one had much to cavil at and much preferred things to stay the way they were.

Unbeknownst to many, the king had recently been struck by a mysterious illness that had left him bedridden, his royal duties mostly having been taken up by his two sons: Crown Prince Dane and Prince Urpo. The fact that King Thad's illness hadn't been officially communicated didn't preclude it from being widely commented on throughout his realm, since a thing like that is very hard to keep a secret. And so, gossip had been circulating, with some speculating that the king's final hour had struck and that very soon now an announcement would be made that Prince Dane had been induced to step up to the plate and was to be crowned the new king and head of state.

But as sunrays fluttered across the noble visage of King Thad, laid up in bed as he had been for the past three weeks, they found the subject of all these rumors and gossip in a most foul mood indeed. Now the king had never been accused of being a ray of sunshine himself, but even for him, his mood today was beyond the pale. His wife, Queen Serena, had entered the royal bedroom with an eye to ascertaining whether the monarch felt up to offering his views on the upcoming Christmas ball, but instead of being enlightened by her spouse's ideas on the matter, she was subjected to the kind of verbal abuse she had come to expect in recent weeks.

"Oh, get lost with your nonsense about the Christmas ball," the king grumbled annoyedly. "Who cares about some stupid ball when I'm about to die, you silly woman!"

"You shouldn't say such things, darling," said the queen, shaken but determined not be browbeaten by her husband. "You're not going to die."

"You're not a doctor, so what would you know?"

Serena had taken a seat next to her husband's bed and now studied the man she had said yes to in an unguarded moment thirty-five years ago. Back then, he had been as handsome and charming as could be, and the whole prospect of being married to an actual future king had momentarily blinded her to the fact that her betrothed possessed a certain meanness of character that she had only caught glimpses of. But as the years passed, she had come to appreciate the real measure of the man, and the results unfortunately weren't much to write home about.

Back then, her mother had warned her that Prince Thad was easily the nastiest of the two princes, but she had thrown caution to the wind, having been swept off her feet by the dashing nobleman who was first in line for the throne. To one day become queen was such an enchanting prospect that it had momentarily made her blind to the man's faults, of which she would soon find out there were many.

"A letter arrived," she now announced primly.

"What letter? What are you talking about?" Thad grunted as he idly played with his phone. He might have been struck down with illness, but that hadn't made him put down tools for a single second. Even though the prime minister had suggested he momentarily place Dane in charge of things, Thad wouldn't hear of it. He might be down, but he wasn't out—not by a long shot.

"A letter from Buffy Kurikka," said Serena. She had positioned her hands in her lap, and it took every ounce of self-control to maintain eye contact with her husband, even as his eyes had suddenly gone a little wary.

"Never heard of her," he blustered.

"She wants to pay us a visit," Serena continued, undeterred. "To introduce her son."

"What son? What are you babbling on about!"

"I probably should have said: your son." Or she could have said: 'Your bastard son.'

For a moment, neither of them spoke, then Thad impatiently motioned with his hand. "Tell her to get lost. Her and that son of hers."

"You better tell her yourself. After all, he is your son, and she was your mistress."

Thad grumbled something under his breath, and for his doing he appeared unusually abashed. This reminder of his infidelity, at a time when Serena was pregnant with their first child, clearly didn't sit well with him.

It was, of course, an open secret that King Thad, who prided himself on being a man's man, had never taken the marital vows he had spoken too seriously. In his view, those vows were more a guideline than a set of rules set in stone. A gentle hint or vague suggestion, in other words. And since he was the king, the man who ruled all and sundry, he felt that he was perfectly entitled to sow his oats wherever he damn well pleased, whether in the nuptial bed or without.

The many affairs Thad had engaged in over the years had driven a wedge between himself and Serena, but that had never stopped him from continuing the much-maligned practice until he was of an age when women started to look at him askance when he made advances. Also, with his sons coming of age, Dane and Urpo had started asking difficult questions, mostly concerned with the impact their father's philandering had on their mother, whom they both loved very much. And so, the affairs had ended, but not the resentment Serena still felt.

It was no big secret that the king and queen occupied separate wings of the castle, and only when in the public eye displayed some token form of affection. Keeping up appearances was important to both of them, if only for the sake of their two sons, who wouldn't have taken kindly to an official separation or, God forbid, an actual divorce.

Only one of Thad's affairs had ever led to actual offspring, and even though he had never officially recognized the boy, his existence was no big secret, even though everyone knew well not to bring it up in conversation with either King Thad or Serena.

She threw the letter down on the bed. "Here. You answer

it. I don't want to have anything more to do with that woman or her son." She got up and prepared to take her leave when a cough from her husband arrested her departure.

"They're trying to kill me, you know," he said.

She glanced down at him with a cold look. "Who is trying to kill you?"

"Well, our boys, of course. They want me dead."

"Oh, nonsense," she said with some vehemence.

"They hate me," he insisted. "I can see it in their eyes. Especially Dane. He can't wait for me to die so he can become king. But I won't let him, you hear."

"Nobody is trying to kill you, Thad," she said emphatically. "You just haven't been taking good care of yourself, that's all. Or did you really think you could eat and drink with abandon and not suffer the consequences?"

In no way did Thad even remotely resemble the man she had married more than three decades before. For one thing, he had tripled in size due to his intemperance, and with the amounts of alcohol he liked to imbibe, his liver had probably gone down the same road. According to the Physician to the King, the only way he might be able to save himself was by going on a very strict diet. That and a prolonged period of complete rest. But of course, Thad would have none of that. He wasn't merely the supreme ruler of the realm but also of his own body, and no silly doctor was going to tell him what he could and could not eat or drink.

He made an impatient gesture. "They're poisoning me!" he insisted. Then he frowned as he regarded her strangely. "My God!" he suddenly cried. "It's you, isn't it? *You* are trying to kill me!"

"Oh, Thad," she said with a shake of the head, causing her platinum tresses to envelop her well-preserved features. Contrary to her husband, even at sixty, she still cut quite a handsome figure and was admired by all for her timeless sense of style, her grace, and her patience and kindness. "You're out of your mind."

"No, but it's true!" he insisted, sitting up straighter. "I thought it was the boys, but it's you, isn't it? You are trying to get rid of me." He picked up the letter and waved it angrily in her face. "And it's all because of this. Revenge!"

"I don't have to listen to this nonsense," she announced, head held high in a regal fashion.

But as she made her way to the door, he yelled after her, "I'm on to you, Serena! And I'm going to beat you at your own game. You hear me? You can't kill me! Not if I get you first!"

CHAPTER 2

*H*aving returned to her own suite of rooms in a private wing of the castle, Serena lost some of her regal fervor. It wasn't that she was about to break down into tears over her husband's latest delusional rant, but the fact of the matter was that they had suffered another security breach last night, this time resulting in the theft of a very precious brooch, one that used to belong to her grandmother.

She entered the sitting room and as she did, her good friend Tiia Pohjanheimo immediately rose from the settee where she had been enjoying a cup of jasmine tea, her favorite.

"And?" asked Tiia anxiously. "How did he react?"

"Badly," said Serena. "As was to be expected."

"He's not going to invite the woman, is he?"

Serena shrugged. "He actually accused me of trying to poison him, can you believe it? I'm telling you, Tiia, the man is becoming more and more delusional with each passing day."

"What do the doctors say?"

Serena had taken a seat next to her friend on the settee, but found she was too wound up to sit still, so immediately she rose again and paced the room, wringing her hands as she did. "They've advised him to go on a very strict low-fat diet. Cut out all alcohol, for one thing, which is exactly what he doesn't want. Oh, Tiia, maybe we should postpone the Christmas ball? With Thad in the state he's in, I don't feel up to it. He seems to be getting more belligerent with each passing day."

"Nonsense," said Tiia, who might look like the sweetest woman in existence but could be quite forceful if she wanted to be. "As far as I can tell Thad only has himself to blame for the condition he is in right now. You can't expect to spend all your life eating and drinking and... to put it bluntly, whoring, and not have your body break down at some point. It's a miracle he's made it this far, considering he's put on about a hundred pounds in the last five years alone. The man looks like a whale, honey. And a very unhealthy whale at that."

In spite of her anxious state, Serena had to laugh at these words. "Thanks for that," she told her friend. "If there's anyone who can cheer me up, it's you."

She had known Tiia longer than she had known Thad, having met in kindergarten. The two had become firm friends from the first day, and even after fifty-five years, that hadn't changed. Throughout it all, they had shared joy and pain, heartache and personal triumphs, and frankly, Tiia was in many respects the best thing in Serena's life, apart from Dane and Urpo and Serena's grandkids.

"It's that brooch, isn't it?" said Tiia, who had an uncanny knack of reading her friend's mind. "Why don't you get the police to investigate?"

"Oh, you know what the police are like. Before you know

it, the story will be in all the papers, and that's the last thing I need right now. More scandal and gossip."

Tiia nodded. "I see. Well, then there's only one thing for you to do."

She looked up in surprise. "There is?"

"Do you remember Opal telling us last year how she was being threatened?"

"Of course. Such a terrible business." Their good friend Opal, who was a big thing in the States, having had her television show for many years and now her own television network, had been plagued by someone sending her threatening letters and messages and even going so far as to try and kill her.

"Then you'll also remember how Opal enlisted the help of a woman named Odelia Kingsley and her husband, who is a police detective. Together Odelia and her husband managed to expose the culprit and bring them to justice. They did what the police couldn't do, and in all discretion. So what I would advise is to get in touch with Opal and ask her to arrange for the Kingsleys to come here and catch this jewel thief for you. That way at least one problem will be dealt with, leaving you to handle Thad without the Tiffany Thief adding to your worries."

Tiia was right. She had enough on her plate right now without the added anxiety over this thief making their lives miserable. So far only a few items had gone missing, oddly enough all of them pieces at one time or another acquired from Tiffany's, one of the jewelry houses the family favored. Which is why Dane's wife Impi had decided to christen the thief the Tiffany Thief. She also had one of her favorite pieces of her collection stolen only a couple of nights ago. In her case, it was her engagement ring that had disappeared. Dane had been on the verge of calling the police when Serena had intervened and told him to wait.

"Maybe you're right," she now told her friend. "If these Kingsleys are as good as Opal believes they are, maybe we should ask them to look into this for us."

"The only problem will be that it's such short notice," said Tiia. "And of course... it's Christmas."

Serena glanced out of the window of her sitting room at the snow carpet covering the ground outside. It had been snowing steadily for the past ten days, and the whole world had suddenly been magically transformed into a winter wonderland. With the castle as its backdrop, the scene now closely resembled a fairy tale. She could see a group of tourists being led through the grounds, eagerly taking selfies with Vaasu Castle as a backdrop. The sleigh that took the tourists around the gardens shimmered brightly, and as the sun hit a patch of snow, it glittered like diamonds. Serena even thought she could hear Christmas music drifting in from down below. One of the tourists must be playing it on their phone.

If only they knew what the actual situation was behind the fairy-tale walls of the castle, they would probably be shocked, she thought with a touch of bitterness. Then she abruptly turned. "Let's do it," she said, displaying her usual knack for making snap decisions. "Call Opal and ask to get in touch with the Kingsleys. If they're available over the holidays, I'll cordially invite them to join us here."

Tiia smiled as she took out her phone. Then she frowned. "What time is it in LA?"

"Better wait until they wake up over there," Serena agreed. The Tiffany Thief might be something of an emergency, but the last thing she wanted was to wake Opal up in the middle of the night. Or the Kingsleys. She just hoped they hadn't planned anything for Christmas. Most people did. And they might not take kindly to having to suddenly change those plans just because some queen on the other side of the world was faced with a problem.

Then again, no doubt Opal would give it her best shot. And knowing the former talk show queen, she could be very persuasive indeed.

CHAPTER 3

The living room was abuzz with activity as Dooley and I rested peacefully on the couch. Our humans were enjoying one of their oft-organized family dinners, and for the occasion had also invited Uncle Alec and his wife Charlene. As it was, it was one of the last times we'd see the new couple for a while, since they were leaving to go on their honeymoon soon.

"Honeymooning in the sun!" Uncle Alec caroled loudly as he raised a glass to his new bride. "Finally!"

It had been a little while since the couple had been married, and except for a brief vacation, they hadn't actually had time to go honeymooning. But now, with a lot of businesses closing down over the holidays, and hopefully criminals deciding to spend time with their families instead of relieving hard-working families of their possessions, they had decided it was now or never.

"So where are you going again?" asked Scarlett Canyon.

"The Maldives," said Charlene with a smile. She looked more relaxed than I'd seen her in a long time. Being mayor of a small town may sound like a great proposition, but

Hampton Cove can hardly be called a typical small town, in that we do get our fair share of trouble and mayhem visiting these shores, causing both Charlene and her new husband to be on their toes. But now it sounded as if they were about to dig those same toes into the warm white sands of a sunny tropical beach.

"God, I'm so jealous," said Marge as she pronged a piece of lettuce with her fork and started eating it with small nibbles. For some reason, she reminded me of a rabbit. "I wish I could join you guys. I could really use a vacation."

"Well, why don't you?" said Charlene.

"Take a vacation, she means," Uncle Alec hastened to add. Clearly, the last thing he wanted was for his family to gate-crash his honeymoon. "Plenty of last-minute destinations to book," he added for good measure.

"As long as they're far away from the Maldives," said Gran with a wink. "Isn't that right, son?"

Alec grimaced. "Oh, you can come if you like," he said reluctantly, making it sound as if the prospect of traveling with his sister was about as enjoyable as having his teeth pulled.

"That's all right," said Marge with a smile. "The last thing I want is to disturb you and Charlene on your honeymoon."

Uncle Alec looked relieved. "I hear San Diego is very nice this time of year. Or what about Puerto Rico?"

"What I would like most of all," said Odelia, "is a nice vacation in the snow. We haven't had snow in Hampton Cove for a while, and I think it would be great if we could build a snowman with Grace and get our sleds out."

"I would love that," her husband grunted. "Christmas isn't really Christmas without a nice thick carpet of white."

"That's the spirit!" said Uncle Alec. There definitely was no snow in the Maldives. Not even a single flake anywhere to be found. "Go up to Canada if you want snow. Plenty to be found there. Or how about Alaska?"

"Or Europe," Scarlett suggested. "Though you'd have to go to the north, of course. I doubt they get a lot of snow in Spain or Italy."

"Oh, but they do," Tex assured her. "They've got some great ski resorts in the Italian Alps if that's your bag."

Judging from the dreamy faces all around the dinner table, it was obvious that a nice Christmas vacation was on everyone's mind. Except mine, of course, or that of my three friends.

"Imagine having to wade through a couple of inches of snow," said Brutus with a shiver. "Yuck!"

"And the slush and the muck it leaves behind," Harriet added.

"Oh, I don't mind snow," said Dooley, offering the contrarian view. "As long as it's still fresh, it's a lot of fun to traipse through it. Though it is a little chilly on the paws."

"It *is* chilly on the paws," I agreed. The moment those snowflakes started to flutter down was the moment I'd hunker down next to the heating and not move an inch until springtime. I don't know about you, but there's something very disagreeable about the cold. I much prefer to stay indoors while all those foolish humans rush to be outside at such a time. But then I guess humans are a little weird. At the first sign of snow, they can't wait to race one another to the door and head out into that world of white. Brrr!

"I hope they won't go anywhere for the holidays," Brutus confessed.

"Same here," I said, adding my voice to the choir.

Unfortunately for us, our most fervent wish wouldn't be answered, for even at that moment, and unbeknownst to us, dark forces were already conspiring to get us out of the safety and comfort of our own homes and into the wild open spaces of the European heartland, where snow and freezing temperatures would await us. Okay, so maybe it wasn't as dramatic as all that. But suffice it to say that the moment Odelia picked up that phone—yes, the phone that you can hear ringing if you pay close attention—our dreams of staying would be rudely interrupted.

"Oh, hi, Opal," we heard Odelia speak into the device.

We shared a look of apprehension. Twice before, this woman had entered our lives, and each time a period of some turmoil had preceded. Once to induce us to pay her a visit in a place called Los Angeles, where we had been instrumental in catching a wannabe murderer, and once when a friend of hers had more or less invaded our home and caused us no small measure of grief.

So it was with a sense of impending doom that we now paid close attention as Odelia exchanged pleasantries with the former daytime talk show host. Before long, she was listening intently, a frown on her face, as no doubt Opal poured yet another story of heartache and sorrow into her ear, requesting her assistance in a matter of the gravest importance and the greatest urgency.

Finally, she nodded and said, "I'll have to discuss it with my family. But I'll let you know as soon as possible—I promise."

That same family was also looking on with a distinct sense of expectancy, and when Odelia hung up, Marge was the first to speak. "And? What did she want?"

Odelia smiled. "You guys, we have all been formally invited by Queen Serena of Liechtenburg to spend Christmas with her and her family at Vaasu Castle! That's in Europe!" she added for good measure.

The four of us closed our eyes in abject dismay.

"I knew it," Brutus grunted. "I just knew it."

CHAPTER 4

"For a brief moment there, I thought Odelia would decide to leave us in Hampton Cove. Put us up at Scarlett's place, for instance, which would have been absolutely lovely, since our good friend Clarice is there, and we could have spent Christmas together. But, unfortunately, this was not to be. She insisted that we join her at this Vaasu Castle, whatever it was, and not only that, but she insisted her entire family travel along on the private jet Serena had chartered to bring us over.

"It's going to be just grand," she assured us. "What better way to celebrate Christmas than in an actual fairy-tale castle, you guys!"

I could have told her there were definitely better ways to spend Christmas. By staying home, for instance. But one thing I've learned from long association with Odelia: when she's got her mind set on something, it's not easy to dissuade her. And apparently Opal has such a strong hold over her that each time she issues a demand, Odelia immediately snaps to attention. Disconcerting, to be sure.

But since there wasn't anything we could say or do to change our human's mind, and the rest of the family all seemed over the moon at this opportunity to enjoy the holidays in a fairy-tale setting—"It will be like a Hallmark Christmas movie!" Marge had exclaimed—we decided just to go along with the whole setup.

"Aren't castles dangerous places for cats, Max?" asked Dooley at one point.

We were watching Odelia pack her bags for the trip, and a lot of bags they were, with our human fretting to some extent that she 'didn't have anything nice to wear!' and Chase assuring her she had plenty.

"Why would a castle be dangerous?" I asked, as I watched the pile of luggage open on the bed and the mountains of clothes Odelia planned on dragging along with her to this strange country in the middle of Europe—that dark continent.

"Well, castles are full of hidden traps, aren't they? And dungeons where they lock people up and torture them with spikes and hot pokers to gouge their eyes out? Not to mention rats, Max." He shivered violently. "We all know that castles are full of rats—millions of them."

"I'm sure that this unfortunate habit of gouging people's eyes out with hot pokers is in the past now, Dooley," I assured my friend. "European royals kicked that habit, as it's probably illegal nowadays to torture one's opponents."

"But what about the rats, Max? What about the rats!"

"I guess we'll just have to wait and see," I said, taking the philosophical view. Then again, if people lived in these castles, they had probably found a way to remedy this rabid proliferation of the rodent element. And if they hadn't, we'd just have to manage to live together with these creatures in some form of peaceful cohabitation, the same way we lived with our humans on a daily basis. You don't always like what they get up to, but you tolerate them to the best of your abilities.

Grace now came toddling up to us. She, too, had been earmarked to be shipped over to Liechtenburg or Luxenstein or whatever this place was called. Unlike us, she seemed overjoyed to be leaving soon.

"It's going to be so great," she announced happily, actually clapping her hands with glee!

"I don't see what's so wonderful about it," I confessed. "It's a cold and drafty castle in the middle of winter, so I can only imagine it's going to be freezing cold."

"And spooky!" Dooley added for good measure.

"Oh, don't be such a gloomy gus, Max," Grace said. "It's a castle! In the snow! How much better can it get?"

"I suppose it can't get any worse," I said, trying to see things from her point of view.

"It could get worse," Dooley pointed out. "If there are ghosts!"

"Ghosts don't exist, Dooley," I said, deciding to stamp out this particular hang-up of my friend once and for all.

"Oh, but they do!" said Grace. "That's what's so neat about going to stay at an actual castle. This place is probably thousands of years old, and so a lot of people must have died there, and all of them are now haunting the place, wandering through its deserted corridors, shrieking and wailing and gnashing their teeth." A sort of exhilarated look had come into her eyes as she spoke these words, and she didn't even notice how Dooley and I were swallowing away lumps of unease at the horrid word picture she was conjuring up. "Ghosts rattling chains. Ghosts carrying their severed heads under their arms. Ghosts with unsightly wounds and ghastly mutilated bodies, bones sticking out at odd angles and eyes dangling from their sockets." She sighed with unadulterated delight. "Best Christmas ever!"

And with these words, she toddled off again, presumably to scare Harriet or Brutus out of their wits. Our friends were next door, where the same ritual was taking place: Marge and Tex and Gran packing their bags for the big trip. The only ones who wouldn't be joining us were Uncle Alec and Charlene, but then they had other prospects to look forward to: their trip to the Maldives.

"Maybe we could ask Uncle Alec to abduct us and take us with him?" Dooley now suggested.

"Dooley, the tropics are not the perfect destination for us either," I reminded him. "Or do you really want to get all that fine white sand between your paws? Or to bake in the hot sun until you're red in the face? No, the best place for us is Hampton Cove. Not too hot in the summer and not too cold in the winter. Moderation, Dooley! That's what it's all about! Moderate climes, moderate intake of foods, moderate everything. It's the only way to live."

All these extremes have never done anyone any good, but then nobody ever listens to a pair of cats, especially not humans, who often suffer from a disease colloquially called 'know-it-all-ism.'

Before long, the bags were packed, travel arrangements had been made, passports had been issued, and our travel carriers had been de-mothballed. And so soon the big day arrived when the whole gang moved out and traveled to JFK Airport to board the private plane at our disposal.

On the trip to the airport, the four of us had already been relegated to our travel carriers, and as things stood, I got the impression that we would remain locked up in them for a little while longer, as apparently cats can't be trusted outside of them.

"I have a strong sense of déjà vu, Max," Brutus confessed.

"Yeah, same here," said Harriet. "Have we made this trip before?"

"All overseas trips essentially come down to the same thing," I said. "You sit in a narrow metal tube for many hours and hope it won't explode, implode, or crash into the ocean. And then if you do make it out alive, you suddenly find yourself in a different part of the world that more often than not is an unsanitary hellhole."

"I just wish they had brought Clarice along," said Dooley. "For the rats," he explained when we questioned his statement. "If that castle is really as infested with rats as I think it is, Clarice would have made short shrift of them."

He was right, of course. With Clarice by our side, we wouldn't have had any trouble controlling a potential rat infestation as she's very fond of rats—as an integral part of her diet, that is.

Before long, we arrived at our destination, and then went through the rather tedious process of having our passports checked—yes, even cats need passports to travel—and then we were ready to go.

The plane was luxurious enough, and once we were in the air, Odelia let us out of our pet carriers, and we were free to roam the plane and stretch our paws. And I have to admit it wasn't too shabby at all. While the human contingent enjoyed the meal that had been arranged, we had our own meals to tuck into, and if the food being supplied was a harbinger of things to come, my mood was improving with leaps and bounds.

European royals may have enjoyed burning people at the stake for centuries, or torturing them on the rack or locking them up in iron maidens and suchlike, but their sense of hospitality seems to have improved since those times.

And after having eaten our fill, we hopped up onto one of

the comfy beds having been put at our disposal and dozed off. If that narrow metal tube went down in a blaze of twisted metal, I wouldn't be any the wiser, for I was soon dreaming of soft meadows of daisies where I pranced about and enjoyed long naps.

CHAPTER 5

I have to say that the castle was pretty spectacular. When we arrived at the airport, an actual limo was there to pick us up, and before long, we were zooming along as the landscape passed by outside our window. Odelia had once again let us out of our pet carriers so we could enjoy the view, and I hadn't actually realized this, but Liechtenburg is one of those countries that are nestled in the Swiss Alps. Though they probably call them the Liechtenburgian Alps, since we're not actually in Switzerland. Which makes me wonder if the Alps, which stretch across different borders, change names each time. Be that as it may, I could see a lot of mountains, a lot of snow, and generally a scenery that was way different from the one we're accustomed to at home. In general: we definitely were not in Kansas anymore!

When I looked down at my friend, I saw he had a smile on his face. "No rats, Max," he said. "So far so good!"

"Lots of mountains, though," said Brutus. "I had no idea they had so many mountains in this part of the world. And they look pretty high, too." He frowned. "I hope we won't be expected to actually climb them?"

"We're here to find a brooch, Brutus," I reminded him. "And unless this brooch thief is in the habit of hiding his loot in some crevasse high up one of them there mountains, I think it's safe to say we won't be going there."

"We're not mountain goats, after all," said Brutus.

"You're right, buddy," I said. "If Queen Serena wanted us to chase this Tiffany Thief up a mountain, she should have asked a band of mountain goats to do the honors, not a clowder of cats!"

"What's a chowder of cats, Max?" asked Dooley.

We all smiled. "Not a chowder, Dooley," I said. "A clowder. Chowder is soup. A clowder is the group name for a group of cats."

"So... we're a clowder?"

"That, we are," I said.

"And proud of it!" Brutus added.

"I could see myself climb one of those mountains," Harriet said now. "High up on a mountain, singing my heart out. Just like in that movie."

"What movie?" I asked, even though I should have known better.

"Why, *The Sound of Music*, of course," she said. Then she seemed to sort of swell up like a balloon and suddenly burst into song. *"The hills are alive... with the sound of music!"*

"Eek!" said our chauffeur, and almost drove the limo into a ditch.

"Maybe better leave the singing for another day," Odelia advised quickly.

But Harriet wasn't deterred. "We'll go up the mountain, and I'll sing my heart out to the birds and the bees and the trees! Oh, it will be just grand, tootsie roll!"

"Absolutely," Brutus grunted but didn't seem fully convinced.

"Maybe they have a cat choir here," Harriet insisted. "And

they can serve as a backdrop to my solo. And if this Queen Serena could assign a film crew to go up with us, that would be amazing. We could shoot our very own musical!"

Somehow I had a feeling Queen Serena had other things on her mind than creating a hit musical for Harriet, but from long association with our passionate friend, I knew it was probably a good idea not to voice these sentiments. The artistic temperament, you see, is very strong in her. So strong, in fact, she might very well smite me, if smite is the word I want.

As I said, the castle, when it finally loomed up large before our eyes, was very impressive indeed. For a moment, there was some discussion about whether it was a castle or a palace, since apparently there is a marked difference between the two, but since it was called Vaasu Castle and not Vaasu Palace, I guess that settled it.

"It's named after Vaasu," the driver explained.

"What's a vase-you?" asked Gran.

"Vaasu is the name of the capital. We're in Vaasu right now."

"Huh," said Gran. "Funny name, that."

"There's a strong Scandinavian influence in the country Liechtenburg," the man said, "which was originally a Norse settlement, over a thousand years ago."

"Norse?"

"Vikings," said the man with a smile. "Hence the 'funny' names, as you so aptly put it, Mrs. Muffin."

"Vikings, huh? So your king is a Viking?"

"No doubt King Thad does have Viking blood running through his veins, and so did his ancestors and his sons."

"Interesting," said Gran as she fingered her chin.

"Viking rats, Max!" said Dooley. "They're probably colossal!"

"There are no Vikings anymore, Dooley," I said. "That's all

24

ancient history. If there are rats at the castle, they'll be contemporary rats. Modern rats, if you will."

"You mean rats who use indoor plumbing," Brutus added with a grin. "And who wipe their little tushies with ultra-soft toilet paper."

"Doe, a deer, a female deer," Harriet murmured softly.

The limo drove across the moat and zoomed through the arched entrance to the castle, and then we were in the cobblestone courtyard. Around us, buildings rose, and I could even see the castle tower with the turrets and such. For a brief moment, I fully expected ladies and gentlemen in medieval outfits to surround us and perform a welcome quadrille, but instead, a liveried servant with a face like a horse's backside joined us. He looked about as old as the castle itself, and he appeared fully devoid of emotion as he welcomed us to Vaasu Castle and inquired if our travel arrangements had been to our satisfaction.

A young man of eager aspect then took charge of our luggage, and before long, we were ushered into the castle proper, where we were met with an astonishing sight: a sweeping marble staircase, stone walls adorned with shields and swords, portraits of bearded men who looked very fierce, a checkered stone floor, and a chandelier that dangled precariously, in my personal view, from the arched ceiling. So much so, I hastened to make sure I wasn't in its flight path if it opted to divorce itself from said ceiling.

A sort of hush suddenly descended upon our collected company, and when I followed everyone's gaze, I saw it had fastened itself upon a figure descending that sweeping staircase, Empress Sisi style.

"It's the queen!" Marge said with unveiled excitement.

And so it was. Queen Serena had deigned to descend from her lofty chambers to meet with us mere mortals and personally welcome us to her humble home. She certainly cut an impressive figure, I thought. She was probably around Marge's own age, perhaps a little older, and had her platinum locks tied back in a loose ponytail. She wasn't dressed in a dress, as I had expected, or to impress, and didn't float down to earth on a cloud of tulle and lace. Instead, she was wearing black pants, black pumps, and a simple white blouse. A modern monarch.

"Probably her day-to-day outfit!" Gran whispered, who had clearly expected something more spectacular. More queen-like, if you will.

"She's not even wearing a tiara!" Harriet cried.

"I doubt queens wear tiaras all day," I said. "They probably only wear them for special occasions."

"Well, this is a special occasion, isn't it?"

I couldn't argue with her there. Though Brutus said it best when he stated, "It may be a special occasion for us, sugar plum, but for her, it's business as usual."

And so it was. Just like the rest of us, queens are regular people, after all, and have a household to run and a lot of stuff to see to. And considering Queen Serena had a gigantic castle to manage, she was probably meeting plumbers all day, and electricians and other maintenance people. I couldn't imagine what it took to keep the place clean. Where does one even begin! When you consider that Buckingham Palace has seventy-eight bathrooms and 775 rooms, it must take a village to clean!

"I'm so glad you accepted my invitation," said the queen once she had successfully navigated the stairs and extended a hand to Odelia. For a moment, our human didn't know how to respond to the proffered hand. But then finally she decided to perform a curtsy, with the others all following her example. A smile of amusement momentarily played about the queen's lips, then she said, "Please dispense with the formalities. I really don't insist on it." She placed a hand on

Odelia's shoulder and gently led her to the stairs. "We're a full house at the moment, and you'll meet the other residents at dinner, but first let me show you to your rooms so you can freshen up and unpack. And then I would like to sit down with you to discuss the matter at hand."

"Ah, yes," said Odelia. "The Tiffany Thief."

The queen grimaced, as if Odelia had struck a painful chord. "Yes, the Tiffany Thief." She glanced down at the four of us and smiled. "I see you have brought along your precious babies. We'll make sure they feel as welcome here as the rest of your family." Then she caught sight of Grace, and her features morphed into a smile of sheer delight. She crouched down and placed a hand on the little girl's cheek. "Ooh, isn't she just the loveliest?"

"She is lovely," Odelia confirmed.

"You must be so proud."

"Very proud," Chase murmured, suddenly looking very bashful for his doing. Clearly, the unusual surroundings were having quite an impression on the hardened cop as well. Even Gran had been left pretty much speechless, which wasn't like her at all.

And then it was time to discover where we would be staying for the next couple of days and 'freshen up,' whatever that might mean. Cats are born fresh, though it's true I wouldn't have minded a little snack and a nap. And so up those stairs we went, with Dooley providing a first expression of his first impressions. "No rats, Max!" he whispered as we mounted the marble stairs. "So far so good!"

CHAPTER 6

"*I*t's the annoyance, you see," said the queen.

"And the sentimental value," her friend added.

We were in the queen's sitting room, where we had been granted an audience with the monarch's wife, with the queen present, as well as Lady Tiia Pohjanheimo, her good friend for the past few decades and the one who had originally suggested Odelia and Chase as a possible solution to unmask this so-called Tiffany Thief.

"Yes, there's the sentimental value as well," the queen agreed. She was showing Odelia and Chase pictures of the brooch that had been stolen on her phone, and as far as I could tell, it was indeed a very impressive piece of jewelry. "It used to belong to my grandmother, you see. So the sense of loss is profound."

"What did the police say?" asked Chase as he studied the picture of the priceless gem.

"We haven't told them," said the queen. "I really don't want to involve them if I can avoid it. The thing is, our police force is highly professional and reliable, of course, and efficient and all of that, but inevitably there will be talk, and before long the story will have leaked to the press. And the last thing I want right now is some scandal engulfing the House of Skingle. Especially now with my husband in the state he is in."

"Thad has been very ill of late," Lady Tiia explained. "We're not sure exactly what is ailing him, but it's bad enough that he's been bedridden for the past three weeks. And now with the Christmas ball coming up, it's looking more and more likely that for the first time since he became king, he won't be able to attend."

"Which is going to raise a lot of questions," the queen added. "Questions about his fitness as king, and inevitably questions about a possible succession. So the last thing we need right now is a scandal involving this thief."

"Do you have any ideas yourself?" asked Odelia. "As to the identity of this thief, I mean?"

"None," said the queen, shaking her head.

"But you have security, correct?"

"Oh, absolutely. It couldn't possibly be someone who walks in here from the outside. No, no, it's an inside job, that much we know. But who?"

"How many people work at the castle?"

"Well, hundreds, as you can probably imagine."

"So it could be any one of them."

The queen nodded. "The problem is, if I were to ask our security team to start looking into possible suspects, we would get the same result as if we talked to the police. People would talk, and before long, this Tiffany Thief would be headline news across the continent. Which is exactly what we don't want. So I would like you to carry out your investigation with absolute discretion. No one is supposed to know."

"Why Tiffany Thief?" asked Chase.

The Queen smiled. "Because he seems to have a penchant for items purchased at Tiffany's."

Odelia and Chase both nodded, indicating they understood their brief and would carry it out to the best of their abilities. Odelia briefly glanced down in our direction, and it was clear that her brief was also ours: talk to any possible pets staying at the castle, and find out what they knew.

Talking about pets, just then I detected movement at the door that led to the next room. It was a tiny Shih Tzu, hair tied back in a high ponytail, who stood staring at us with a look of surprise on its furry face. Then it yapped once and joined us, jumping straight into the queen's arms.

"Oh, look who's here!" she said, her face, which had been wreathed in an expression of extreme concern, immediately breaking into a delighted smile. "This is Ariana," she said, introducing the tiny mutt. "My very own sweet baby and queen of her own realm!"

"And who are you?!" this queen of the realm now demanded as she studied us with a curious eye.

"Max," I said. "And these are my friends Dooley, Brutus, and Harriet. We're here to catch the person who stole your human's brooch."

"Oh, phew," said the doggie. "I thought you were here to replace me!"

I smiled an encouraging smile. "I'm sure no one will ever replace you, Ariana. Your human seems to love you very much."

"She does," said Ariana with a sigh of relief at this good news. "Though not as much as I love her, of course."

"Of course," I murmured. Dogs often have this whole 'I love my human so much I will follow them to the ends of the earth and back' thing going on. Cats are more laid-back in that sense. Less uptight, if you know what I mean.

"So Ariana," said Dooley, "I have a very important question for you."

"Yes?" said Ariana, her eyes widening in suspense.

"Where are the rats?" asked our friend.

"Rats? What rats?"

"Well, the castle rats, of course. I know they're here, since this is a castle, and all castles have rats, just like all castles have ghosts, but if you tell me where they are, I'll make sure never to go there."

Ariana, who had jumped down from her human's arms and had joined us on the floor, now frowned. "I don't think I understand the question," she admitted.

"Just tell us where the rats are, so we know where not to go," said Dooley, trying to make this as clear as he could.

"But… as far as I know, there aren't any rats in the castle," she said. "At least I haven't met any, and I've been here for three years now."

Dooley's face was something to behold. Elation competed with incredulity at these words straight from the horse's mouth, so to speak. "No rats?"

"No rats," said Ariana. And considering she was a royal dog, I think we may assume she spoke with a sense of authority.

"Oh, phew!" said Dooley. "Oh, phew, phew, phew!" But then his expression clouded again. "What about ghosts?"

"No ghosts," Ariana said. "Though we do have a minor mouse problem. But then our mousers take care of those, so I wouldn't worry about that if I were you."

"Mousers?" asked Harriet. "What are those?"

"Well, the king's brother Asko has cats, and cats being cats, they make sure the mice infestation doesn't get out of control."

"And who are these royal mousers?" asked Harriet. I could

see that her eyes had turned a little glittery, which is never a good sign.

"Their names, you mean? Julie and Anne. They're Asko's favorite cats and live with him in his chambers. I don't see much of them, as they like to keep themselves to themselves, but they seem to be doing a good job, as I almost never trip over a mouse. Though the cook is always claiming they're all over her kitchen, which may or may not be true. Cook is a little... eccentric." She shrugged. "But then I guess that can be said about a lot of the castle inhabitants."

"Tell us about these inhabitants," I said, happy at this opportunity to hear an insider's account about the goings-on at Vaasu Castle. Inside information, in my experience, is always crucial.

"Well, there is King Thad and Queen Serena, of course," said Ariana as she settled down with us. "She's the sweetest, kindest person in the whole world, whereas he's something of a brute, I have to say."

"A Viking," Brutus suggested.

"Something like that," Ariana agreed. "And since he got sick, his temper has become even worse. He has always been verbally abusive to his wife and the staff, but now he's positively vile at times." She scrunched up her face and stuck out her tongue. "Not my favorite person!"

"So what about the rest of the family? Do they also live here at the castle?" asked Harriet.

"Yes, so Serena and Thad have two sons, Crown Prince Dane and Prince Urpo. They both live in separate wings of the castle with their respective families. Dane is married to Princess Impi, who used to be his fitness instructor at his local gym. They have two daughters, Ainikki and Hely. And Prince Urpo married his high school teacher Kami, though so far their union hasn't been blessed with offspring, unfortunately. But then they only married last year, so there's still time."

"A fitness instructor and a teacher," said Brutus. "Isn't that... unusual?"

Ariana made a face. "Highly unusual! When Dane announced his engagement, he and his dad had a flaming row. You could hear them screaming all the way to the queen's quarters."

"The king and queen don't share the same set of rooms?" I asked.

"No. They don't get along all that well, and for their own benefit they've decided to put a little distance between themselves. So now the king does his thing, and the queen leads her own life, and there have been a lot fewer noise complaints since they did, which is good for everyone involved."

"Not really a tight-knit happy little family, then," said Brutus.

"Not exactly," Ariana agreed. "First Dane married his fitness instructor, much against his father's wishes, and then Urpo married his high-school teacher, which caused an even bigger scandal." She lowered her voice. "They met when Urpo was sixteen and Kami twenty-two, and according to the rumors, it was love at first sight. They only started dating many years later, though, when Urpo was in college and he happened to bump into Kami again, who had just gone through a pretty nasty break-up. Urpo was her shoulder to cry on, and then one thing led to another and now they're married."

"Against his father's wishes," I said.

"Exactly!"

"And what does Queen Serena think about her sons' marriages?" asked Harriet, intrigued by this peek into a royal family's internal kitchen.

"She wasn't happy about it, but at least she didn't get into a screaming match with her sons and instead tried to be as supportive as she could."

"Does she get along with her daughters-in-law?"

"She does, but I think it's safe to say they'll never be great friends. There's the age difference, and also the difference in class. Impi and Kami may be nice girls, but they both come from very different worlds and have little in common with Serena. But she tries, she really does. She wants to make it work, if only for the sake of her grandchildren, whom she absolutely dotes on."

"That would be…" I said, trying to remember all of the names mentioned.

"Ainikki, that's the eldest—she's seventeen now—and Hely, who just turned ten. Sweet girls, both of them," she said with a smile of affection. Clearly, she also doted on the queen's granddaughters.

"So… the queen told us that her husband is ill?" I asked.

"Yes, he hadn't been feeling well for quite a while now, but then three weeks ago he got really sick and hasn't left his bed since. The Physician to the King is doing what he can, but even he is stumped. And Thad is refusing to be admitted to a hospital, figuring it will damage his reputation as a virile and in-charge monarch, so this hampers his treatment to some extent. What his illness hasn't done is change the cantankerous nature of his personality. Like I said, the yelling is worse now than ever." She shook her head. "Poor Serena. She's the one who bears the brunt of her husband's foul moods. And his two sons, of course, who never seem to be doing anything right in the eyes of their dad."

"So… Dane is the crown prince, right?" I said, trying to keep all of this straight in my head.

"Yes, Dane will be the new king when his father passes away or decides to abdicate. But only if he stays married."

"What do you mean?" asked Harriet.

"Well, the succession rule that governs the House of Skingle says that the monarch's oldest son is in line to the throne, but only if he's lawfully married. If the oldest son isn't married, his younger brother becomes eligible—if he's married."

"So no women?" asked Harriet, sounding disappointed.

"No women," said Ariana.

"But what if neither of the sons is married?" asked Brutus. "Then who becomes the new king?"

"Or what if the king doesn't have male offspring?" I asked.

"If the king's sons aren't married, the throne goes to the king's brother, or to Prince Asko's descendants. But again, only if he's married."

"Very complicated," I said.

"Yeah, it's a little tricky," Ariana agreed.

"Not to mention archaic!" Harriet added.

"There are plans to change the royal line of succession," said Ariana, "but thus far they haven't gotten around to it. Maybe Dane will take care of it once he ascends the throne."

"So... Dane has two daughters, right?" I said.

Ariana smiled. "Very clever, Max. Yes, unfortunately, Dane and Impi's marriage has only been blessed with two daughters so far, which has been another bone of contention between father and son."

"And between son and wife, I imagine."

Ariana nodded. "It is a very sensitive subject, which is why Dane will probably change the system the moment he becomes king, much against his dad's wishes, by the way. King Thad is very old-fashioned and believes the system shouldn't be tampered with. He's a big believer in tradition, and if it was good enough for his forebears, it should be good enough for another thousand years or so."

"Is that how long the House of Skingle has ruled Liechtenburg?" asked Dooley, fascinated by this glimpse into history.

"That's right. There have been Skingle kings for the past thousand years, and if all goes well, it should extend into the future. Though of course, you never know." She sighed deeply. "One thing I can tell you: it's not easy to be the king— or the queen, for that matter. And I'm glad I don't have to do it!"

"Can you imagine, though?" said Harriet. "Queen Ariana. Does have a nice ring to it, doesn't it?"

"Well, it does, but—"

"Or Queen Harriet?"

"Cats can't ascend the throne, sugar lips," Brutus pointed out.

"But if they could, I think I'd make a great queen. And you a great king, of course," she added as an afterthought.

This was all moot, since the only reason we were there was to catch the person who had stolen the queen's brooch. Which reminded me... "How often has this Tiffany Thief struck so far, Ariana?" I asked.

"Well, let me think..." said Ariana, and closed one eye while directing the other at the ceiling. "Um, this is probably the fifth time in the past two months or so?"

"Five times!"

"That's correct. So far he's targeted all the different members of the royal household: Crown Prince Dane's expensive watch was stolen—one he was very attached to, apparently. Then Princess Impi's necklace, Princess Kami's engagement ring, Grant Chubb's mother's ring, and now Queen Serena's brooch."

"Grant Chubb?" asked Harriet. "Grant Chubb is staying at the castle?"

"That's right. He's a close friend of the family and has

been staying with us for the past three weeks or so, along with his mother, as Queen Serena's honored guests."

The fact that the famous actor was staying at the castle clearly impressed Harriet, for her jaw had dropped, and she made no attempt to reel the mandible back in.

"Those are the five incidents we know of," Ariana continued. "Though it's possible members of staff were also targeted, of course. But if that's the case, so far no one has come forward or alerted our security team."

"So they have been informed, correct?"

"Yes, they have, but Serena asked them to hold off on conducting a full-scale investigation."

"Because word would get out."

"Exactly. And now that you guys are here, you're going to catch this thief posthaste, aren't you?"

I grimaced. No pressure!

CHAPTER 7

*W*hile Odelia and Chase were being brought up to speed on all things Tiffany Thief, Marge and Tex were in the room that had been assigned to them and marveling at the stunning view from their window.

"Isn't it amazing?" asked Marge as she pointed to a bird flying overhead.

"It is pretty amazing," the doctor agreed. The panorama was indeed one they hadn't often seen before, with the full array of mountain tops lined out in front of them as if made just for their enjoyment. But then the castle itself had been constructed on a hill, possibly because it offered certain advantages in ancient times when fortifications were important to defend oneself from invading armies, and so the vantage point was ideal.

"I'm so glad we'll be spending Christmas here," said Marge. "Can you imagine sitting by the fire with the king and queen and telling Christmas stories?"

"Um... I'm not sure we'll be doing a lot of sitting by the fire," Tex said. He hated to rain on his wife's parade, but as far as he had understood the program, there would be a big banquet and subsequent ball on Christmas Eve, with hundreds of invitations having been sent out, so the intimate and homely atmosphere Marge was hoping for probably wouldn't come to pass.

"But Christmas Day won't be the same, will it? I'm sure even the Skingles celebrate Christmas Day amongst themselves as a family."

"Even if they do, I'm not sure we'll be invited, honey. We're not family, after all."

"Oh," said Marge, but then quickly recovered. "We're still going to have a good time, aren't we?"

"Absolutely," said Tex. "I mean, we're staying at one of the finest castles in Europe, as guests of the royal family. How much more Christmassy can Christmas get?"

She placed her head on his shoulder, and he placed an arm around her as they stood admiring the scenery. He just hoped that Odelia and Chase wouldn't catch this thief too soon. A week or two spent in Liechtenburg would be perfect. Then he'd have to get back to his patients, and Marge to her library. But at least for the next two weeks, they'd make the most of it. Have the perfect vacation!

"I wonder if there's a Christmas market in Vaasu," said Marge, voicing his thoughts exactly.

"Let's head into town now," he suggested. "And explore."

"Good idea," Marge said. "We can always unpack later."

And he was just checking on his phone where the center of town was and all the local touristy highlights were when a deferential knock sounded at the door, and the oddly stony-faced majordomo who had greeted them in the courtyard entered. "King Thad would like a word," he now announced, making it sound as if they'd been invited to attend a funeral, which, considering the rumors they had picked up about the king's condition, might very well be the case.

"Oh, that's so kind of him," said Marge, and made for the door.

The majordomo produced a soft cough, then said, still speaking with a voice as if from the tomb, "Only the doctor, please, madam."

Tex exchanged a look of surprise with his wife. "The king wants to speak to me alone?" he asked for good measure.

"That's correct. If you will follow me, sir."

And after giving Marge an apologetic shrug, he hurried after the man. It took a while to get to their destination as the corridors and hallways in the palace were of the Byzantine variety, but finally, they arrived where they were supposed to be. All the while, the servant hadn't uttered a single word, which was more disconcerting than Tex had expected. He would have liked to pepper the man with a thousand questions, but could sense that each one would be met with the same stoic silence, so he didn't bother lobbing even a single one.

At long last, the majordomo halted in front of an ornately carved wooden door and opened it, then gestured for the doctor to pass through, closing the door again once he had.

He discovered he was on familiar terrain, standing in a bedroom that was perhaps a little more luxurious than most bedrooms he had frequented in his long career as a small-town physician but had in common with the ones he had seen in that it contained a single large bed in which a single large man lay. Next to the bed, a doctor stood, wearing a frown of concern on his face. He was a smallish man, with a head that was entirely too large for the body that supported it.

"Ah, Doctor Poole, I presume?" asked the doctor, his expression morphing into one of delight at making Tex's acquaintance. "My name is Eerikki Storrar, and I'm the personal physician to His Majesty the King."

"Tex Poole," he said as he approached the monarch's sickbed. What struck him was the wild red beard the king sported, which seemed to sprout from the lower slopes of the man's face and extended in all directions in a haphazard sort of way, as if having been left to its own devices by a careless gardener, unwilling or unable to rein it in.

"They tell me you're an American doctor," said the king in a booming voice that belied the gravity of his illness. A pair of icy blue eyes zeroed in on Tex and seemed to hit him like a laser beam. "Is that correct?"

"I am a doctor, and I am an American," Tex confessed. "So I guess in a sense that makes me an American doctor."

The King produced a sort of deep rumble, which belatedly Tex interpreted as a noise of approval. "I like American doctors," the wild-bearded ruler announced. "American doctors are good. They are modern." At this, he directed a vicious look at his own doctor, who was decidedly not American.

Doctor Storrar's frame quivered for a moment as he took the frontal assault in his stride, then settled down again. "I would very much like to consult with you, Doctor Poole," he said. "In other words, get a second opinion."

"Since the first opinion is lousy!" the King exclaimed with more forcefulness than Tex had expected.

"I'm doing all I can," Doctor Storrar protested.

"Not enough!" the King boomed. "Three weeks, Storrar. Three weeks I've been confined to this bed. While I could be out there—hunting and shooting and..." He frowned, which involved a pair of bushy brows descending over those icy blue eyes, only slightly lessening their impact. For a moment, Tex got the impression that the King would have liked to hunt and shoot his doctor, but of course, that couldn't be right.

"So what seems to be the problem?" he asked now, in his usual practical manner. "Symptoms?"

And as Doctor Storrar started rattling off the symptoms that seemed to be troubling his patient, the king's jaw worked, and his face turned almost as red as his beard until he suddenly thundered, "Poppycock!"

Both doctors looked up in surprise. "Poppycock?" asked the personal physician to the King.

"Balderdash! You have no idea what's wrong with me. Admit it, you incompetent nincompoop!"

The doctor bridled a little at this, giving the impression of a much-put-upon scrawny chicken trying to act like the ruler of the roost but failing miserably. "I must protest, Your Majesty!" he said in a high, reedy voice. His face, too, had turned a dark shade of crimson.

"Get out!" the king yelled. "Get out, dum-dum! And don't come back!"

And after darting a look of apology at Tex, and before the latter's surprised gaze, the Physician to the King hurried out and carefully closed the door behind him.

The moment he was gone, the king visibly relaxed. "My apologies," he said as he lay back against the pillow. "But that man has been getting on my nerves for weeks. Always beating about the bush and spouting a lot of nonsense while he has no idea what's going on, the idiot. If it was up to me, I'd have his head chopped off and put on a stake as a warning to other quacks like him. But apparently, I'm not allowed to do that anymore." He fixed Tex with a serious look. "Can I rely on your discretion, Doctor Poole?"

"Well, yes, of course," said Tex.

"See, the thing is that I know what's wrong with me. The only problem is getting that nincompoop that just left to accept it."

"You know what's wrong with you?"

"Absolutely." He lowered his voice, forcing Tex to come closer. "I'm being poisoned, Doctor Poole."

Tex stared at the man. "P-p-poisoned, Your Majesty?"

The king nodded slowly. "It's my wife, you see. She hates me and wants me dead." He suddenly clutched the doctor's sleeve and pulled him even closer until they were almost nose to nose. Tex gulped a little. "You have to expose her, Doc. You have to prove that my wife is trying to kill me. Will you do that for me?"

Tex blinked. "Well…"

"Promise me."

"Um…"

"Promise me!"

"I promise!" he said quickly, visions of his lopped-off head on a stake decorating the castle ramparts suddenly floating before his mind's eye.

Abruptly the king let go of his sleeve, thereby returning the good doctor to perpendicularity. The effect of this was that he stumbled back a few paces before recovering his balance.

"Or it could be my sons," said the King with a dark frown. "Either way, my family wants me dead. And you're going to reveal the conspiracy and save my life. Is that understood?"

"Y-yes," he said.

"Good," said the king and closed his eyes.

Tex stood balancing from his left to his right foot for a few moments before coming to the conclusion that his audience was over, and retreating to the door and back to safety, away from this madman.

As he approached the door, it noiselessly swung open, operated by the same majordomo who had brought him there, and as the man closed the door again, he spoke.

"Congratulations, Doctor Poole. You are now the official Physician to the King. You will find your office in the next room. If His Majesty's health were to further decline..."

There was menace in those words and in that cold gaze, and Tex swallowed a few times before nodding his agreement. And as he was led into his new office, which indeed located right next to the king's bedroom, he wondered what he had done to deserve this.

One thing was for sure: there would be no Christmas market in his immediate future.

CHAPTER 8

*S*ince her husband had disappeared for some urgent meeting with the king, and her daughter and son-in-law for an urgent meeting with the queen, Marge decided to take Grace for a walk through the royal gardens, which were rumored to be absolutely worth a visit. So she took her granddaughter by the hand and together navigated the maze that was the royal castle until they found the exit and entered the gardens, which were indeed lovely.

The carpet of snow felt crunchy under their feet, and Grace squealed with delight as she pranced about in her rubber boots. And as they walked along, they passed by a small brook that wasn't frozen yet, proving once and for all that the rumors of Liechtenburg being a world of ice and snow were greatly exaggerated. Which was just as well, since it also meant the temperatures were quite balmy for the time of year and the sun was out, covering the world in sparkly hues.

They soon arrived at the royal stables, and Grace was over-joyed to take a closer look at the horses, so for a few moments, they admired the noble animals. There was quite a lot of activity at the stables, with several riders riding out on their horses while others were being groomed inside the stables by stable-hands. Marge had lifted her granddaughter up so she could put her pudgy little hand on one of the horses and carefully pet it.

"I wouldn't do that if I were you," said one of the stablehands.

"Oh, and why is that?" asked Marge.

"That's Princess Ainikki's horse," said the young man, who couldn't have been older than seventeen or eighteen. "She doesn't like it when people touch it."

"I'm sorry," said Marge. "I didn't know."

Just then, a teenage girl approached, dressed in riding gear. When she saw Marge and Grace, she hesitated for a moment, then walked up. "It's all right, Eloy. I can take it from here."

Eloy glanced up at her for a moment, his face coloring, then quickly retreated, leaving Marge and Grace alone with the girl.

"Is this your horse?" asked Marge.

The girl nodded as she stroked the horse's nose. "Gilly, yeah. I've been riding her for three years now." She directed a smile at Grace, who seemed intimidated by the strange world they had entered. "Don't worry, she won't bite. Here, you can touch her nose. She likes that."

"Very gently, honey," said Marge as Grace reached out a hand to touch the horse's nose. "So you're Princess Ainikki?" asked Marge.

"Yeah, that's right. And you are one of my grandmother's guests?"

"Marge Poole," said Marge. "I arrived just now with my family."

"Quite a big party, from what I could see."

"Yes, we're six people."

"Will you be staying here for Christmas?"

"I think so. I'm not sure how long we'll be staying."

The girl nodded. "My mom says it's got something to do with the thief that's been active at the castle. Your daughter, she's a private detective of some kind?"

"Of some kind," Marge admitted. "And her husband is a police detective back home, so they're well placed to find out what's going on with this thief of yours."

The girl smiled. "I hope you catch him. He's been stealing a lot, and people are all in a tizzy over it. He stole my dad's expensive watch and my mother's necklace, which she was very fond of. He hasn't stolen anything of mine yet, or my sister, but it's only a matter of time. He's very clever, you know. In and out of rooms like a ghost. Oh, and he's stolen something very valuable from Grant's mother, which she's very upset about."

"Grant?"

"Grant Chubb. The famous actor." A dreamy look had stolen over the teenager's face. "He's absolutely gorgeous, isn't he? Even more handsome in the flesh than in the movies. His mother is related to my grandmother somehow. Don't ask me how, it's all very complicated. I wasn't even going to be here this Christmas, you know," she said as she idly played with her horse's mane. "I was supposed to stay with a friend in Finland, but when I heard that Grant was going to spend the holidays at the castle I simply couldn't stay away. Just to be near that man…" She sighed happily, then seemed to realize she was discussing her private thoughts with a total stranger and gave Marge an awkward smile. "Anyway, I better don't keep you. You have a thief to catch, after all."

And with these words, she mounted her horse and was off at a light canter.

Marge stared after the girl and Grace burbled a few words that she didn't understand.

"Yes, that was a nice horsie, wasn't it?" she said. "But there are plenty more. Do you want to see them?"

Grace nodded in agreement, and so they ventured deeper into the stables in search of more horses. Before long they had found another prime specimen for Grace to admire, and as the toddler made happy sounds, she rubbed her hand against the horse's nose, like the queen's granddaughter had taught her.

Marge now saw that the same stablehand was busy shoveling something that looked a lot like horse manure from behind the horse in question. When he rose, he wiped the back of his hand across his sweaty brow, and caught sight of Marge and Grace.

He gave them a smile. "I'm sorry about that," he said, referring to the earlier incident. "Usually Princess Ainikki hates it when people handle her horse, but I guess she decided to make an exception for you."

"You know her well?" asked Marge, who hadn't missed the odd sense of befuddlement that had assailed the young man upon the arrival of the princess.

Once again, his cheeks colored. "We're friends," he said curtly. "I'm Tiia Pohjanheimo's grandson," he added. "She's the queen's best friend. So I spend a lot of time here at the castle, but whereas Ainikki is a princess, obviously I'm not a prince, so…"

Marge thought she did see, and she gave the young man a look of encouragement. "You like her, don't you?"

He grinned sheepishly. "Is it that obvious?"

"Pretty obvious," Marge agreed.

"The problem is this actor," he admitted. "Ever since he arrived he's all she talks about. It's always Grant this and

Grant that. The guy is old, for crying out loud. Old and boring. So I really don't know what she sees in him."

"He's a famous actor," Marge said. "So he may be old and boring to you, but to young girls like Ainikki, he represents glamour and glitter and excitement."

"He's just about as exciting as that stuff over there," he said, gesturing to a bucket filled with horse dung.

"I wouldn't worry about it too much, Eloy," said Marge. "It's just a teenage crush. It will pass soon enough. The moment he's out of your lives, she'll forget all about him."

"I wouldn't be too sure about that," said the kid. "She's been like that since the guy first came to stay with us, and that was three years ago. Three years of having to listen to her going on and on about how amazing he is, and how generous and talented and handsome." He sighed. "It's been hell, Mrs…"

"Poole," said Marge. "Marge Poole, and this is my grand-daughter Grace. Who fortunately is too young to have a crush on Grant Chubb. And I'm too old," she added with a smile. But then she turned serious again. "If you like, I could talk to Ainikki? Find out what's going on?"

"You can try," he said. "My grandmother has tried to talk some sense into her, and Ainikki's own mother, but so far she's convinced that one day she'll marry Grant and he'll take her to Hollywood, and they'll be happy together forever. I keep telling her that these Hollywood marriages never last, and that Grant isn't even remotely interested in her, and nor should he be, since she's entirely too young for him, but then she just gets upset with me." He had been gesticulating, and now gave the bucket a kick, which caused it to topple over and its contents to spread across the stable floor. And as he started to collect it again, he said, "I'm sorry for bothering you with this, Mrs. Poole. You probably have other things on your mind."

"No, it's fine," said Marge. "My daughter is busy, my husband is busy, so it's perfectly fine. I'll talk to your friend— if she'll talk to me, of course." He nodded, and she gave him a smile of encouragement. "It'll be fine," she assured him. "Just you wait and see."

* * *

FROM THE WINDOW of her room at the castle, Tiia Pohjanheimo looked on as Odelia Kingsley's mother walked into the stables with Odelia's daughter. Tiia's room might not offer the same stunning view that her good friend Serena's did, but since she loved horses, and always had, she was perfectly happy with her view. A nice bonus was that Eloy now worked there, so she could keep an eye on him from a distance.

It hadn't escaped her attention that her grandson was madly in love with Ainikki and had been for a long time, with the girl completely oblivious that her dear friend harbored feelings towards her that were deeper than mere friendship. And even though at first it had amused her and Serena, now they were a little concerned. What if Eloy's feelings were never reciprocated? What if he never got over it?

Even as young girls, the two women had entertained an idle wish that one day their respective offspring would marry and strengthen the bond of their friendship by crystallizing it into that of an actual family connection. But now that her grandson appeared to have fallen in love with Serena's granddaughter, the only thing she could think was that he might end up with a broken heart.

She had already tried to play matchmaker, and so had Serena, but the girl seemed to have her mind set on Grant Chubb, of all people, a man who was old enough to be her father! At least Chubb didn't seem to have any designs on the girl—thank God for small favors.

She watched as Ainikki rode out of the stables on her horse Gilly, going for her daily ride, and expressed a silent fervent wish she would finally see the light and give Eloy as much attention as she did that horse of hers—or Grant Chubb.

She turned away from the window and picked up her phone to check her messages. One was from Serena. A link to an article about the Kingsleys and how well they had handled that Opal business at the time. She nodded approvingly as she quickly scanned the article.

The meeting with the couple had gone well, and Odelia and Chase had made a great impression on both her and Serena. Opal had been right in her assessment. They knew their stuff, and if anyone could end the reign of terror this Tiffany Thief had brought, it was them. She just hoped they'd manage without alerting the media, which was the bane of Serena's existence, with their constant need for scandalmongering and screaming headlines.

It was one of the reasons Serena had asked her to come and stay at the castle for the holidays, even though Tiia had plenty of things to do in town, where she had her own apartment where she lived. But with Thad's mystery illness and this thief running amok, her friend's needs were obviously greater than hers, and so she had put her own life on hold for the moment and accepted Serena's invitation to be by her side at this moment of crisis.

That's what friends are for, and she'd never have a greater friend than Serena. When Tiia's husband had fallen ill, Serena had also dropped everything so she could be with her and hadn't left until after the funeral, something Tiia would forever be grateful for. So now that she could finally return the favor, she was more than happy to. She just hoped that

Thad's sickbed wouldn't stretch too far into the future, as it was wreaking havoc on his entire family, with everyone in a tizzy. Either the man got well again soon or…

She caught herself harboring ill thoughts about Thad again and knew she shouldn't. It wasn't Christian. But with him being the kind of person he was and treating Serena the way he did, it wasn't difficult to wish him dead. Now he was even accusing Serena of trying to poison him! The man was becoming more delusional with each passing day. But then there was a streak of madness that seemed to run through the House of Skingle, affecting some more than others.

And in Thad, it was stronger than in most.

CHAPTER 9

*I*t isn't every day that you encounter a stable full of horses, and so after we decided to trail after Marge to see what she was up to and take in some of the scenery, it came as something of a surprise when we found her entering the royal stables, which were, no doubt, filled with royal steeds and mares. For some reason, kings and queens have always been closely associated with horses, and clearly the House of Skingle was no exception.

"Is there a horse for every member of the royal family, Max?" asked Dooley as we marveled at the sheer size of these animals. They pretty much towered over us, and we were careful not to get too close lest we get trampled underhoof.

"I'm not sure," I confessed. "But I imagine so."

"So the king has a horse, and the queen has her own horse, and the princes and their wives and their offspring," said Brutus as he sidestepped what looked like a giant poo one of the horses must have left as a souvenir.

"Yeah, and probably all of the servants as well," Harriet said. I could tell that she was scanning the place for mice, hoping to establish a name for herself as a royal mouser. She might have a point, for catching mice is probably a lot easier than catching horses, who are too big to snugly fit between our sharp teeth.

Marge was chatting with some girl who turned out to be a princess, and then she proceeded to chat with a young man, who wasn't a prince, per se, but could have been. I got the impression that you couldn't swing a stick in this place without hitting at least a dozen royals.

As far as I had followed the conversation—we were a little distracted because of the powerful scent emanating from the horses surrounding us—the girl was in love with a famous actor named Grant Chubb, and the boy was in love with the girl and upset that she was in love with the actor. It all sounded very complicated, and I got the impression that Marge intended to play matchmaker to try and align the stars for this ill-matched couple.

"Feeding all of these horses must cost a lot of money," Dooley said as he marveled at a giant stack of hay.

"Well, since horses only eat grass," I said, "it probably doesn't cost that much."

"But what do they do when there is no grass?" asked my friend. "Like now, for instance, when snow covers the ground?"

"In case you hadn't noticed, snow doesn't actually cover all of the ground, Dooley," said Brutus. "Contrary to what we've been told. There is still some grass left to be eaten."

"It doesn't look very appetizing," said Harriet with a look of distaste.

She was right. The parts of the grounds that weren't fully covered in snow didn't look as if they would provide a gourmet meal for any royal horse.

"Horses eat hay," I told my friend. "Which is dried grass, basically. So the stable owner collects grass in the summer months, when it's nice and fresh, and then dries and stores it for the winter months when there is no grass. That way, the horses always have something to eat."

"They could eat kibble," Dooley suggested. "Just like the rest of us." He seemed to resent these horses for acting holier than thou, with their habit of refusing to eat like normal pets and insisting on eating grass instead.

"I guess horses aren't carnivores like us," said Harriet, who made a face as she sniffed the air. "Let's get out of here, you guys. This place isn't sanitary in my personal opinion. And the last thing I need right now is having to lick all of that horse manure off my paws for the rest of the day."

"Yuck," said Brutus under his breath.

And since Marge's business appeared to be concluded anyway, we followed our human out of the stables and back into the open, where we filled our lungs with some fresh air. Marge continued her stroll around the grounds, this time sticking to the snow-cleared path, and we soon found ourselves approaching a very pretty pavilion or gazebo built in a classic style. Two men were convened there, and so Marge decided to turn back so as not to disturb them. We felt no such qualms, and instead approached the duo to listen to what they were discussing. Cats are sneaky like that.

"How much longer, do you think, Prince Dane?" asked one of the men. He was of the smallish variety, with a beak for a nose and a bald dome liberally sprinkled with freckles, while his counterpart was tall and handsome, with lush auburn tresses and a noble visage. What struck me about him were his icy blue eyes.

"It won't be much longer now, Prime Minister Saffman," said the prince. "So it's imperative we make sure everything is in place. The moment my father abdicates, we immediately implement the succession plans we've decided on."

"Of course. Absolutely," said the prime minister in a soft and groveling tone. "Anything you say, Your Highness. The problem is that we've got an election coming up, and if your father decides to hang onto the throne until after the election, there's no telling what the next government will do."

The prince eyed him sternly. "You will lead the next government, surely?"

"That's not how democracy works," the prime minister explained. "It's the people that decide. Of course, I'm hoping I will be in a position to lead the next government, but it's not a given."

"Nonsense. I want you to lead our next government, and I'll make sure that's exactly what will happen. If necessary, I'll make the necessary interventions on your behalf."

"I don't think that's such a good idea," said the politician, looking a little alarmed.

"If I can't use my influence for good, then there's no point in having a monarch at all," the prince stated firmly. "So when the time comes, I'll address the nation and tell them that you are the best guarantee we have for leading Liechtenburg into the future and beyond."

"Well…" The man didn't seem entirely happy with this, but since effectively he was talking to the future king, he probably needed to be careful what he said.

"Too bad we don't have a clear timeline," the prince continued. "If only we knew how much longer my father plans to hang on, but we don't. Though I can't imagine he'll stick it out much longer. Weeks, maybe. One month at the most."

"That's good," the prime minister murmured. Then he glanced up at the prince. "Have you given some more thought to the issue we discussed last time?"

"I have, and I don't mind confessing that it's been preying on my mind, Efrain. The trouble is that there's no easy fix. My wife doesn't seem to be able to produce male offspring, and that's the long and the short of it. The only solution I see is to get a divorce and find a woman who can. But then I'd have to do so before the coronation. It doesn't do for a king to divorce his queen. Gives the wrong impression. So if I were to go through with this, I'd have to do it now, before my father passes away."

"But how can you be sure that your new wife will be able to give you a male child?" asked the prime minister.

"Ah, now therein lies the rub," the prince said with a dark frown. "Unfortunately there are no guarantees, Efrain. No guarantees at all. Unless…"

"Unless?" asked the prime minister hopefully.

"Unless we could procure a male baby from some other source."

The prime minister frowned. These were deep waters. "Some… other source?"

"Yes. Imagine I were to remarry a woman who's already with child, the doctors being in a position to give their absolute assurance that the child is not only male but also in good health, well, that would be fine, wouldn't it? Would suit our purposes perfectly."

"You mean… you have already impregnated some other woman, Your Highness?" asked the prime minister, looking entirely bewildered now.

The prince turned on him with a frown. "Don't talk nonsense, man. Of course I haven't impregnated some woman. This child doesn't necessarily have to be mine is what I'm saying." When the politician continued to look puzzled, he sighed deeply. "Do I really have to spell it out to you?"

"Well…"

"We both agree that in order to secure the future of the House of Skingle, there's an urgent need for me to produce male offspring, agreed?"

"Agreed."

"And we also agree that Impi has failed in this important task."

"Yes."

"Adoption is out of the question."

"Okay."

"So what I need right now is a woman who is with child—a male child. Doesn't matter if this child is mine or not, as long as the child is male and the woman is my bride and therefore the future queen. Problem solved."

"But… won't the baby's real father protest to this state of affairs?"

"We pay him off. Or we find a pregnant woman whose baby's parentage is… opaque, shall we say."

"Oh, right. I see." But it was clear that he didn't.

"Anyway, you don't have to concern yourself with that, Efrain. I'll take care of that side of the business. You just make sure that you keep your end of the bargain. A great coronation for me. National holiday and all of that."

"Of course, of course," said the politico.

The meeting had come to an end, and as the prince walked back to the castle, with the prime minister heading in the opposite direction, we also commenced the relatively short trek back to our new home away from home for the holidays.

"I wonder how the prince's wife feels about all of this," said Harriet. "Do you think she knows she's about to be replaced as wife and future queen?"

"I very much doubt it," I said. "Judging from the way they were discussing these plans, I got the impression it's all very hush-hush."

"I'm sure they don't want anyone to know that their future king will not be Prince Dane's actual son," said Brutus. "If news leaked about that, there probably would be some kind of scandal."

"Oh, absolutely," I said. "Royals are very big on bloodlines and all of that."

"There is a simple solution," said Harriet. "All they have to do is change the law and make it so that girls can also accede to the throne. That way, one of Prince Dane's daughters can become queen, and he doesn't have to divorce his wife and put some non-family member on the throne."

"It seems logical," I agreed. "But apparently that's not how they do things here in Liechtenburg."

"Feels very old-fashioned to me," said Harriet. "As if a woman can't be a perfectly fine monarch." She sighed deeply. "By the same token, they should consider putting some other species on the throne. I mean, why does it always have to be humans who run countries? Why can't they put a cat in charge, for instance? In other words, why don't they put someone like me in charge?"

I would have laughed at this if Harriet hadn't been perfectly serious. "Cats can't rule nations, Harriet," Dooley said, just as seriously.

"Oh, and why not? Don't you think we've got the skills?"

"Well, there's the language barrier, for one thing," said Dooley, who must have given this some thought when we weren't looking. "Humans don't understand cats, so how would you tell them what to do? They'd simply think you're asking for more kibble when you're trying to explain to them they should invade some neighboring country."

Harriet smiled at this, and so did Brutus and me. "You're right, Dooley," said Harriet. "I hadn't thought this through. But I'm sure our scientists, who are very intelligent and ambitious, will invent a device at some point in the future that will make it possible for humans to understand cats. And when that happens, I will simply give my orders, and the machine will translate them."

This gave us all some food for thought. I still saw one

minor problem, and that was that of heritage. Kings and queens usually leave their empires to their own personal offspring, except, apparently, Prince Dane, who was thinking about outsourcing this important task to some unknown individual. And as far as I could tell, no human has ever given birth to a cat, so that made Harriet's dream scenario highly unlikely indeed.

We had arrived back at the castle just in time to find Odelia in something of a tizzy. "Where were you guys!" she said. "We have to talk to the staff about this Tiffany Thief business."

And so once again, we were drawn into the maelstrom of this ongoing investigation and soon forgot all about Prince Dane's personal struggles with his succession.

CHAPTER 10

$\mathcal{W}$e were in the kitchen, where Odelia and Chase had set up an interview with three members of the royal household staff: the maid, the cook, and the majordomo. And if you think this is the premise of a joke, I'm afraid I have to disappoint you, for the queen took the theft of her precious brooch very seriously indeed.

The cook, a middle-aged rather small and stout lady named Tilly Möttönen, was the first to speak. "I had nothing to do with this," she said with vehemence. "And if Serena really thinks I did, she should get it over with and fire me now!"

"Nobody is accusing you of anything, Mrs..."

"Tilly," said the cook.

Odelia smiled. "All we're trying to do is find out who did. And since you have worked here the longest, the queen figured there was a good chance you might have some ideas."

"Oh, I have some ideas, all right," said the cook. "This is all down to bad security." She turned to the majordomo, a man whose face was so expressionless he could have been a waxwork dummy. "Haven't I said it all along, Oskari? Security at this place is absolutely terrible. You mark my words, any old person could walk in from the street, and no one would stop them."

"It's true," said the majordomo. "You have voiced this opinion many times before."

"And I'll keep saying it until someone does something about it!"

"How about you, Miss...Lovelass?" asked Chase, addressing the maid.

Miss Lovelass looked startled at being addressed, and her cheeks colored prettily. She was around Odelia's age, I would have said, and was a little plump but with a very kind face. She also seemed extremely shy. "M-me?" she stuttered.

"Just tell these detectives what you told me, Heljä," said the cook, adopting a more kindly tone. "About the windows?"

"Y-yes," said the maid. "Well, the windows don't lock very well, sir," she said in deferential tones. "I've noticed it many times. They're old and should probably be replaced."

"Anyone could climb in through those windows is what she's saying," said the cook, taking over. "Just one push and you're in. Locks don't work, wood is rotten, window panes rattling around in there. What this place needs is a renovation. But of course, renovations cost money, and Thad would much prefer to throw another big party than do what needs to be done." She shook her head. "If this keeps up, this whole place will fall down around us one day—you mark my words."

"There is a certain element of neglect," the majordomo agreed with a straight face.

"So what all three of you are saying," said Odelia, recapitulating, "is that security is lax, the castle's windows are broken, and anyone could walk in off the street, and nobody would stop them. Is that a correct representation of your statements?"

"Absolutely," said the cook. "Take last week, for instance. I was going about my business here in the kitchen when all of a sudden, there's this strange noise. I look up, and there's this old guy seated at this here kitchen table, sticking his fork into a nice turkey stroganoff I'd made for the staff! Brazen as can be! Obviously, I chased him out. Turns out he'd joined one of the tour groups and decided to go on a little excursion."

"It has been known to happen," the majordomo murmured.

"Security is lax," the cook stressed. "Criminally lax. So if I were you, I'd talk to the king and get him to fire his head of security and hire a new team. Cause if this goes on, accidents are going to happen—you mark my words."

I had a feeling a lot of the cook's words needed to be marked—possibly all of them—and Odelia and Chase were doing the marking with a lot of attention, judging from the way they were filling up their respective notebooks.

They thanked the three members of staff, gave them their cards in case they remembered anything else, and said they'd convey their remarks to the powers that be and took their leave. We decided to stick around a little, cause you never know if the cook had more words she wanted us to mark.

She seemed extremely satisfied with the words she had already produced, though, and said as much to the others.

"I gave them a piece of my mind, didn't I?" she said, settling back. "Though I very much doubt they'll actually tell Thad. And even if they did, that stubborn old buffer wouldn't do anything about it anyway."

"King Thad is rather stubborn," the majordomo admitted stoically.

"Do you think they'll find the thief?" asked the maid,

looking even more like a scared little mouse than she had before. She was chewing her fingernails and sitting hunched over as if a great weight pressed down on her.

"Oh, that would surprise me," said the cook. "And why Serena would feel the need to hire a bunch of Americans to find a thief is beyond me. As if we don't have perfectly capable people right here in Liechtenburg."

"Maybe they're friends of hers?" the maid suggested.

"Could be," the cook admitted. Then she slammed the thick wooden table with her meaty fist, causing us all to jump. "Wouldn't surprise me if they think one of us did it. Why else talk to us and not any of the others?"

"I'm sure they'll talk to everyone," said the majordomo.

"Why pick on us?" the cook demanded, pretending not to have heard the majordomo's comment. "Because they're still feeling so high and mighty they think they can accuse us of all kinds of stuff and get away with it!"

"Do you think they suspect us?" asked the maid in nervous tones.

"Of course they do! We're their number-one suspects, that's obvious." She rolled up her sleeves, and a sort of angry look came into her eyes. "Oh, just wait until the revolution rolls over these lands, and the gutters are awash with royal blood, the streets littered with their mutilated corpses. I'll be laughing my ass off! When that guillotine chops off Serena's head, I'll be standing first in line, and when her head hits that bucket, I'll spit right on top of it, you mark my words!"

The maid wrinkled up her nose. "You don't really think that way, do you, Tilly?"

"Of course I think that way! The only good royal is a dead royal, and I can't wait for the day they'll all be cut down by the mighty sickle of the worker's revolution!"

The four of us winced a little at these words, and inadvertently I touched my own neck with my paw. The last thing I wanted was for the mighty sickle of the worker's revolution to cut my head off. Then again, I wasn't a royal, so maybe I was safe?

"She's a little unhinged, isn't she, Max?" Dooley whispered as we decided to make ourselves scarce.

"She does seem to harbor a particularly powerful aversion to royals," I agreed.

"Mark my words," said Brutus, "but that woman strikes me as a good candidate for the Tiffany Thief."

"Didn't you hear what she said?" asked Harriet. "She wants to murder royals, not steal from them."

"Maybe she's stealing from them so she can fund the great worker's revolution?" Brutus suggested.

It certainly was a possibility that shouldn't be discarded, I thought. And as we made our way back to safety, I thought we should probably inform Odelia about what we'd overheard after the interview had concluded. Then again, the remarks the cook had made, and also the maid, about the lack of security measures at the castle, were certainly things to look into as well.

All in all, a very instructive interview, albeit a little scary!

CHAPTER 11

*W*hile Chase had a chat with the head of security at the castle about the allegations the cook had made, Odelia decided to step out for a moment to get some fresh air. When she accepted this assignment, she hadn't thought it would be so time-consuming and had secretly hoped she would be able to spend some time with her family. Visiting Vaasu, maybe go hiking in the mountains or even do some skiing. But it now looked as if this case of the Tiffany Thief might take up all of their time. She wasn't even sure she would get a nice story for the paper out of it. After all, who in Hampton Cove would be interested in some kind of cat burglar causing a headache at a kingdom far away?

She looked behind her for a moment, fully expecting Max to be trailing her with his friends, but to her surprise her cats were nowhere to be seen. Maybe they had decided that the case didn't really hold their interest and wanted to take it easy for the next couple of days. She couldn't blame them. The case didn't even hold her own interest all that much, and the only reason she had accepted it was that Opal had been so insistent. That, and the opportunity to spend Christmas at a fairy-tale castle in the heart of Europe. Though with the king on his sickbed, it didn't look as if there would be much of a Christmas atmosphere at the castle at all.

And she had reached a fountain with a statue that looked a lot like the queen when a man approached her. He looked oddly familiar, but it took her a moment to realize that there was a reason for this: she had seen his face in many movies.

"Mr. Chubb," she said, much surprised. It's one thing to know in an abstract sort of way that a famous celebrity is staying at the castle, but another to actually come face to face with the man.

"Just call me Grant," said the actor, who looked exactly like he did in the movies, only perhaps even more appealing in the flesh, if that was possible. At one time he had been famous for his babyface looks, but over the years he had grown into a handsome man and had made quite the career for himself as a character actor who could tackle any part, no matter how challenging. He was taller than she had imagined, and when he smiled, it was as if the world lit up.

"Odelia Kingsley," she said, extending a hand.

He took it and pressed a kiss to it, which almost made her giggle in sheer delight. She had interviewed quite a few celebrities in her time, but had never had the opportunity to sit down with Grant Chubb.

"I've heard Serena brought you in to tackle the Tiffany Thief?" he said with a twinkle in his eye. He seemed to find the whole episode highly entertaining, which perhaps it was.

"And I've heard that you are also one of the victims of this thief?"

"Not me, personally, no. My mom. She had her ring stolen. Or at least one of her rings."

"When was this?"

"Oh... three nights ago? Something like that? She wanted

to report it to the cops, of course, but Serena wouldn't let her. Said they liked to keep things on the down-low for reasons of privacy, which I can totally understand. The moment the media vultures get a whiff of this we'll be tabloid fodder for the next couple of weeks, until the circus moves on." He gave her a dazzling smile, showing off perfect rows of brilliantly white teeth. "Has anyone ever told you that you've got a very engaging smile, Odelia?"

"Well…"

"I'm sorry, it's just that you're very pretty for a private investigator. When Serena announced she had engaged the services of a private dick, naturally I assumed she had hired some unshaven wino in a trench coat with a trilby hat and an attitude problem. Imagine my surprise when you showed up."

"I think you have some very old-fashioned ideas about what constitutes a private detective, Mr. Chubb."

"Grant, please. No one calls me Mr. Chubb, except maybe my bank manager, and the tax man, of course."

"So do you have any idea who could have stolen your mother's ring?"

"No idea whatsoever. She was sound asleep in her room, the ring in her jewelry box as usual, and when she woke up in the morning, it was gone. The whole thing reminds me of that Cary Grant movie. The one with Grace Kelly?"

"*To Catch a Thief.*"

"That's the one. So I'll bet it's some kind of cat burglar doing this stuff, since I can't imagine any of the royals themselves robbing their guests." He suddenly took her hand in his. "Do you know I'm very good at palm reading? I picked it up when doing research for a movie." He traced the long line of her palm. "Long life line, which is good. See this line here? That means you've got a pleasant, kindhearted demeanor, which I don't need to tell you, obviously."

"Grant!" Suddenly a voice sounded behind them.

The movie star looked up as if caught with his hand in the cookie jar and immediately let go of Odelia's hand. "Mom," he said. "This is Odelia Kingsley. She's here to look into the theft of your ring?"

The woman who had arrived was a full head shorter than her son and had a sort of squarish face that now spelled storm. She was dressed in a pink padded jacket with a bright yellow cap protecting her head from the cold. She now turned to Odelia. "And? Have you found my ring yet?"

"Not yet," Odelia confessed. "But we're working on it."

"Mom, Odelia just got here. You can't expect her to get results this quick," said her son.

"Grant, I've forgotten my gloves in my room," said the woman in measured tones. "Can you get them for me?"

Grant sighed but did as he was told. They watched him stomping off towards the castle.

"You better have no designs on my son," said his mother, immediately getting down to business. "He's the best son a mother could ever hope to have, but I'm not blind to his many faults, one of which is that he has a habit of chasing anything in a skirt."

Even though she wasn't wearing a skirt at that moment, Odelia got the message. "My interest in your son is of a purely practical nature," she assured the woman. "As a possible witness to a crime. I'm a happily married woman, Mrs. Chubb, and the mother of a daughter I adore, so you don't have to worry about me."

The woman visibly relaxed. "Oh, God," she said. "You probably think I'm some kind of ogre. But the thing is that Grant is very popular with the ladies. He practically has to fight them off with a stick. And in the past he has been burned on more than one occasion, which is when I decided to keep a closer eye on him."

"I take it he's not married?"

"Hasn't found the one yet," said his mother. "Oh, and the name is Jo." She stuck out a hand and shook Odelia's with some vigor. "Apologies for my rudeness."

"That's all right. I can imagine it's not easy being as famous as your son is."

"Oh, it's quite a challenge, I won't lie," said Jo with a smile. "And it's not as if he can help it, the poor boy. His dad was just like him. Always chasing skirts and turning heads wherever he went."

"His father didn't join you here?"

"He passed away, and since we didn't have more kids, now it's just me and Grant. He looks after me, and I look after him, and that's the way it's been for years."

"So about that ring of yours."

"I don't know what Grant told you, but I'm fine with it, really. It wasn't even all that valuable, and it certainly wasn't a big heirloom or something, or held any sentimental value to me. So if it's not found, it's no big deal. Though from what I've heard, Serena suffered a much greater loss?"

"She did. The brooch that was stolen used to belong to her grandmother, so it's quite a big loss for her. Which is why my husband and I have been talking to members of the staff, trying to get to the bottom of this unfortunate business."

"I can see that you're obviously a very clever young lady," said Jo as she patted her arm. "So I know you'll figure it out. You and that husband of yours. Is it true that he's a cop?"

"He is. Chase works as a detective back home."

"And where is home for you, Odelia?"

"Hampton Cove, in the Hamptons."

"Oh, fancy."

"Not really. I guess we're a part of the Hamptons that the tourists haven't discovered yet. Or not as much."

"Good for you. We live in the Hollywood Hills, and I can tell you it's not always as fun as you'd think. We do get our fair share of problems up there."

"You live with your son?"

"I do, yeah." She gave her a wink. "Someone needs to keep an eye on that boy, and who better to do it than the person who loves him the most? Like they say, a boy's best friend is his mother."

CHAPTER 12

One of the main disadvantages of living in a castle is the distances you have to travel to get anywhere. That, and the maze of corridors and rooms. So it was no surprise that after we decided to linger in the kitchen after Odelia and Chase's departure, we couldn't find them anymore, and so we ended up wandering the hallways in search of a familiar face or place. Which is how we found ourselves on unfamiliar terrain but on the trail of a very familiar scent: that of a clowder of cats!

"We're close," Harriet announced as she stuck her nose in the air. "Very close!"

A certain sense of excitement had gripped her since she had been very anxious to meet the famous royal mousers ever since mention of these very special cats had been made. And since we were now on the trail, we decided to follow through and make their acquaintance.

We had arrived at a part of the castle we hadn't seen before, which wasn't difficult since we hadn't yet explored the entire castle yet, having only arrived in the country that morning.

"This must be where the king's brother lives," said Brutus as we came to a halt in front of a locked door, behind which Harriet was convinced the royal mousers resided. "He's the one in charge of these mousers, right?"

"That's correct," said Harriet with unveiled curiosity as she tried to stare a hole in that door.

"I feel bad for the mice," said Dooley. "It can't be a lot of fun to have to live in the company of a pair of mousers."

"The whole idea of a mouser is to keep out the mice," I pointed out.

"Yeah, if those mice know what's good for them, they'll find some other home to infest," said Harriet with barely concealed disdain. Once upon a time, a family of mice had humiliated her by locking her up in the basement of her own home. The experience had made her feel less than friendly toward the entire species.

The door suddenly swung open, and a liveried servant appeared, carrying a tray. And since we saw our opportunity, we decided to take it and slipped through the door and into the room on the other side. Which is when we discovered that it wasn't a room as such but an entire suite of rooms, just like the queen's quarters.

"This castle consists of a series of houses that are all connected," said Dooley, describing the phenomenon well. "Just when you think you've seen it all, there's another part of the castle that opens up and is full of surprises."

This particular segment was certainly surprising to us, in the sense that it seemed to be entirely devoted to cats. The room we were in was the entrance hall, but even here there was a lot of artwork adorning the walls devoted to the feline species: busts of cats, paintings of cats, wallpaper with little cats, even the carpet on the floor depicted a group of cats looking quite regal indeed.

"I think we're on the right track, you guys," Harriet whispered. "We're in the presence of the royal mousers!"

"I think you're right," said Dooley. "I don't see a single mouse."

Mice would probably think twice about trespassing here, that was for sure. We moved along and soon found ourselves in what I assumed was the living room, since I detected quite a few couches—no less than half a dozen, in fact. A woman was meticulously vacuuming the couches, presumably getting rid of all the cat hair and cursing a lot as she did. Another cleaner was busy cleaning the windows, against which I saw several climbing contraptions that cats can use to pretend they're in a forest climbing a tree.

"No cats!" said Harriet with a frown.

"Yeah, where are all the cats?" asked Brutus.

"It's the vacuum cleaner," I said, having to shout to make myself heard over the noise. "If these royal cats are anything like us, they hate vacuum cleaners."

We decided to move along and go in search of the kitchen. If this section of the castle was home to the royal mousers, the best place to find them was where the food was. And it didn't take us long to ascertain that we were right on the money.

The kitchen was located on what I assumed was the perimeter of the king's brother's quarters, and contrary to the rest of the place, it was of quite modest proportions. Then again, when you have an actual private cook who makes sure you're well fed, there's no need for a kitchen. So this kitchen was probably added for when Asko Skingle was feeling peckish or when he wanted to feed his cats.

When we arrived in the kitchen, for a moment all activity halted, almost as if we had stepped into an Old West saloon. I counted no less than a dozen cats of different sizes and descriptions, and as we sized them up, they obviously sized us up as well. They had been in the process of having a bite to eat, and at the center of all this activity a man stood ladling food from a can into a bowl. It took him a moment to catch on, but when all the cats turned to face us, finally he did too.

"Now where did you come from all of a sudden!" he exclaimed, his face morphing into an expression of pure delight.

"You belong to those detectives, don't you?" asked one of the cats. This was a phenomenally handsome specimen—a Persian, of course. "The ones that are looking for the queen's brooch?"

News obviously traveled fast at Vaasu Castle, and since there was no sense denying it, I nodded. "That's right. We've been charged by Queen Serena to find her brooch, as well as the rest of the items that were stolen by the Tiffany Thief."

"Did you walk in off the street?" asked Asko Skingle as he approached, still clutching the spoon and the can of food. He walked with a slight stoop and wasn't dressed as one would expect a royal to be. Instead of some fine and expensive threads, he wore a simple pair of jeans that had seen better days, and a fleece sweater that looked old and ratty. Even his hair looked as if he hadn't washed it in days, and he sported a thick dusting of stubble on his jowly face. All in all, he had all the hallmarks of a bum.

"They're guests of your brother, Asko," said the Persian. And for a moment, I wondered if this man spoke our language. But his next words confirmed that he didn't.

"Walk in off the street, did you? Well, you certainly picked the right place," said the man as he took another bowl from one of the cabinets and placed it on the floor in front of us. "You're welcome to stay as long as you want." He eyed Harriet with pleasure. "My, my, aren't you a pretty one? Almost as pretty as my Anne."

"I'm Anne," said the Persian curtly. "And I can't believe Asko would compare me to you." She gave Harriet a nasty look of pure disdain.

Under normal circumstances, Harriet would have taken offense to this, but we were far away from home, and also, this whole royal mouser business intrigued her. So she swallowed her pride and said, "Is it true that you're the kingdom's official mouser?"

Anne scoffed lightly. "Oh, please. Who told you that?"

"Oh, don't be rude, Anne," said a second cat. This one was smaller and gray. She smiled. "I'm Julie. What are your names?"

"Max," I said. "And these are my friends Dooley, Harriet, and Brutus."

"Nice to make your acquaintance," said Julie. She was more soft-spoken than her fellow mouser and a lot friendlier.

"How does one become a royal mouser?" asked Harriet.

"Don't answer that," Anne snapped.

"Dig in," said Prince Asko encouragingly. "It's good stuff. I get it from Switzerland. Drive over there myself once a month to get it. Best stuff in the world. Healthy, too."

"Don't eat it!" Anne snarled. "That's ours!"

"Oh, but Anne, we have to learn how to share," said Julie.

"Yeah, Anne," said one of the other cats. "Sharing is caring."

More of the troupe insisted that Anne was being entirely too selfish, with one of them even calling Anne unwelcoming and nasty. And so finally, she gave in.

"Fine. You can have a taste. But don't you dare fill your tummies! You've got your own humans for that."

"Go on," said Prince Asko encouragingly. "Lots more where this came from."

And so we decided to take a nibble. And I have to admit it

was some pretty tasty grub. Not as good as the stuff we get at home, of course, but still really good. Before long, the only sounds that could be heard were over a dozen cats enjoying their meals, with Asko looking on like a proud father.

There are probably worse ways to spend your day.

CHAPTER 13

*C*hase had just finished talking to a woman who said she was the queen's dresser when he received an intriguing message on his phone. He frowned at the message.

'I have some very important information for you regarding the Tiffany Thief. Meet me in the car park (it's in the basement).'

Odelia hadn't returned from her stroll, so he had a snap decision to make: wait for her to return and risk that this person would have left by then, or go and meet the mystery informant alone. He glanced out of the window and saw that his wife stood chatting with a dumpy middle-aged lady dressed in a pink down jacket.

"Okay, let's do this," he told himself and wondered who this mystery person could be. But if they had vital information for him pertaining to the case, he shouldn't postpone but meet them posthaste.

It took him a while to get to the car park, but after receiving directions from several people who were all most helpful, he finally took the elevator down and stepped out into what looked like a typical concrete underground space where several cars stood parked. Since several hundred people worked at the castle, it stood to reason they'd have to park their cars somewhere, and this was it. He glanced around for a sign of his mystery contact, but when he couldn't find him, typed a message.

'I'm here. Where are you?'

'B-52,' the prompt reply came.

The concrete columns did indeed carry numbers, which is how he discovered he was on the A level. This time using the stairs, it didn't take him long to find this 'B-52' his contact referred to, and saw that it was located in the far corner of the car park. It was a little darker there, and a lot more spooky, and for a moment, he wished he had been allowed to bring his gun into the country. Still, he couldn't imagine that this person would have set a trap for him.

"Psst!"

He wheeled around, and soon located the source of the sound. "What do you want?" he asked, keeping a safe distance.

"I've got some information for you!" a loud whisper came.

And now he saw it: a person dressed in a trench coat stood half concealed behind one of the thick concrete columns, and if he wasn't mistaken, it was the majordomo.

"Oskari? Is that you?" he asked.

"No," said the person after a pause. "It is I. Deep Throat."

Chase had to suppress a light chuckle. Deep Throat, right. "Okay, what is it you wanted to tell me?"

"I will now reveal the identity of the Tiffany Thief to you, Detective Kingsley."

"Great. Who is it?"

"Grant Chubb."

"The actor?"

"That's right."

"But why?"

"He's a star, Detective Kingsley. And we all know that stars are fickle. Fickle and thrill-seekers at heart. So Grant is bored, and he decided to have a little fun at our expense. So he becomes a cat burglar and steals. Just a fun game for him. Something to occupy his time. While away the long evenings."

"Do you have any evidence to back up your accusations?"

"I don't need any evidence, detective. It's all about the psychology of the individual. And in this case, I have studied this particular individual intensively and have come to the conclusion that he is the Tiffany Thief. Search his room, and you will find the loot, as you Americans like to call it."

"Okay," said Chase, who had to admit there was a certain logic behind the majordomo's words. "The problem is that I can't just go around searching people's rooms. I'm not a cop. Well, I am, but I have no jurisdiction here."

"Then I will do it," said Oskari.

"Please don't. It will only lead to trouble."

"Fine. I will not search his room. But I will keep a close eye on the man. And if he strikes again, I will catch him."

"Please don't catch him. If he really is the thief, he might be dangerous."

"So what do you want me to do, Detective Kingsley? I can't let him rob more people."

"Just send me a message, and I'll catch him in the act, all right? But please don't go around playing the hero. It never ends well. Can you promise me that?"

No response followed.

"Deep Throat?"

But when he stepped forward, he saw that the majordomo had vanished into thin air.

"Huh," he said as he scratched his head.

It was a pensive Chase who returned from the car park. And so when he almost bumped into Odelia, the latter asked if he had seen a ghost.

"Not a ghost, no." And he told her all about his strange encounter with the majordomo.

"Are you sure it was him?"

"Oh, absolutely. He probably thought I couldn't see him, concealed as he was behind that column. But I could see him fine enough. It was definitely him."

"I talked to Grant just now," said Odelia as they walked along the downstairs hallway back to the main entrance hall. A series of windows offered a stunning view of the terrain that stretched out as far as the eye could see. "He didn't strike me as a thief. And besides, why would he need to steal anything? He's probably one of the richest actors on the planet."

"Oskari claims he does it for the kicks. Because he's bored. And he may have a point. A lot of these guys probably love a challenge. And what better challenge than to rob your own host of their valuable jewelry?"

"He did make a reference to that old Cary Grant movie," said Odelia with a pensive frown. "*To Catch a Thief*?"

"I remember. Cary Grant plays a retired cat burglar when all of a sudden a string of break-ins that have all the hallmarks of his previous career puts him in hot water, making the police suspect he may have decided to come out of retirement and pick up his old trade again."

"Oskari wouldn't go around accusing the guests of his employers," Odelia argued. "If he thinks Grant is the Tiffany Thief, maybe it's true?"

"We'll find out soon enough," said Chase. "He said he's going to keep an eye on the man. And if he makes a move, he'll send me a message so we can catch him in the act."

"I hope he's wrong. I kinda like his movies."

"Me too. But stranger things have happened, babe."

"Unless of course Oskari himself is the Tiffany Thief, and he's trying to throw us off the scent."

"My thoughts exactly."

CHAPTER 14

That evening dinner was being served in the main dining room, indicating there were others, which didn't surprise me. It was a pretty grand affair, with a lot of people present, a lot of servers making sure that things ran smoothly, and the four of us relegated to the sidelines as it wouldn't do for a couple of cats to sit in with the guests.

Queen Serena was there, of course, and also her sons Dane and Urpo, their respective wives Impi and Kami, and Dane and Impi's daughters Ainikki and Hely. Next to Serena, her friend Tiia had taken a seat, and also Tiia's son Eloy, and guests Grant Chubb and the actor's mother Jo. And then finally the King's brother Asko had decided to put in an appearance, and for the occasion had dressed up, ditching his threadbare threads and putting on a nice suit.

"He dresses up really well," said Harriet as she regarded Asko with affection. Anyone who feeds us well gains our everlasting respect and admiration—or at least until our next meal.

"Yeah, he does," I agreed.

"Where is the king?" asked Brutus.

"Still too sick, I guess," I said.

Ariana, who had joined us, also looked on. "The king hasn't joined these family dinners for the last three weeks," she informed us. "Ever since he fell ill."

"We overheard Prince Dane discuss his father's illness with the prime minister," I said. "And he seemed to think it won't be much longer now before he dies."

"I hope not," said Ariana. "Thad may not be a nice man, but neither is Dane. In fact, he may be even worse than his father, if that's possible."

"In what sense?" I asked.

"Well, he's very mean to his wife, for one thing," said Ariana. "So in that sense he takes after his dad. I overheard them arguing only last night—one of their epic fights."

"What about?" asked Harriet.

"Dane is very upset that Impi hasn't been able to give him a male heir," said Ariana. "And he personally blames her for that. He wants her to have another baby, but she feels she's past the age where it's safe to become pregnant again. After she had Hely, she was sick for a long time. That pregnancy hit her really hard, with the doctors even telling her that if she got pregnant again, she might not survive. But that hasn't stopped Dane from putting a lot of pressure on her to try again—he must have a son."

"The man is a monster," Harriet determined, and so we told Ariana all about what we had overheard.

"So he would divorce Impi just because she can't give him a male successor? The man is even worse than I thought."

"What about Urpo?" I asked. "Doesn't he have kids?"

"No, he doesn't. But then he only married last year, so they may have decided to wait."

"If Urpo has a male child, will he be eligible to succeed his father on the throne?"

"I'm not sure," said Ariana. "Maybe? It's a complicated business. He is very popular."

"Who, Urpo?" asked Brutus.

"Yeah, a lot more popular than his brother."

"He's more handsome, too," said Harriet.

We studied the two brothers, and I could see why Harriet would say that. Dane gave the impression that at one point a stick had been firmly inserted in his behind, while Urpo seemed kinder and more fun to be around. He laughed easily and appeared to be a warmer person.

"Both princes are pretty popular," Ariana said. "Because they both married commoners, which makes the population feel they're just like them, you know. But for some reason, Urpo's wife is the most popular of the entire royal family."

"That would be the former teacher?" I said.

"That's right. She's an absolute sweetheart."

"So have you found our thief yet, Detective Kingsley?" asked Urpo now.

Chase shook his head. "Not yet, Your Highness. Though we are following some promising leads."

"Is that right? And what are they, can you tell us?"

"Now darling, you can't expect the detective to give away the game," said his wife as she gently chided him. A server poured her more wine, and she took a sip. "Is it true that he broke a window to enter the castle?" She had directed this question at Odelia.

"I couldn't possibly say," said our human.

"Oskari assures me that no windows have been broken," said Serena. "Isn't that correct, Oskari?"

She had to repeat her question, for the majordomo had been intently studying the back of Grant Chubb's head, and only looked up now. "Mh? Oh, absolutely, Your Majesty. We've checked all the windows and none of them appear to have been broken anywhere."

"He doesn't have to break a window to get in," said Dane grumpily. "The locks on most of those windows are broken as it is. A simple push and he's in."

"Dane is right," said Impi. "In our rooms, the wood on two windows is so rotten that you can practically feel the draft. Which can't be good for your heating bill, Serena."

"Or your ecological footprint," said Impi's daughter Ainikki, earning herself a smile from her mom.

"What this place needs is a complete overhaul," said Dane. "Top architect, top project manager, designers, the works."

"That will cost millions," said his mother. "And you know your father won't allow it. The last thing we need right now is an expensive renovation that will knock the bottom out of the treasury."

"We shouldn't have to pay for it," said Dane. "The taxpayer should. Vaasu Castle is, after all, the most important landmark Liechtenburg has. What good would it do if it crumbles into a pile of rubble? No, we should really work with Efrain's government and get things moving in that department. And I think it's possible."

Urpo studied his brother with a half-smile on his face. "You and Efrain seem to get along really well."

"Only to be expected," said Dane as he pronged a piece of rosti and popped it into his mouth.

"Dad isn't dead yet, brother," said Urpo, an expression of anger suddenly flashing across his face.

"I didn't say he was," said Dane with a shrug. "Just that we need to be proactive, and building a good working relationship with the ruling party's leader is important. Not just for us but for the whole country."

"Oh, please," said Urpo, rolling his eyes. "Don't pretend you're cozying up to Efrain for the good of the country. You're only doing this for yourself."

"What gave you that silly idea?"

"You can't wait for Dad to die, can you?"

"Boys, boys," said Serena. "Let's keep it civilized, shall we? We have guests." She shot a warning look at Urpo, who glanced over to the Pooles, who were all listening intently, and quickly simmered down. Serena's implication was clear: don't wash your dirty linen in public.

"I, for one, think Vaasu Castle is absolutely wonderful," said Gran. "It's so big and so beautiful. And the view!"

"Yeah, the view is amazing," Marge agreed.

"At least we don't have to pay millions to renovate the view," said Dane with a grin.

"I took a walk to the stables today," said Marge. "And you have so many amazing horses, Your Majesty."

"We're very fortunate in that regard," said Serena. "Though I can't take any of the credit. The horses are entirely my husband's domain."

"And mine," said Ainikki quietly. Like the majordomo, she hadn't been able to keep her eyes off Grant Chubb, though presumably for entirely different reasons. Odelia had told us about Chase's meeting with Oskari, and it was clear that the man took his mission to watch the actor like a hawk very seriously indeed. So much so that Grant, who had caught the man's eye a couple of times now, was starting to shuffle a little uneasily in his chair.

"What has Gran been up to?" asked Brutus now.

"She went for a long walk," said Harriet. "I think she misses Hampton Cove, and Scarlett most of all."

There had been talk about inviting Scarlett along for this trip, but Queen Serena had vetoed it, which was probably understandable. All she had wanted was Odelia and Chase, and she had received Odelia's mom, dad, and grandma as part of the bargain. So to invite even more people to the party was where she had put her foot down.

"She's probably jet-lagged," Dooley said, and he was probably right. Even I was feeling the strain from crossing different time zones, and I was looking forward to a nice long uninterrupted nap.

"Those cats over there," said the king's brother. "Are they yours?"

"Yes, they are," said Odelia. "Well, mine and my mom and grandmom."

"They're gorgeous, aren't they?" said Prince Asko. "They paid me a visit, you know. I thought they had wandered in from the street, but then I remembered Serena mentioning something about a family coming to visit and bringing their cats along with them. So I figured they must be yours." He pointed to Harriet. "That one looks just like my Anne. Is she also an excellent mouser?"

Odelia suppressed a smile at this. "Um… not exactly."

"Asko's cats catch every mouse that happens to wander in," said Serena. "It's almost uncanny."

"They're vicious killers," said Hely, Dane and Impi's youngest daughter. "And I hate them!"

"Darling, you shouldn't say that," said her mother. "Mice are not welcome here, and you know that."

"Well, they should be," the girl said stubbornly. "Mice are nice. They're cute and cuddly, and I love them."

Her mother gave Odelia a look of apology. "They organized a play at her school last month," she explained. "And Hely got to play one of the mice. And since then she's crazy about mice and has been bugging us to adopt one."

"Please don't adopt a mouse," said Asko. "Get one mouse today and find a thousand crawling all over your kitchen tomorrow, eating all of your food and making a mess. And besides, if Anne or Julie find a mouse, they will catch it, and they will… get rid of it."

"How will they get rid of it?" asked Hely.

"Well… they'll put it outside, of course," said Asko.

"They'll pick it up ever so gently between their teeth, and then they will carry it out and leave it there."

"But… Won't the poor mousies be cold outside?"

"Of course not," the king's brother assured the little girl. "They'll move into the stables and be nice and warm in there."

The girl seemed appeased by this. "I still want a mouse," she said. "Daddy, can I have a mouse?"

"Not now, Hely," said her dad, who was checking his phone.

"But when!"

"Maybe after Christmas," said her mom, shooting her husband an angry look.

"I gotta take this," the prince murmured, and got up from the table, his phone pressed to his ear. "Yes, Efrain?"

"Always busy busy busy," Urpo said, earning himself another warning look from his mother, the queen.

"Okay, so what is your problem?!" suddenly Grant exclaimed, throwing down his napkin and facing the major-domo. He turned to Serena. "This guy," he said, jerking his thumb at Oskari, "has been breathing down my neck all through dinner!"

Oskari, standing stiff as a board, directed his gaze at the ceiling and announced, "Merely making sure that everything is to your satisfaction, sir."

"Well, it's not," Grant said. "Sir."

"My apologies," said Oskari.

"You really shouldn't shout at the help, Grant," said his mother as she lightly slapped her son's arm. "He's only doing his job. Making sure your wine is topped up and all of your rostis in a row. So pipe down already, will you?"

"I'm sorry," Grant said. He turned to Oskari. "I'm sorry, all right? We good?" He held up his fist.

Oskari stared at the fist. "Sir?"

"Just hit me, buddy."

"Hit you, sir?"

"Don't leave me hanging, bro. Hit me!"

"Fist bump him, Oskari," Eloy said with a smile. The stablehand had also cleaned up pretty well, though of course, he wasn't actually a stablehand but the queen's best friend's grandson. "Just bump your fist against Grant's."

With reluctance and a face that revealed his extreme unease, the majordomo touched his fist against the actor's, who gave him a pat on the back for his trouble, causing the faithful servitor to retreat whilst shaking his head at such a display of folly. At least he would be out of the actor's hair for a while.

Which is why we were all surprised when ten seconds later he returned, head held high, and loudly announced, "Miko Kurikka, Rena Kurikka, and Buffy Kurikka, Your Majesty."

He stepped aside, and indeed, three more people were ushered into the dining room. Oddly enough, Miko Kurikka, whoever he was, shared a remarkable resemblance to both Prince Dane and Prince Urpo. But before we could ascertain who these newcomers were, there was a commotion at the head of the table.

Queen Serena had fainted.

CHAPTER 15

$\mathcal{W}$ith the assistance of Tex, Serena had been revived and had retreated to her quarters with her good friend Tiia. The new arrival, Miko Kurikka, whoever he was, had left the scene, accompanied by the princes Dane and Urpo, and they were now ensconced in a room nearby. Judging from their raised voices, a sort of argument had broken out, and clearly the meeting didn't proceed along lines of cordiality and hospitality.

For a moment, an air of awkwardness reigned in the dining room, but then one of the new arrivals decided to break the ice by introducing herself. "I'm Miko's mom," she said in kindly tones. It was a little hard to determine her exact age, as her skin had the consistency of leather and had taken on an orange hue, possibly due to a prolonged and ill-advised exposure to the sun. "And this is my daughter-in-law Rena."

Rena resembled her mother-in-law to some extent. Rail-thin, just like Buffy, with the same skin tone, but a more supple type of leather. Less tanned.

Taking Buffy's cue, the other remaining inhabitants of the

dining room introduced themselves, and before long, conversation was flowing pleasantly, with Buffy proving to be quite the conversationalist.

"I couldn't stay away, you see," she explained. "When I heard how poorly Thaddy was, I simply had to be near him. Serena may have banned me from the kingdom, but I never stopped loving my sweet teddy bear."

"You and Thad... were an item?" asked Marge.

The older lady cast down her eyes in a coy look and flashed her lashes. "We were, yeah. Quite inseparable. Until Serena decided to put an end to things."

"Oh, so Thad was already married at the time?"

She pouted. "He wasn't happy in his marriage, the poor thing. That was the tragedy and what struck me the most. He always said the only time he was truly happy was when he was with me in my little room above the Fuzzy Peach."

"The Fuzzy Peach?" asked Odelia.

"The club where I used to work."

"Was this..." Gran cast a quick look to Ainikki and Hely, then lowered her voice. "An exotic club?"

Buffy smiled. "You could say that. Or you could say that I'm an *artiste*, and that's what attracted Thaddy to me."

"What is an exotic club, Mom?" asked Hely.

"It's a club where the atmosphere is... exotic," said her mother with a touch of helplessness.

"You mean like with palm trees and such?"

"Absolutely," said Impi. "Lots and lots of palm trees." She seemed to wonder if it was at all advisable to keep her daughters present for this conversation or to send them up to their rooms, but in the end decided to let them stay. After all, I think we could all sense that something momentous was taking place—something that would affect the future of the House of Skingle, for better or for worse.

"So what you're saying is that you're a stripper," said

Grant, not beating about the bush.

Buffy bridled a little, Impi and Kami directed irate glances at the actor, and Hely turned to her mom to ask her what a stripper was. But before she could explain, Buffy's daughter-in-law intervened. "Buffy is an artist, Mr. Chubb. A great artist in the tradition of Mata Hari and Josephine Baker. And you'd do well to show some respect to the mother of the future king of Liechtenburg."

There were gasps of shock around the table, and it wasn't hard to see why.

"Your son is…" Marge said.

Buffy nodded modestly. "That's right. Miko is Thaddy's son, and the only rightful heir to the throne. As the eldest, he's first in line, you see."

"But surely that's impossible," said Impi, and I could see why she would be upset. If this Miko was Thad's firstborn son, Impi's husband Dane would be cut from the roster, and Impi could kiss her chance of becoming queen goodbye.

"Not only is it possible, it's the way it is," said Buffy with a shrug. "Not that Miko is all that eager to become the new king, you know. He's a very successful businessman in his own right. But like his father, he's blessed with a strong sense of duty. And if his country calls upon him to take his responsibility, he can't say no."

"But…" Impi looked around the table for support. "But that's… I mean, your son was born out of wedlock."

"So? That doesn't make him any less of an heir. And it's not as if dear Thaddy hasn't recognized my boy's rights. Even after Serena kicked us out of the country, Thaddy still kept supporting us and sending us money. At least until Miko was of age, at which point it was no longer necessary, and he made a remarkable career."

"Miko is so clever," Rena gushed. "So very clever."

"What does he do, your son?" asked Marge.

"He sells yachts," said Buffy proudly. "In Hong Kong, which is where we live. Thaddy even came to visit us a couple of times, so Miko would have a bond with his daddy. I doubt whether he told Serena, though," she added with a smirk.

Impi and Kami shared a look, and it was obvious that this whole business with the illegitimate child of the king had hit them out of left field. "We had no idea," Kami revealed.

"Of course you hadn't," said Buffy. "And that's because Serena forbade Thaddy from ever mentioning me or our affair ever again. Persona non grata, that's what she called me." There was a lot of bitterness behind these words, I saw, but also a sense of triumph that she had burst onto the scene once more, to take up her rightful place at the heart of the king's court.

For a moment, no one spoke, then suddenly the king's brother rose. "It's all a load of nonsense!" he vociferated with a gesture of disgust. And then he stalked off and left the room, presumably to return to his beloved cats. And I had to commend him for this. It is true that cats never cause as much trouble as humans seem to do. Faithful companions is what we are, definitely averse to a lot of this type of drama.

"So why did you come back now?" asked Jo Chubb. "If Serena expelled you years ago, why return now?"

"Because I was invited!" said Buffy.

"You were invited?" asked Impi. "By who?"

"Why, Thaddy, of course. When I found out how ill he was, and that he might not survive, I sent him a letter suggesting he see his son one last time before he died. He immediately sent me a message on my phone. Said there was foul play at work here at the castle, and he could use a friend. Said he was being poisoned!"

"Poisoned?" asked Impi.

"Absolutely," said Buffy. "And by his own family, no less!"

CHAPTER 16

After the stunning events at the dinner table, I think we all needed some time for reflection and repose. So, after Buffy Kurikka had delivered her shocking remarks, the company had decided to part ways, and everyone had returned to their respective rooms. Dooley and I decided to spend the night curled up at the foot of Odelia and Chase's bed, with Harriet and Brutus deciding to do the same but in Marge and Tex's room. Gran, meanwhile, had gone for a midnight stroll of the grounds—possibly to contemplate a past that was notoriously devoid of affairs with kings of any description. But then Gran has never been an exotic dancer like Buffy, of course. A gaping hole in her resume, I would have said.

"Poor girls," said Odelia as she turned down the bed.

"You mean Prince Dane's daughters?" asked Chase.

"Yeah. All their lives they were told that their daddy one day would be king, and now all of a sudden here arrives this interloper, and he will be the new king. It's a nasty trick Thad has played on his family."

"I don't think Miko will be the new king. Unless I've

missed something, there are probably laws about this kind of thing, and sons born out of wedlock are excluded from the line of succession. Otherwise, every two-timing king would have a serious problem to contend with, and I'm guessing there are a lot of those."

"I guess," said Odelia, but she didn't seem convinced. And as she slipped between the covers, the frown on her face told me this problem was seriously vexing her. Perhaps even more than the Tiffany Thief. "My dad says the king is suffering from some mystery illness—at least according to the Physician to the King. Though now it seems that Dad is the Physician to the King, so I don't know."

Chase laughed. "Tex is Physician to the King? When did that happen?"

"Oh, sometime today. The king said he wasn't happy with the old physician, and he believes an American doctor is better equipped to deal with the kind of illness he's been contending with."

"But he believes he's being poisoned by his own family, right?"

"Yeah, that seems to be the gist of the thing. He's not sure who's trying to poison him—either his wife or his sons—but he is convinced they're trying to kill him. Dad discussed things with the King's doctor, and he says that he fell ill about three weeks ago. Suddenly felt very weak and couldn't stand on his legs. He advised him to go to the hospital, but the king refused. Says he doesn't trust hospitals as he will be even more vulnerable to attack there."

"Sounds to me as if the guy is a crackpot."

"He is... eccentric," Odelia agreed.

"But did they test his blood?"

"They did."

"And?"

"No poison was found. The doctor thinks he's simply

suffering from extreme fatigue, brought on by bad dietary habits and a penchant for alcohol. He's put him on a very strict no-alcohol and low-fat diet, but the king has decided to throw caution to the wind and continues to live life on his own terms, as he calls it."

"He probably thinks that because he's the king he can cheat death," said Chase. "But at the end of the day, he's just a guy, and not a very healthy one, apparently."

"Poor Serena. As if she hasn't suffered enough, now she has to contend with her husband's mistress and his illegitimate son."

"She'll deal. After all, she has been living with this dude for thirty years or however long they've been married, so she probably knows how to handle the guy."

"Is Tex going to live here at the castle from now on, Max?" asked Dooley.

"I doubt it, buddy," I said.

"But he's the official Physician to the King now."

"I'm sure it's just a temporary posting. Once the king is feeling a little better, he'll thank Tex for his services, and we can all go home."

"Or maybe the king will die, and then Tex will be sentenced to death for gross negligence."

I shivered. Dooley could have a point. In the States, if a doctor is negligent to a patient, he has to pay a fine. But here in Liechtenburg, they'd probably lock him up in the deepest dungeon or the highest tower and then chop his head off.

"All we have to do is catch this Tiffany Thief, Dooley," I said, determined not to lose focus, what with everything that was going on. "That's our brief, and we should stick with it."

Next to Odelia and Chase, Grace had also turned in for the night in her own cot, but if we thought she had gone to sleep, we were mistaken. Even as I was starting to doze off, I could see her head appear over the parapet, so to speak, and eye me with interest.

"Maybe we could stay here forever, Max," she suggested.

"And why would we do that?" I said, yawning a little.

"Why not? We're in a royal castle, living our best lives. And you said yourself that the food this Prince Asko gave you is the best food you've ever tasted. So why not stick around a little longer? Or even indefinitely? I could go to school here, Mom could become a lady-in-waiting, Dad could take over security duties, Grandpa will be Physician to the King, and we will all live happily ever after!"

"What is a lady-in-waiting?" asked Dooley.

"I guess she's a lady... who waits for something?" I suggested.

Grace laughed. "Silly Max. A lady-in-waiting is a woman who takes care of a queen or princess. It's a very high position and very rewarding because you spend all of your time taking care of Queen Serena."

"Pretty soon this lady-in-waiting won't take care of Serena but of Buffy," said Dooley.

"Well, not exactly," said Grace, who had obviously given this whole royalty business some thought. "If Prince Miko becomes the new king, his wife Rena will become the new queen, and so the lady-in-waiting will be waiting on her."

"What about Buffy?" asked Dooley. "Will she become a queen, too?"

"Not likely," said Grace, our resident royal expert. "She'll probably get some title, but not that of queen or even queen mother."

"Why not?" asked Dooley. "She will be the mother of the queen, right?"

"No, she will be the mother of the king, but not the queen mother. The title only goes to a mother of a monarch if she has been a queen consort herself."

"Huh," said Dooley, clearly not following.

As for myself, I had lost the thread of the conversation a long time ago. All this royal stuff sounded very complicated to me, and not even all that interesting. But Grace lapped it all up, clearly excited to be living at the castle at this time of great upheaval.

"Though I very much doubt that Miko will be the new king," she said, endorsing the view her dad took. "He's not the official heir. And unless they change a few laws, he never will be."

"Oh, phew," I said and closed my eyes.

"On the other hand, if the king really wants him to succeed him, he might find a way."

"Is that a fact?" I said, yawning widely to indicate it was time for beddy-bye.

"And if the king believes that his wife and sons are trying to murder him, he might cut them all out of the line of succession and make Miko his one and only heir."

"Queen Buffy," said Dooley. "It does have a nice ring to it."

"Oh, Dooley," said Grace with an eye roll. "Haven't you listened to a single word I've said?"

CHAPTER 17

*C*ats are light sleepers, and so when a sudden noise sounded in the middle of the night, it only took me a fraction of a second to be wide awake. I glanced around the room in search of the source of the sound, and then I saw it: a dark figure was rooting through the suitcase that Odelia and Chase had left unpacked.

"Dooley," I whispered. "Are you awake?"

Of course he was. "It's the Tiffany Thief, Max!"

But before we could wake up our humans, the thief must have become aware that he was being observed, for all of a sudden, he froze, glancing in our direction. Cat's eyes have a habit of glowing in the dark, at least if there is some light source available, and when confronted with this eerie phenomenon, the thief uttered a soft cry of alarm and hurried off in the direction of the living room.

"Let's catch him!" I said and jumped down from the bed.

Dooley followed my lead, and moments later, we were streaking across the room in pursuit of the nocturnal marauder. The odd thing was that the moment we arrived in the next room, of the thief, there was no trace! I cast a glance at the window but couldn't see him. He wasn't at the door either, and try as I might, I couldn't see any sign of him in the room.

"Where has he gone?" I asked.

"He's vanished, Max!" said Dooley.

"What's with all the racket?" suddenly a voice sounded behind us. The light was switched on, and we saw we had been joined by Odelia and Chase, who stood yawning on the threshold of the room.

"The Tiffany Thief was here," I announced. "He was searching your luggage."

"My luggage?" asked Odelia.

"What's going on?" asked Chase.

"It's the Tiffany Thief," said Odelia. "Max says he was going through our luggage."

"When?"

"Just now," I said.

"Where is he?" asked Odelia.

"He's gone!" said Dooley. "We followed him into this room, and suddenly he disappeared. Like a ghost!"

Odelia and Chase briefly searched the room, but couldn't find the thief either. Then they hurried to check their luggage, but as far as they could tell, nothing was missing. Oddly enough, Chase's police badge was lying on top of the luggage, as if the thief had been studying it.

"This is so weird," said Odelia, scratching her head. "One moment he was here, then he was gone."

"He really is a cat burglar," said Chase. "Too smart even for our own cats to catch him!"

"But we did catch him," I said stubbornly. "But then he got away." I felt this was like a personal insult to my professional pride. Cat burglar is a profession that should only be carried out by an actual cat, not by some human who pretends to be one. It's called catwashing and is a big no-no. So this whole episode hit me hard.

"He probably wanted to snatch me," said Grace, who had followed the whole thing from the safety of her cot.

"Now why would this thief want to snatch you?" I asked.

"Because I'm cute," said Grace with a gummy smile. "And we know he's someone with a taste for the good stuff. And what more precious treasure to snatch than the cutest kid on the block?"

In spite of my misgivings, I had to laugh at this. "I think you're quite safe, honey," I said. "This thief is only interested in gems that are sold at Tiffany's. And since that doesn't apply to you, he won't try to steal you."

"Well, he could," Grace insisted. "And he might have if you hadn't stopped him. So thank you, Max. And thank you, Dooley. My very own personal guards."

"You're welcome," I said.

"I wonder why he targeted us," said Odelia. "Unless he thought we were rich?"

"Did you recognize him, Max?" asked Chase.

I shook my head. "He was wearing a mask."

"Are you sure it was a he?" asked Odelia.

I wavered. "I wouldn't swear it was a he. It could have been a she. But he seemed to move like a man."

"Was it Grant Chubb?" asked Chase.

"I'm not sure," I said. "It could have been."

The episode had definitely given all of us a scare. If this thief was now targeting our family, that meant we should probably take measures to stop that from happening. Then Odelia suddenly got an alarming thought. "Mom and Dad!" she said.

And since her parents occupied the next room, she immediately set foot for the connecting door and opened it. Next door, everything seemed quiet, with Tex and Marge sleeping peacefully, Harriet and Brutus occupying the space at the foot of the bed.

"What's going on?" asked Harriet. "What's with all the noise?"

"It's the thief," I told her. "He just broke into our room."

"Oh, no!" said Harriet, immediately wide awake.

Tex and Marge must have become aware of strange goings-on and also woke up. And after Odelia had told them about our discovery, they inspected their room and their personal belongings, making sure nothing had been taken. And since we were all up anyway, they decided to apply the same procedure to Gran's room, which was next to Marge and Tex's.

The old lady had been reading a book and looked a little disturbed when we all came barging in unannounced. She held up the book, which was called, 'The Liechtenburgian Monarchy for Dummies.' "Very enlightening," she said. "Did you know that there has been a king in this country for the past thousand years? Amazing, huh?"

But after Odelia had informed her that we had received a nocturnal visit from the Tiffany Thief, she put down her book and joined the impromptu brainstorming session on how the thief could have gained access to our room and then left without being seen. It was a mystery, for sure.

"There's only one solution," said Gran. "He must be a ghost." She pointed to her book. "There have been rumors that Vaasu Castle is haunted, you know. At least a dozen sightings have been reported over the years by many of the guests. Most of the ghosts are servants who fell down the stairs and broke their necks and then forgot they were dead, so they continue their service as if nothing happened. Or prisoners who were thrown into the dungeons and then forgotten about. Though there is one incident written about in the book that refers to a lady in white, a former queen who was cast aside by the king when he decided to remarry a younger model when the previous queen couldn't give him the heir he wanted."

"Sounds a little bit like what's going on right now," said Marge.

"Yeah, history has a habit of repeating itself," Gran confirmed. "Though I doubt whether the king will murder his wife so he can marry Buffy."

For a moment, speculation was rife, but in the end the general consensus was that the Tiffany Thief couldn't be a ghost since ghosts don't actually steal stuff. Which still didn't solve the mystery of how the man had gained access to our room, but since everyone was too tired to think things through, they decided to return to bed and look into this most baffling case again in the morning.

And so we all said goodnight once more and retired for the remainder of the night. Tomorrow was another day—and another chance to catch the Tiffany Thief.

CHAPTER 18

*J*t took Chase a little while to wake up, and when he did, at first he couldn't remember where he was. But then it all came back to him: Liechtenburg, Vaasu Castle, the Tiffany Thief, and the weird dinner that had descended into vaudeville.

No, he definitely was not in Hampton Cove anymore!

When he finally returned to full wakefulness, he discovered that it was actually his phone that had dragged him from the land of dreams. He picked it up from the nightstand and saw that 'Deep Throat' had sent him another message.

'We have to meet.'

Oh, God. Not again. But since he couldn't deny that a man who was integral to the inner workings of the castle might have some interesting information to share, he replied that he would be there in ten minutes.

At least if he could find the way to the underground parking garage again.

And since he didn't want to wake up Odelia, who was still sound asleep, he snuck from between the covers and tiptoed to the armchair that he had used as a receptacle for his clothes.

As was to be expected, Max was eyeing him intently, so he put his index finger to his lips and whispered, "I'm going to meet the majordomo again."

Max seemed to nod, which was the strangest thing, then closed his eyes again.

As it was, he found the entrance to the car park easily enough, and when he arrived there, discovered that the majordomo had picked the same spot for their secret meeting: the concrete column marked B-52.

"This better be good," he said.

"Oh, it's very good," said the informer. "I searched Grant's room last night while you were all having dinner and couldn't find a thing. No jewelry, no brooch, no evidence that he's the Tiffany Thief at all. What I did find was a large box of contraceptives—family pack edition—and what's more important: love letters."

"Love letters?" asked Chase, who wondered if he really wanted to know what the actor was up to.

"Love letters to and from Grant, and I think you'll find that his correspondents are two ladies who probably shouldn't be engaged in this type of activity."

"Who are the ladies?" he asked, intrigued in spite of himself.

"The princesses Impi and Kami."

"Grant is having an affair with the two princesses?"

"Affirmative, detective. I've taken pictures of the letters. If you care to see them?"

"No, that's fine," he said, not all that interested in the love lives of the members of the monarchy. "But no evidence that Grant is the thief?"

"Grant returned before I could finish. I only made it out

in the nick of time. I'll do a proper search later on when he and his mother are having breakfast."

"Or maybe he's not the thief."

"I refuse to believe that, detective. He's still my prime suspect, and I will catch him. It's only a matter of time before he slips up and makes a mistake."

"He was in our room last night," Chase revealed.

"He was?"

"Yeah, but he got away before we could stop him. Almost as if he vanished into thin air."

"I see," said the majordomo carefully. "Mr. Chubb has been a frequent guest at the castle for many years, so he knows his way around the place."

"Look, I really think you're barking up the wrong tree here, pal. Why don't you look at some of the other principals, huh?"

"Like who?"

"Your fellow servants, of course. You know all of them, so you're probably best placed to figure out which one of them might be doing this."

"How do you know I know the servants?" asked the majordomo with a touch of suspicion.

"Oh, let's cut the crap, shall we? I know who you are, Mr. Deep Throat. Or should I say Oskari?"

At this, the informer became very quiet, and when the silence dragged on, Chase stepped to the fore. Only when he reached the spot where the majordomo had been standing, once again it transpired that he had vanished into thin air.

"Christ," said Chase. It seemed to be a habit for people to simply disappear!

* * *

MARGE STUDIED her reflection in the vanity mirror and wondered if she should do something different with her hair today. Being surrounded by queens and princesses all day long had established in her a sense that she probably should try harder to look her absolute best. Both Princess Impi and Princess Kami looked as if they had just stepped out of a beauty parlor, and Marge wondered how they did it. Their skin was so peachy and so fresh that they almost appeared ageless. Even Queen Serena didn't look her age at all. Even though the woman was older than Marge herself, she looked years younger.

Then again, these royals probably had a team of beauticians standing at attention and waiting on them hand and foot. A mere mortal like Marge couldn't afford that kind of treatment, even if she had the time to spend, which she didn't.

Her husband was pottering about the room looking pensive, and finally she asked what he was thinking, which was always a dangerous course of action, for her husband's thoughts were often a jumble of incoherency.

"Well, I'm still trying to figure out what King Thad is suffering from. As far as I can tell, and Storrar agrees with me, it's all in his head."

"Who is Storrar again?" Ever since they had arrived, she had a hard time remembering the names of all of these people.

"Eerikki Storrar. The king's personal physician. Though now it looks as if he's not his personal physician anymore—I am."

"So this Doctor Storrar thinks the king's illness is entirely psychosomatic?"

"He does, since he can't seem to find an actual physical cause of the symptoms."

"How does he feel about this whole poisoning business?"

"He thinks the king must have lost his marbles. Well, that's not the technical term he used, of course, but that's certainly what it boils down to. And now the king has asked me to conduct another blood test. Only this time in secret, and to send it to a different laboratory, one that isn't 'controlled' by Storrar."

"He thinks his own doctor is trying to poison him?"

"Something like that. Sometimes it's hard to know what the king is thinking, exactly. He has a tendency to get a little incoherent, not to mention belligerent."

"Tough patient, huh?"

"Oh, honey, you can say that again."

"So, are you going to have his blood tested again?"

"Well, yes. Yes, of course. Though it's not going to make much difference. The king is going to believe whatever the king wants to believe. And if I tell him that there's nothing inherently wrong with him, he'll simply fire me and hire a different doctor. He seems determined to keep looking for a doctor who will agree with his own diagnosis. Or I should say his personal delusion."

"Maybe it's a good thing," said Marge. "If he fires you, we can all go home." Though first Odelia would have to catch this thief, of course. But she didn't think that would be so hard. After all, they had almost caught him last night. So if he tried again, maybe the next time they would get lucky—and the thief unlucky.

She stretched out her forehead and wondered if the queen used Botox to get rid of those annoying wrinkles. She wanted to ask her, but didn't know if she should, not unless first she got to know her a little better. Maybe today she'd try to spend more time with the woman, become her confidante. And to that end she could drop by the queen's chambers and ask if she was all right. After last night's fainting spell, it was the least she could do for the poor woman.

* * *

BRUTUS WATCHED HIS MATE CLOSELY. He could tell when Harriet was brooding on something, and she was definitely brooding on something now.

"What are you thinking, starshine?" he asked therefore.

"I'm trying to figure out how I can become the official royal mouser," said Harriet.

Brutus smiled. "You should probably start by catching a mouse," he pointed out. "It's the main job description of a mouser, after all."

"And therein lies the rub, sugar britches," said Harriet. "I don't like to go anywhere near a mouse. I don't even like to touch the foul little creatures!"

"I know, but if you want to become a mouser, you will have to. There doesn't seem to be any other way."

"Oh, I know," said Harriet. "Don't you think I know? I've been wracking my brain all night trying to come up with a solution, and I still haven't found it."

"But why do you want to become a mouser?"

"Because mousers are famous, sweetums. Look here." She had drawn his attention to the tablet Marge liked to drag around for her cats' enjoyment. Brutus jumped up onto the bed and studied the website Harriet had clicked. It was a page dedicated to Anne and Julie, and they both looked absolutely amazing.

"It's a portrait by the official royal photographer," said Harriet, a touch of envy in her voice.

"I didn't even know they had a royal photographer at the castle."

"Oh, they have everything. A royal baker, a royal butcher, a royal shoemaker, a royal dressmaker. I guess when you provide a service to the royals you automatically become a royal whatever. So if I were to become a royal mouser, they would take my picture and put me on the website also. And look here."

She switched to another tab in the browser, which showed an article written about Julie and Anne. It was a so-called interview with the two of them, and was very funny, with the answers obviously having been supplied by the reporter.

"And look at this," she said. Another tab and another website, this one Wikipedia. "They have an actual Wikipedia page dedicated to them! Can you believe it? They're famous, teddy bear. World-famous!"

"Or at least famous in Liechtenburg."

"Oh, no, there are hundreds of articles devoted to them, with millions of hits on Google. Anne and Julie are celebrities. Worldwide celebrities!"

He suppressed a sigh. If he'd hoped for a little bit of peace and quiet and a nice pleasant family Christmas holiday, it was starting to come home to him that this wasn't in the cards. With this thief running riot, turmoil in the royal family, and now Harriet wanting to become a royal mouser, he could tell that peace and quiet were the last commodities they would find at Vaasu Castle.

"Will you help me?" asked Harriet.

"Of course. What's your plan?"

"That's just it. I don't have one. Do you?"

"Um…"

CHAPTER 19

*O*delia and Chase had been summoned to the queen's quarters to give her an update on their investigation, and Marge had asked to accompany them as she was worried about Serena's state of mind after last night's shocking arrival of Buffy Kurikka.

We found the queen looking in excellent fettle, and clearly she hadn't suffered any adverse reaction after her malaise. Tiia was also present, and of course Ariana, who was seated on a silk pillow surrounded by a cloud of pink tulle that presumably had been made especially for her.

"Hey, you guys," said Ariana the moment we walked in. "So nice to see you again."

The queen inquired about the state of the investigation, Marge inquired about the queen's health, and before long a lively conversation ensued, with Odelia and Chase revealing how they had almost caught the thief last night, but that somehow he had managed to get away.

"That's very worrying," said the queen with a frown. "That means he knows about the hidden passageways."

"Hidden passageways?" asked Odelia.

"Yes, the whole castle is a maze of secret passageways. They lead from room to room and floor to floor and are only accessible if you know how to find them. Which can only mean that the thief is an insider who knows his way around the place."

"What are these hidden passageways?" I asked Ariana.

"Oh, you want me to show you?" asked the little doggie. She had hopped down from her perch, so she was at our level, and now led us to the wall of the queen's sitting room. "You have to press a hidden section of the wall," she explained.

"Ooh, isn't this exciting, twinkle toes?" asked Harriet.

"It is. Very exciting," said Brutus, even though he didn't sound all that excited.

"Okay, so you have to press the flower," said Ariana. "Always press the flower, and then only the middle flower. Like so." The wall had been decorated with a frieze that ran all the way along, both vertically and horizontally, and was interspersed with flowers in the four corners. Ariana now pressed the center of the middle flower with her paw, there was a soft click, and a tiny crack appeared in the wall.

"It's a panel," said Harriet. "An actual panel."

"Not all the walls have them," said Ariana, "but in every room there is at least one that does." She now stuck her paw in the fissure and opened it further until it was a crack wide enough for us to pass through.

"Lead the way!" said Harriet, who was almost giddy with excitement. When I stared at her in wonder, she explained, "Mice, Max. Mice!"

It didn't make me any the wiser, but as first Ariana and then Harriet disappeared into the wall, and also Dooley, Brutus explained, "She got it into her head that she wants to become a royal mouser. But to be a mouser, first you have to catch a mouse. And now I guess she hopes to find a mouse in these secret passageways."

"But I thought Harriet was afraid of mice?"

"She is, but she's prepared to make the sacrifice if it will make her famous. These royal mousers have their own Instagram, Max, with millions of followers."

"Of course they do."

We followed Ariana into the wall and found ourselves in a place of relative obscurity, which was probably to be expected, as no lights had been arranged inside the walls, and no light penetrated there. Still, if the thief had a flashlight, he could easily travel these passageways and go from room to room in his quest to relieve as many palace inhabitants of their jewelry as possible.

"It's very dusty in here," I told Brutus.

"And very dark," he grumbled, clearly not a big fan of these passageways.

The dust was getting into my nostrils, and I sneezed.

"Not long now," Ariana announced as she led us up a wooden staircase. "As you can see, these lead all over the castle, behind the walls of the different rooms. You can go from one part of the castle to another without being seen."

"I just hope we won't find a dead person behind these walls," said Brutus.

"A skeleton!" said Dooley. "Imagine finding a skeleton here."

"No skeletons," said Ariana. "And I would know, since I like to use these passageways when I don't feel like taking the regular stairs or the elevator. And of course, when the castle is full of guests, it's an easy way to move around without being disturbed or some of Serena's guests picking me up and petting me."

"Does that happen a lot?" asked Harriet.

"Oh, you wouldn't believe. Whenever there's a big social

happening going on, I can't move ten steps without being picked up at least a dozen times. Sometimes I wish I was a Dobermann, you know, or a Rottweiler? I'm sure people wouldn't pick me up if that were the case."

"They would probably be worried about losing a finger," I said.

We had arrived on the next floor, but Ariana showed no sign of stopping. After what felt like hours, she finally came to a full stop. "Now this is the tricky part," she said. "See that little button there?"

We all stared at where she was pointing. A faint light trickled in from somewhere above, which I assumed was a skylight at the top of the castle, and so we managed to make out what she was pointing at. It was indeed a small metal button.

"Push it once and..." She did as she said, and the panel clicked open, just like before. She pushed it open further, and suddenly we found ourselves... in Gran's room!

The old lady, who had emerged from the bathroom, a towel wrapped around herself, uttered a shriek of surprise when she suddenly saw four cats and a dog emerge from behind the wall.

"My God, you almost gave me a heart attack!" she cried. Then she moved closer. "Is that what I think it is?"

"A secret passageway," Harriet announced. "Isn't it way cool?"

"It is," Gran confirmed. "So this is how this thief has been getting around, is it?"

"It is," I said. "Another mystery solved."

"Now all we need to find out is who this thief is," said Ariana. "But that's your job, not mine," she added blithely.

CHAPTER 20

*E*ver since she had arrived at Vaasu Castle, Vesta hadn't been feeling like herself. She didn't know whether it was the jet lag, the change in climate, food, or the people at the castle, but she was having trouble finding her groove. And the worst part was that she was suffering from an acute sense of homesickness, something that had never troubled her before. Even when she had joined her family on a Caribbean cruise, she had been in her element. But now... not so much.

She decided to go for a walk, as only when she was out and about did she start to feel a little better. And she had just set foot for the stables so she could say hi to the horses and feed them some carrots, like that nice young man had encouraged her to do the day before, when she came upon that funny-looking Prince Asko, who probably had the same idea she had and was on his way to the stables.

He was dressed in sturdy rubber boots, a cable-knit long cardigan sweater that had seen better days, and a peaked cap. As usual, he wore his face in a frown, as if he harbored a personal grudge against the whole world.

"Hey there," she said by way of greeting. When he gave her a blank look, she added for good measure, "Vesta Muffin. I arrived yesterday? My granddaughter is looking into this whole thieving business."

His face relaxed as recollection returned. "You were at dinner last night," he said curtly.

"I was! And what a dinner it was, huh? People shouting, long-lost secret heirs suddenly showing up, the queen almost suffering an aneurysm. I gotta say that life is never boring around this family of yours."

"My best advice is not to get involved in any of that nonsense," he said gruffly. "I don't, and it's the only reason I've managed to hold on to my sanity."

"Things did get a little crazy last night," she agreed.

"Not crazier than usual," he grumbled. "Though it's true that we thought we'd seen the back of that Buffy person. Horrible woman."

"Yeah, she does seem like quite the character."

"Vulture," the prince said. "Circling the carcass of my brother."

"He's not dead yet, though, right?"

"I hope he's not! The moment Buffy takes over, that will be the end of everything. She'll kick us all out of our home and destroy the monarchy with her cockamamie ideas. She did it once before, you know."

"I thought her relationship with your brother was of the hush-hush variety?"

"Oh, no. Buffy isn't the type who will be hushed up. She made quite the splash back in the day. Pictures all over the papers, making sure that she tipped off every paparazzo to get the best shots. She was hoping to get rid of Serena, but then she didn't realize that Serena may look like an angel, but that woman is tough as nails. How she managed to get rid of Buffy, I still don't know, but I suspect she strong-armed my brother to get her banned from the kingdom. So off she went, and good riddance, too."

"Until last night."

"If what she said is true, my brother personally invited her and that son of hers."

"Do you think that's possible? That your brother went against his wife's wishes to invite his former mistress back here?"

"Who knows? My brother has been getting wackier with each passing day. Wouldn't surprise me if he ends up divorcing Serena and marrying Buffy."

"And what about you?" asked Vesta, who found this old bird a very fascinating character indeed. "No plans to get married?"

A look of absolute horror passed across the man's face. "Absolutely not! Women are the devil's spawn—no offense."

"None taken," she said, curious about this highly original point of view. "So you never got involved with some pretty lass in all those years living under your brother's roof?"

She must have said something insulting, for the man now waggled a pair of phenomenally expressive eyebrows at her. "Vaasu Castle belongs to the entire family. It is *not* my brother's personal property."

"I'm sorry. My bad. As you can probably tell, I don't know a lot about your royals and the monarchy in general."

"Well, that's only to be understood, as you Americans don't have a royal family."

"We have the Kardashians," Vesta quipped, but when he gave her a blank look, she added, "Never mind."

"I saw you brought your own cats," said the prince.

"That's right."

"And some very fine creatures they are too. Especially the Persian."

"Yeah, Harriet is gorgeous, isn't she?"

"She reminds me of my Anne."

"Anne?"

"Here, I'll show you." And he proceeded to take out his phone and show her pictures of his cat brood. "This is Anne," he said, and it was true that she resembled Harriet to some extent, though of course Harriet was much prettier. Not that Vesta said as much.

"Gorgeous," she murmured approvingly.

"And this is Julie," he said, showing her a picture of a small gray cat who looked a little like Dooley. "Anne and Julie even have their own Instagram."

"Is that right?" she said. She loved her cats dearly, but the last thing she wanted was to set up an entire website in their honor. That was overdoing things a little. But it was true that Anne and Julie's Instagram was nicely done and got a lot of responses from followers.

"I want to marry them, you know," said Prince Asko fervently.

"Come again?"

"Marry my cats. Of course, my brother told me I can't, but I think I'll do it anyway. I already talked to the arch-bishop, and I think he's ready to see things from my point of view. I mean, if a person can marry another person, why can't I marry my cats?"

"I guess so," she said, wondering if insanity ran in this family. First, the king behaving like a lunatic and now his brother.

"Not a big ceremony, mind you. I'd keep it small and only invite a couple of close friends and family. Not my brother, obviously, because he's dead set against the whole thing. But I talked to Impi, and she understood. And also Kami. My nephews... not so much. But then they're hard men, especially Dane. He takes after his dad in that sense. Thad is also a hard man. Always has been. Even as kids, we used to butt heads a lot. One time he even split my head right open. We were playing by the lake, and he had dragged along some ancient sword that he could barely lift. Only he did lift it, but couldn't hold it up, and so he hit me over the head with it. I spent two weeks in the hospital. The doctors thought for sure I was a goner, but I pulled through."

"Oh, my," said Vesta, who figured she had discovered why Prince Asko was a little nutty.

"Yeah, I still got the scar," said the prince and took off his cap to show her. The scar ran all along his scalp, from his forehead to the back of his head.

"Looks pretty serious," she commented, for lack of anything else to say.

"I'll say it does. It felt pretty serious," said the prince with a chuckle. "What did you say your name was again?"

"Vesta Muffin."

"Well, I like you, Vesta Muffin. You're very easy to talk to."

"Likewise, Your Highness."

"Oh, none of that nonsense, please. Just call me Asko since that's my name."

And so they headed to the stables, talking pleasantly, and Vesta had to say she already felt a lot better than before now that she had found a friend. Though if this guy was going to marry his cat, they would probably lock him up in the local loony bin soon, so maybe she should befriend someone who wasn't nutty.

Judging from the rest of the roster of inmates, that was a tall order.

CHAPTER 21

*O*delia felt for Serena. Even though she was trying to stay strong, it was obvious that last night's arrival of her romantic rival had come as a big shock to her. Seated on the queen's sofa while she discussed these recent events, Odelia could clearly tell that she still wasn't fully recovered from her husband's betrayal.

"I can't believe he would invite the woman to the castle," she said. "After I had specifically told him never to lay eyes on her again and ban her from the country."

"Thad seems to believe that you're trying to murder him," said Tiia. "Which of course is ridiculous. But it does explain why he would ask Buffy to come here with her son. He probably wants to cut you off and also his own sons, and make Buffy's boy his son and heir."

"But he can't do that!" said the queen. Then she reconsidered. "Can he?"

"I guess he can. He is still the king, so if he wants to change the rules of the game, that's his prerogative."

"Doesn't the government need to approve such a decision?" asked Marge.

"I guess so," said Serena. "But since my husband has Efrain in his pocket, that wouldn't be a problem."

"Your son was talking to the prime minister yesterday," said Odelia. "I saw them from my window," she explained. "And they seemed very deep in conversation."

"Yes, Dane has been working closely with Efrain for the last couple of years. My husband has been handing him more and more responsibilities, you see, making sure he's ready when the time comes to take the reins. So maybe I should talk to Dane. Ask his opinion about all of this. Though he'll probably tell me to stay out of it. Sometimes I think he's almost as bad as his father."

"I'm sure things will work out," said Tiia consolingly.

"I hope so. I still can't believe that Thad would humiliate me in this way. Sneaking this woman in here behind my back. And promising her son that he'll become our next king. What was he thinking!"

"Clearly he's not well," said Chase.

The queen nodded. "So about the Tiffany Thief. The passageways that run all across the castle are the only way he could have gained access to your room and then abruptly vanished again. So what I would advise is to search those passageways and maybe find a clue?"

"We're on it," Odelia assured the queen. "The last thing you need to concern yourself with right now is this thief. You've got more important things to deal with."

"You can say that again," said Serena. "And I feel like I owe you an apology. If I'd known that my husband would pull this stunt, I would never have invited you here, thief or no thief. I feel so embarrassed that you had to witness all of that."

"It's fine," Odelia assured her.

"You will be discreet about this?" asked Tiia.

"Of course. You can count on our discretion."

Serena looked thoroughly relieved. "It's bad enough that I have to contend with my husband's foolishness, and now I have to worry about the story leaking to the press as well. Though it's probably unavoidable, as Buffy will be eager to stake her claim by using her old contacts in the media. But at least I'll be able to deny everything."

"That's it, Serena. Deny, deny, deny," said Tiia. "That's the only way to deal with this dreadful woman."

"You know Buffy well?" asked Marge.

"Oh, do I know Buffy?" Tiia exclaimed. "I was there when this whole thing went down, wasn't I, honey?"

"You were," Serena confirmed. "And just like now, you were a great support. My only support, in fact."

"Nonsense. The entire population stands behind you like one man—or woman. Buffy may think she's popular, but she's not. She's just a common little hustler who's trying to boost her own self-worth by tearing other people down. But she won't succeed."

"She wants money," said Serena. "Last time she demanded one million dollars in exchange for leaving my family in peace."

"Did you pay her?" asked Marge.

"No, I didn't. I simply sent her packing and told her that if she ever set foot across the border again, I'd have her arrested and thrown in jail for the rest of her life. Though now it transpires that my dear husband kept in touch with her all this time. He even paid her the occasional visit in Hong Kong to meet the boy."

"And all behind your back," said Tiia. "It's disgusting."

"Oh, well," said the queen, plastering a brave smile on her face. "I beat Buffy then, I'll beat her again. Or die trying."

"Let's hope not!" said Tiia. "If anyone deserves to die, it's that horrible grafter!"

Odelia decided to pretend she hadn't heard that. She

understood, of course. This Buffy person seemed to hold the power to destroy the lives of a lot of people living at the castle right now. Though she couldn't imagine King Thad would allow her to kick out his entire family. He might believe that his wife was trying to poison him, or his sons, but surely reason would at some point reassert itself and return to the throne?

Then again, if what her dad had told her was true, Thad's state of mind was far removed from reality already, and getting worse and worse every day. Which made her wonder if their arrival at the castle had come at a precipitous time or the worst possible time of all. They were complete outsiders, and there wasn't a lot they could do. Oh, they could try and catch this mysterious burglar, but they were powerless in the face of the family drama that engulfed the monarchy. Not even Max with his big brain could turn around that particular avalanche as it started making its way down the mountain and destroyed everything in its wake.

"What is that horrible noise!" suddenly Serena exclaimed. Odelia, awakening from her musings, realized that her cats were yelling at her from behind the wall.

"Oh, dear. I think they're locked in," said Tiia.

"Ariana didn't head into those passageways again, did she?" said Serena. "She should know it's dangerous to go there."

She hurried to the spot where the meowing was coming from and pressed a part of the panel near the floor. Immediately the wall opened up, and four cats and one dog poured out.

"We were stuck!" said Max, looking extremely perturbed. "The mechanism broke."

"Ariana, I told you not to go in there, sweetie," said Serena. "Didn't I tell you?" The Shih Tzu had jumped into her arms and allowed herself to be cuddled, clearly grateful for having been saved from her predicament.

"We went all the way up to Gran's room," said Dooley. "But when we tried to get back, we couldn't get out."

"Poor dears," said Marge as she picked up Dooley from the floor and gave him a good cuddle. And as Odelia did the same with Max, and Chase did the honors with Brutus, there was no one left to console Harriet, which the Persian responded to by producing a loud wailing sound.

Finally, Tiia picked her up and gave her fur a stroke, causing the pretty Persian to start purring up a storm.

And as peace finally returned to the sitting room, suddenly there was a loud scream that pierced the air. It seemed to come from somewhere outside. And as they all hurried to the window, at first Odelia didn't know what she was seeing. But then she realized that it was Kami, Prince Urpo's wife, screaming her head off as she stood next to the inert body of a woman half concealed in the bushes.

CHAPTER 22

Kami had stepped out of the house and onto the terrace for an urgent smoke. In all the years that she lived at the castle, she had never experienced a more tense time than she was experiencing now. It was almost as if things were all coming to a head. This thief who kept harassing them with his habit of absconding with their most prized possessions, the king's health suddenly declining, and now the arrival of Buffy Kurikka, after everyone thought they'd finally seen the back of the woman.

The most shocking part was, of course, the sudden decline of the king's health. Her father-in-law had always been one of those larger-than-life figures with the most robust constitution she had ever seen in a man. He had often reminded her of a Norseman, and she had even named him Hägar the Horrible, after that funny cartoon with the red-bearded Viking. He looked a little like Hägar, with his wild beard and hair and his penchant for a good meal and a glass of wine.

Contrary to some, she actually liked her father-in-law. He might be one of those people that were an acquired taste, but to her, he had always been very kind. Even when she had first started dating Urpo and a wave of criticism had threatened to engulf them, one of the only people in the kingdom who had offered them some support was actually Thad. Even Serena had told her son not to go through with the marriage, but Thad had told his son that if he truly loved her, he should marry her, and he had. She knew that he wasn't happy that their marriage hadn't been blessed with offspring yet, but they were taking their time and wouldn't be pressured into starting a family before they were good and ready.

The thing was that Urpo was still something of a kid himself, and even though Kami wanted kids, she didn't think it was a good idea to have them when their dad clearly wasn't ready to handle the responsibility. She thought Thad understood, though she wasn't sure. It had been a while since they had last had a good talk, and in the state her father-in-law was in right now she didn't want to bother him with her personal stuff.

She lit her cigarette and wandered off in the direction of the lake, but even before she got there, suddenly she thought she saw a foot sticking out of the bushes nearby. As she drew nearer, figuring it was a little chilly to have a nap in the bushes, suddenly she saw the person hidden there and saw her fully.

And that's when she started screaming, for it was the only thing she could do when confronted with the most terrible sight she had ever witnessed.

THE POLICE HAD ARRIVED, and when they discovered that Chase was a police detective in his own right, they naturally assumed that he would assist them in their inquiries. And so it wasn't long before Chase and the detective in charge of the

127

case stood conferring while the rest of us watched from a distance.

It was soon determined that the dead person found by Princess Kami must be her sister-in-law, Impi. You may wonder why there was any doubt, but then the state of the body was such that identification proved a little tricky. The thing was that whoever had murdered the poor woman had utilized a method that was both brutal and very effective. According to the police, the murder weapon must have been what is commonly called a tenderizer—an instrument used to tenderize a slice of beef or a steak to soften the fibers and make it more digestible.

In this case, the common kitchen implement had been used on the murder victim.

"What a terrible thing to do," said Harriet.

"Whoever did this must be a monster," said Ariana, who had joined us at the perimeter of the crime scene.

"Do you think it's the Tiffany Thief, Max?" asked Dooley. "Maybe Princess Impi refused to give up her bracelet, and he got mad?"

"There's a big difference between sneaking into a person's room at night to steal their Tiffany jewelry and murdering them with a meat tenderizer, Dooley," I said. "To me, this seems like the work of an entirely different person."

The police detective, whose name was Eric Storrs—no relation to Doctor Storrar—watched on as the crime scene people performed their tasks. Of the murder weapon, there was no trace, but they did manage to lock down a time of death: between nine-thirty and ten, when the unfortunate victim had been discovered.

"Where were we at nine-thirty, Max?" asked Brutus.

"In the secret passageways, sneezing up a storm," I said.

"Darn it," said Harriet. "We should have been out here, making sure that this poor woman wasn't murdered!"

This seemed like a tough proposition since only the killer would have known when he was going to strike, but it was a strange feeling to know that while we were stuck in those walls, the murderer was out there doing his dirty deed.

According to preliminary witness statements, the victim was last seen leaving the breakfast table at nine-thirty to go for an after-breakfast smoke, as was her habit. She was found half an hour later by her sister-in-law, hence the pinpoint accuracy of the time of death.

"And now what?" asked Harriet. "Are we involved in a murder investigation on top of this Tiffany Thief business? If this keeps up, we'll never be able to get home again, you guys. We'll be stuck here in this weird kingdom forever!"

If Ariana was insulted by this, she didn't show it. "It is a weird place, isn't it?" she said. "Though I have to say I like it and always felt very happy here. But if they're going to start *murdering* people..."

Odelia gestured for us to join her and Chase.

"Looks like the game is afoot, you guys," I said.

"Oh, dear," said Harriet. "Here we go again."

CHAPTER 23

*E*ric Storrs, the detective assigned to the case, had confessed to Chase and Odelia that he didn't have a lot of experience with murder cases. Normally, another detective handled those, but he was sunning himself on a beach in the Maldives, possibly sharing a cocktail with Uncle Alec and exchanging war stories while they were at it. That didn't help us, of course, but at least Chase was on the case, an experienced detective with many investigations under his belt, and Odelia, who was no slouch at this game either.

The first thing the investigating team did was line up the different witnesses-slash-suspects to try and find out what exactly could have happened. Meanwhile, Detective Storrs's officers combed the scene in search of evidence and, most importantly, the murder weapon.

And since things were a little confused in these first instances of the investigation being set up, the good detective didn't seem to mind when Odelia added the four of us to the roster. Which is how we came to sit in on the series of interviews that were conducted in the aftermath of this most heinous of crimes: the taking of another human being's life.

The first person the team spoke to was, of course, the king, as royal protocol demands. The king was in excellent fettle for a man allegedly knocking on death's door. He was sitting up in bed, a healthy color on his cheeks, and received the news with customary good-natured bonhomie and compassion.

"So the witch is dead," he said, nodding approvingly. "Finally, someone had the guts to drive a stake through her heart. Find out who did the deed, and I'll get out the medals."

"You... would offer a medal to the murderer?" asked the detective, sounding shocked.

"Of course! Dane married beneath him, that's a well-known fact. He married the first girl who caught his eye. Not that I can blame him, of course. Whatever her faults, Impi was a looker. A fitness girl, you know. Always pumping up the jam and all that. Seducing young men with her bendy body and curvaceousness. But as I told him from the start, he shouldn't have married her. Date her, sure. Keep her on the side while he married a girl of his own class, absolutely. But why marry her and spoil the bloodline? That's just ridiculous. Bad judgment on his part."

"So... you feel that the murderer did the world a favor?" asked Odelia, not fully on board with these sentiments and finding it hard to hide her shock and dismay at the king's words.

"Absolutely," said the king happily. "And I sincerely hope he gets rid of the other one as well. The teacher. She's even worse than the fitness girl. Seducing her pupils and tricking them into marrying her. Disgusting, and probably illegal as well. But to get back to Dane's wench. He had the pick of the litter, you know. Eligible young royals chomping at the bit to marry the lad, but oh no. He had to go and marry his fitness instructor! Terrible taste, detective."

The detective blinked a few times. "So... do you have any idea who might have killed her, Your Majesty?"

"No idea. Though if I were to hazard a guess, I'd say my money is on Dane. That marriage was rotten to the core, you see. As I could have told them when they plighted their troth. They had terrible fights—screaming rows. I could hear them all the way to this very bedroom! Dane's quarters are right next to mine, you see, so I had a front-row seat to some of their epic fights, unfortunately."

"When... when did they fight, would you say, Your Majesty?"

"Last night, for instance. You should have heard them. Big, big fight. No idea what it was about. Probably the fact that she tricked him into matrimony. All I can say is that if I were a betting man, my money would be on Dane holding the... what did you say the murder weapon was?"

"I didn't, but..." He glanced at Chase and Odelia, then coughed. "We think it was probably a kitchen utensil called a tenderizer."

For a moment, the king merely stared at the man, then he burst into a booming laugh. "A tenderizer! Why, that's priceless! Our killer is inventive. A tenderizer!"

"Can you account for your whereabouts this morning between nine-thirty and ten, Your Majesty?" asked Chase curtly. Clearly, he wasn't happy with the ruler's outrageous statements.

"Why, in bed, of course. Hasn't that father-in-law of yours told you? I'm bedridden, fellow. Do you understand the meaning of the word?"

"Yes, Your Majesty, I do," said Chase tersely.

"Well, there you go. And now get lost. I feel my strength fading." And as the trio left the room, he added, "And send Tex to me, will you? The only honest doctor in the world!

And catch that killer so I can pin a medal on his chest! Commend him for a job well done!"

I think it's safe to say we were all a little discombobulated after our meeting with Liechtenburg's supreme ruler, and I felt for Tex, who had to spend so much time with the man.

"He is really sick, isn't he, Max?" asked Dooley.

"Yeah, I would say he is," I confirmed.

"He's evil, that's what he is," said Harriet.

"Not a very nice man," Brutus determined.

"If I didn't know any better, I'd say we've found our prime suspect," said Harriet. "That man hated that poor woman so much... How sure are we that he is unable to leave that bed?"

"We'd have to ask Tex to be sure," I said. "But as far as I can tell, he hasn't left his bedroom in three weeks, so chances are he's innocent."

"Too bad," said Harriet. "He certainly has an excellent motive."

"I wouldn't be so sure," I said. "He seems to hate his son as much or even more than he hated the man's wife. And if he thought that Impi was as bad for Prince Dane as he said she was, he would have let her live as punishment for Dane being fool enough to marry her. And also, he seems to believe that Dane is trying to poison him, so if he was going to murder someone, wouldn't he try to murder his son instead?"

It certainly gave us food for thought, and if the frowns on the faces of our three detectives were anything to go by, they were of the same opinion.

CHAPTER 24

The next person on the list of the investigative team was Prince Dane himself. We found the prince in his chambers, which were indeed located right next to his father's. Unlike his father, Dane was clearly impressed by the death of his wife, and judging from the dark rings under his eyes, mourned her departure.

"It's a tragedy," he said. "Who would do such a terrible thing? Impi had her faults, to be sure, but she was a good woman, a good wife, and a loving mother to the girls." He directed a pained look at us. "Please catch the person who did this, and I will personally mete out the appropriate punishment."

I exchanged a worried look with my friends, and visions of torture chambers and dungeons once more made their way to the forefront of our minds. Too bad Ariana had decided to return to her own quarters and keep her human company, or she could have enlightened us in this regard and put our minds at ease.

"According to certain witness statements, you and your

wife had an argument last night, Your Highness," said Eric Storrs. "Can you tell us what this argument was about?"

The prince made a vague gesture with his right hand. "Oh, just the usual, you know. Impi felt that I was acting too much like a pushover, allowing my father to walk all over me. Especially with the arrival of this bastard son of his, she was afraid my dad would decide to change the law and hand the crown to Miko. I told her there was absolutely no way that was ever going to happen, but she said my father was capable of anything, and we should be prepared. Hire a lawyer or be ready to defend our rights some other way." He sighed. "She often accused me of being too weak, and maybe she was right. But of course, no man likes to listen to his wife accusing him of being a weakling. A mussel. A spineless insect. And so we fought. But that doesn't mean I wanted to kill her, if that's what you're implying, detective." He pounded his chest. "I loved my wife."

"Where were you this morning between nine-thirty and ten o'clock, Your Highness?" asked the detective.

"I was in a meeting with Prime Minister Efrain Saffman, discussing the succession. If my father abdicates—or rather when he does—a lot needs to happen in a short space of time. Not just the succession but also certain changes need to be made to the government, and Efrain has been helping me with that."

"We'll have to confirm this with the prime minister, of course," said the detective.

"Be my guest," said the Prince, suddenly sounding tired. "And now please leave me. I will be alone."

And so we left, wondering how he was going to tell his daughters that their mother had been brutally murdered. I would not like to be in his shoes.

The next people we spoke to were Prince Urpo and his

wife Kami. We met them in their chambers, which were much lighter and brighter than the ones we had visited so far. Clearly, these were people of a younger generation and had a more modern approach to interior decoration. Whereas both the king and Prince Dane's rooms had been steeped in antique furniture and furnishings, Urpo and Kami's suite was a breath of fresh air with its concessions to modernity.

"It's a terrible thing," said the prince, who welcomed us seated on his couch alongside his wife. The couple were holding hands in a display of unity and mutual support, and we could tell that Princess Kami had been crying. Since she was the one who had found the body, that was understandable. "I was very fond of my sister-in-law, as I think we all were."

"Except your father," Kami said.

"Well, yes, that's probably a given. Then again, my father doesn't love anyone except himself, so there's no mystery there."

"Now that your brother is a widower," said Odelia, "you're the only one who is married. And forgive me for being so blunt, but doesn't that make you the legal heir to the throne now?"

Urpo smiled a charming smile, and the dimples in his cheeks added to his image as the most handsome of the two brothers. "That *is* very blunt, Mrs. Kingsley. But I guess you're right. I hadn't really thought of it that way, but now that Dane is no longer married, as you say, he has become ineligible to follow in my father's footsteps and will have to renege his claim on the throne." He darted a curious look at his wife. "Which makes me the next king, I suppose."

"I guess it does," Kami said, looking confused. She turned back to us. "The laws of this country are a little hard to follow sometimes."

"Very medieval, I'd say," said Urpo. "But then I guess that's a good reason for me to assume the position of the next king, so I can change all of that."

"You would abolish those old laws?" asked Kami.

"Of course, darling. When we decide to start a family, and we are blessed with only girls, like my brother, I'd want them to be eligible to succeed me."

Kami seemed pleased by this, if her smile was anything to go by.

"Look, I can see what you're thinking," said Urpo, as he dragged a hand through his floppy mane. "I had an excellent motive for murdering my sister-in-law, but I can assure you that I'm not a murderer. I didn't even want to become king. If you've been the spare for as long as I have, you've learned to mitigate your expectations of what you will get out of life, and so I've created a life for myself that is as fulfilling or even more so than that of my brother, who was raised from the moment he was born to become the next king. I'm perfectly happy in my own role as second fiddle."

"We have created a life that's deeply satisfying," Kami confirmed. "In fact, I'm not sure if I even want you to become the next king, darling. Maybe you can refuse?"

"I'm not sure if that's possible," said her husband. He gave us a grin. "You see, you really caught me by surprise with this."

"Where were you this morning between nine-thirty and ten o'clock, Your Highness?" asked the detective.

"I was having breakfast with my wife," said Urpo as he thought for a moment. "That's right, isn't it, darling?"

Kami nodded. "We were in the breakfast room, and we weren't alone either. My nieces were there, Ainikki and Hely. Oh, and Grant and Jo Chubb, of course. You can ask them—they'll confirm it. Impi left at some point to go for a smoke, and I followed her soon after, which is when I found her—as you know."

It all seemed straightforward enough, and so the detectives thanked the couple for their time, and we left them to contemplate the news that they might be the new king and queen of Liechtenburg soon.

"I don't believe for one second that they didn't know they were going to inherit the throne if Impi died," said Harriet as we walked out of the prince's suite of chambers. "They must have known."

"I agree," I said. "Something monumental like that must have crossed their minds long before. And they probably discussed it many times."

"But that doesn't mean they murdered Impi," Brutus pointed out. "Though it certainly gives them an excellent motive. And Kami could have snuck out of that breakfast room, murdered her sister-in-law, and then started screaming her head off."

"But if she did, where is the murder weapon?" I asked. "it wasn't found, and she didn't leave the scene of the crime at any point before the police arrived. So she never had the opportunity to get rid of the weapon."

"Mh…" said Brutus as he thought about this. "She could have handed it to her husband? They could have set this up together?"

"Someone would have noticed," I said. "A tenderizer is not a small weapon. It has heft and size, and if she passed it on to her husband at some point, it would be hard to do so unnoticed."

"Unless they practiced the move. Used sleight of hand?"

It certainly gave us something to think about while we proceeded to the next suite of chambers to talk to our next potential witnesses.

"Good news about their plans to have babies, though, isn't

it, Max?" asked Dooley, always eager to focus on the positive rather than dwell on the negative. "A new baby will bring much happiness to the House of Skingle, wouldn't you say?"

I gave my friend an appreciative smile. "Absolutely, Dooley."

CHAPTER 25

e found the Kurikka family in the lodgings the royal staff had set up for them in the same wing of the castle we ourselves were staying in: the guest wing. If they were to be believed, though, they wouldn't be staying there long but very soon now would be moving into the main wing, with Miko and Rena the new king and queen. Before that happened, a few minor technicalities had to be overcome, like the fact that the current king was still in office and wasn't the kind of person to abdicate, and then of course the fact that Miko wasn't the official heir.

But that didn't stop them from celebrating, if the bottle of champagne cooling in an ice bucket was anything to go by.

The trio seemed less affected by the sudden death of Impi Skingle than the rest of the family, but then they probably had never met the woman until last night.

"Look, I had nothing to do with any of this," said Miko, who was lying stretched out on the couch, his feet up on the coffee table and dressed in silk pajamas and velvet mono-grammed slippers. His wife, also dressed in similar garb, sat next to him, her feet curled up underneath her, looking like the cat that got the cream. "I mean, why would I want to kill a woman I've never even met before?"

"To get rid of the competition?" Chase ventured. "With Princess Impi dead, the throne automatically shifts to the youngest son Urpo."

"Not true," said Miko, waving his index finger in a negating fashion like a school teacher. "I am the heir to the throne, and I was from the moment my father invited us here."

"This isn't official, though, is it?" asked Odelia.

"Oh, but it is. Or it will soon be, once all the documents are signed and whatnot, and the politicians give the deal the seal of approval. Look, I'm the oldest son, and I'm married, so that makes me the only heir to the throne and gets rid of my two loser brothers. The one with the stick up his butt and the playboy. They are out, and I am in. So why would I murder Dane's wife? That makes no sense."

"My husband is not a murderer, detectives," said Rena. "But he will be a very great king. The greatest in the history of Liechtenburg. And I will be a great queen."

"And I will be the greatest queen mother," said Buffy croakily. Clearly, she hadn't slept a lot last night—too busy partying, no doubt. She did look a little bleary-eyed, I thought, and it wasn't because she had been crying over the death of Princess Impi.

"I already told you, mother, you won't be queen mother," said Miko. "To be a queen mother, you need to be married to the previous king."

"Who cares? Laws are made to be changed, and I'm sure Thaddy will take care of all of that. I'm a queen mother, and I'll be the best queen mother this pitiful little kingdom has ever seen. I'm going to rock this place. Shake its foundations until it doesn't know what hit it! That will teach them to make fun of me and ban me!"

"Mother is very excited," Miko said with a grin. "She has been waiting a long time for this, and so who can blame her for expressing herself a little forcefully? But you can rest assured that Liechtenburg is in good hands with me at the helm."

"My Miko is a very successful businessman," said Rena. "He sells yachts. Many, many yachts. He even sold a yacht to the prince of Brunei. For two hundred million dollars!"

"That's great," said Chase, not at all impressed. "So can you tell us where you all were this morning between nine-thirty and ten?"

"I was in bed making love," said Miko, his grin spreading to shit-eating proportions. "To the sexiest woman on the planet: my wife."

I exchanged a look of concern with Harriet, and for a moment, we contemplated distracting Dooley, but that hardly seemed feasible.

"Miko is a great lover," Rena added for good measure. "A very generous and skilled lover. The things he can do with his tongue…"

Miko extended his tongue, possibly to lend credence to his wife's words. I didn't see anything special about the appendage, though. It was just a tongue like any other.

"And where were you, Mrs. Kurikka?" asked Odelia.

"I was in my room, and if you think I wasn't, I've got two words for you: prove it!"

"My mother was in her room," Miko was quick to confirm. "We ordered breakfast, and we ate it in our respective rooms. We in ours—"

"Before making more sweet love," Rena added for good measure.

"—and my mother in hers. We had nothing to do with this murder business, detectives. Nothing whatsoever."

"I think Serena did it," said Buffy now. "She's the one who hated her daughters-in-law so much she couldn't stand the sight of them. It was common knowledge. She thought her sons married beneath themselves and couldn't wait to get rid of them. So she got rid of the yoga teacher first, and it wouldn't surprise me if the other one is next. The teacher who seduced Prince Urpo when he was just a young boy. And I can't say I blame her. If my boy married a woman I didn't approve of…" She dragged a finger across her neck, and for a moment, Rena stared at her mother-in-law with a frozen look on her face. "But lucky for me my Miko married a most wonderful girl. The best daughter-in-law I could wish for."

Rena relaxed and smiled.

As we left the trio to celebrate their good fortune, I couldn't help but notice that Dooley had a pensive air.

"What's wrong, buddy?" I asked.

"What was all that about that man's tongue? What does he do with it, exactly?"

"Um…"

Lucky for us, Harriet had the answer. "He tastes all the food before he gives it to his wife," she said. "You know, to make sure it's all up to snuff? And of course, she's very grateful for that."

Our friend's face cleared. "Oh, of course! Wow, that's very nice of him." Then he frowned again. "So why doesn't Chase do the same thing? Making sure that no rotten food ever reaches Odelia's lips?"

"We'll have to make the suggestion," I said.

"Let's do that," Dooley agreed. "Then Odelia can say that Chase has the most skilled tongue in all the world."

Somehow I wasn't sure our suggestion would be met with Odelia's approval, but at least for now, the danger to Dooley's innocent mind had been averted. I just hoped we wouldn't have to listen to any more of this couple's shenanigans.

CHAPTER 26

"𝒩o, of course I didn't murder my daughter-in-law!" Serena said when Detective Storrs gently insinuated such a scenario. "Are you crazy?"

"But isn't it true that you weren't happy when your son married Princess Impi?" asked the detective, probing the matter further.

"Oh, not with this old saw again! Okay, so maybe when Dane first introduced her to us we weren't happy with his choice of partner, since we felt he could have done so much better. But over the years, Impi has really grown on all of us. Of course, she was fully aware of all the stuff that was being said about her, and she was determined to prove us wrong. And she did. She was an amazing woman, who overcame serious hardship to really make something of herself, and in that sense, I can say I was proud of her and became very fond of her."

"Your husband doesn't seem to have gone through the same process," said Odelia. "When we talked to him just now he told us he wants to give Princess Impi's killer a medal."

Serena's expression hardened, and she shared a look with her friend Tiia. "Sometimes I think the man is mad," she confessed. "Did he actually say that?"

The detective flipped through his notepad. "The witch is dead," he read from his notes. "Finally, someone had the guts to drive a stake through her heart. Find out who did it and I'll get out the medals." He cleared his throat as the queen stared at him with piercing eyes. "Um… there was also talk of a bendy and curvaceous body… pumping up… the jam… spoiling the bloodline… and words of admiration for the killer's choice of weapon, which he liked very much."

"Oh, God," said Queen Serena as she closed her eyes in dismay. "I hope you won't mention this to the media? They'll think my husband has gone completely off his rocker, which clearly he has."

"So you didn't feel the same way about Princess Impi?" asked Chase.

"No, I did not! Like I said, I had my reservations when Dane first introduced her to us, but over the years, Impi removed all of those and managed to win me over. Whatever else you can say about her, she was a wonderful mother to the girls—absolutely devoted to them."

"Was she also a good wife to your son?" asked Detective Storrs.

"Absolutely. She loved my son, and he loved her."

"They had some epic fights," Odelia said.

"Last night, for instance," Chase added.

"Every couple fights. I mean, you probably fight."

Chase and Odelia shared a look. "Rarely, actually," said Odelia, as if surprised by this fact.

"Yeah, I think I can count the number of times we had a fight on the fingers of one hand," said Chase.

"Well, good for you," said the queen with a touch of acerbity. "I can tell you that I can't count the number of times I've fought with my husband. But that doesn't mean I want to kill him."

"Besides, Serena was having breakfast with me," said Tiia. "And then afterward you were here, talking to us, when Kami found the body. So she couldn't possibly have murdered the poor woman."

That was true enough. Unless she had snuck out shortly before Odelia, Chase, and Marge arrived, of course. But if her friend had been with her, that was impossible—unless Tiia was lying, which was also a possibility, considering how close these two were, and how protective Tiia obviously felt towards her friend.

"Look, I think we need to consider the fact that the Tiffany Thief may be behind this dreadful business," said the queen. "I was discussing the murder with Tiia just before you arrived, and I was just telling her that maybe Impi had managed to discover the identity of the thief and was threatening to report him to the authorities. And so he saw no other recourse than to silence her."

"We considered that possibility," said Chase. "But there's a big difference between stealing a few baubles and murdering a person in cold blood."

"And in such a gruesome way, too," Odelia added.

"I know that what you're saying is true, but I still would like to urge you to think about this," Serena insisted. "Just take it into consideration," she said, and rose imperiously from her position, a clear sign that the interview was at an end.

And so we took our leave, wondering where this left us. We had talked to all the different family members, and so far I couldn't say I was satisfied to point the finger at any of them. The most likely candidate for the murder was King

Thad, of course, since he seemed to have harbored an almost visceral hatred towards the dead woman. But if it was true that he was bedridden, that left him out of it.

Obviously, we still had a lot more people to talk to, but so far my money was on the king. He could easily have fooled everyone—his doctors included—and in actual fact be as nimble as could be. Hopping and tripping across the castle's hidden passageways when nobody was looking, nipping out to murder this unwanted daughter-in-law of his, and be back in bed in time to deny all accusations.

He certainly was one of the most mean-spirited individuals I had ever met.

"This tongue business, Max," said Dooley once we were out of the queen's quarters and walking along the corridor once more. "Are you sure Miko was talking about his habit of being a taster for his wife? They did also mention they spent the morning in bed, kissing. And she said he was the best kisser in the world. So maybe he likes to add some tongue action to his kissing?"

The three of us stared at our friend. "What do you know about tongue action?" asked Brutus, much surprised.

"Well, I talked to Shanille last week, and she mentioned that Father Reilly took Scarlett's confession. And Scarlett said she was very much into French kissing lately, and Father Reilly said she should probably say three Hail Marys and ten Our Fathers. So I asked Shanille what this French kissing was all about, and she said the French like to kiss with their tongues. She wouldn't explain, claiming that if she did, she would have to say three Hail Marys and ten Our Fathers herself, but it got me thinking. How do you kiss a person with your tongue? Isn't kissing usually done with the lips?"

"Um..." I said, while casting about wildly for the exit from this conversation.

"It's very simple," said Harriet with a quick glance at me, indicating that she had it covered. "So kissing is done with the lips, see?"

"Yes, I do see," Dooley confirmed.

"You put your lips on the lips of the other person. But the lips have this tendency to become dry and chapped, and then the whole thing becomes extremely uncomfortable."

"Not to mention unsanitary," Brutus added.

"Not to mention unappealing," I added.

"And so a good rule of thumb is to moisten your lips from time to time," Harriet continued. "To keep them wet."

Dooley's face cleared. "Of course! Like you put oil in a car engine."

"There we are," said Brutus happily. "You need to make sure that your engine keeps ticking over, so you need to keep the whole thing lubricated."

"And that's where the tongue comes in," said Harriet with satisfaction.

I gave her a nod. 'Great thinking,' that nod said.

"But... why does it have to be a French tongue?" asked Dooley.

"Because... the French are more health-conscious," said Harriet.

"Or maybe their lips are drier than their American counterparts?" I suggested. "The climate probably has a lot to do with that."

"The air in France is very dry," Dooley commented. "So it stands to reason that people's lips would become chapped much quicker."

"See, Dooley?" said Brutus. "There's a simple explanation for everything."

And as we walked on, Dooley asked, "So is Hong Kong very dry also, Max?"

"Extremely dry," I confirmed.

"Then why don't they call it Hong Kong kissing?"

"Well…"

CHAPTER 27

*S*omehow Marge seemed to find herself in the role of babysitter and comforter of Princess Impi's two daughters. She had no idea how this had come about, but it came as a shock to her that nobody seemed to give even the smallest thought to the two girls. When she arrived downstairs, she found Ainikki and Hely in one of the drawing rooms, where they sat looking absolutely shell-shocked by what had just happened. Of their father, there wasn't a single trace, and apart from a servant who had brought them tea and cookies, nobody paid them any attention.

And so she had taken it upon herself to sit with them and try to comfort them. Especially the youngest one seemed to be most affected by her mother's sudden death and was weeping softly while her sister held her in her arms. Feeling helpless to say anything that would be of any meaning, Marge had joined them, and her presence must have helped, for before long she was holding both girls.

"Who did this, miss?" asked Hely. "And why?"

"I don't know, honey," she confessed. "But I'm sure my daughter and her husband will find out. They're very good at that sort of thing, you know. Back home where we live, they do this all the time."

"It's probably someone who wanted to take her money," said Ainikki. "And when she wouldn't give it, they killed her."

"But don't you have security here at the castle?" asked Marge. "Aren't they supposed to keep you safe?"

"They are, but since my grandfather became ill, things have been unraveling," said Ainikki. "Almost as if he held everything together, and now that he's not there to look after us, it's all falling apart. First with these people arriving last night, and now Mom."

"I want my mama," said Hely, and Marge hugged the little girl close.

"Your mama is in heaven now," she said. "And she's looking down at you and loving you very much."

"But I want her here."

"I know you do, honey," said Marge, and her heart broke. What a dreadful business. And somehow, she couldn't escape the thought that all of this had something to do with the arrival of this Buffy Kurikko and her son and daughter-in-law last night. She didn't know how or why, but she thought they probably had something to do with what had happened.

"Where is your daddy?" she asked now.

"Outside," said Ainikki. "Talking politics as usual."

She glanced over to the window and caught a glimpse of Dane, talking on the phone, as Ainikki had indicated. Probably arranging the succession, she thought. Which was important, but not as important as being a father to his daughters.

Just then, Eloy walked in, and when he saw the trio seated on the sofa, he hesitated for a moment. But when Marge beckoned him over, he approached.

"Terrible business," he said shyly.

Ainikki didn't respond but stared moodily before her.

"I'm very sorry about your mother," Eloy added as he stood there, awkwardly taking up space.

"Thanks," said Ainikki. "Did you see her?"

"From a distance. The police were everywhere."

"They wouldn't let me see her," said the girl.

And a good thing, too, Marge thought. It was a sight no kid should ever be confronted with.

"Who do you think did it?" asked Eloy.

"No idea. Probably some crazy person. Who else would do a thing like this?"

Screwing up his courage, Eloy took a seat on the other sofa. And before long, he and the princess were in conversation. Which was good, since the girls could use every friend they had. The last thing they needed was to be alone at such a difficult time.

"Where is your dad?" asked Eloy.

"Out there, plotting to take over the kingdom," said Ainikki.

"Business as usual then," said Eloy.

Ainikki nodded. "Mom just died and all he can think about is how he can use this to increase his chances of becoming the next king. Politics is horrible, isn't it?"

"It's pretty intolerable," Eloy agreed.

"Frankly, I hope he won't be king. It's only going to attract more crazies, and then maybe we'll all be killed next."

"Don't say that," said Eloy. "Nothing's going to happen to you."

"Oh, no? Mom said the same thing, and look what they did to her."

"No one will touch you," said Eloy, his cheeks coloring. "Not as long as I'm around," he added softly, causing Ainikki to emit a giggle.

"My hero," she said in a gently mocking tone but still seemed to appreciate the gesture.

"I don't think Daddy should be the king," said Hely. "I think he should tell Grandpapa that he's going to resign and then take us far away from this place. Maybe to where you live, miss."

"Marge," said Marge.

"Is it nice?" asked Hely.

"It's pretty nice," said Marge. "I like it."

"Then let's go," said Ainikki. "I want to go now."

"But what about Daddy?" said Hely. "And what about Grandpapa and Grandmama? And Uncle Urpo and Aunt Kami?"

"They can all come, too," said Ainikki magnanimously. "We can all go and live in a nice big house, and we'll never have to look over our shoulder ever again."

Marge wanted to mention that people got murdered in Hampton Cove, too, but decided not to. Instead, she smiled and said, "If you want, I'll show you where I work."

"Where do you work, nice lady?" asked Hely.

"I work at the library," Marge explained. "And my husband is a doctor, my daughter works at our local newspaper, and her husband is a policeman."

"Sounds terrific," said Ainikki. "I can't wait to leave."

"I'm not sure that's such a good idea," Eloy said tentatively.

"And I think it's the best idea I've had in a long time." She directed a curious look at Marge. "Does Grant Chubb live there?"

"It's possible that he has a house nearby," she said.

Eloy's face had darkened. "Grant Chubb won't be able to save you," he said. "He couldn't even save your mom, could he?"

Ainikki bridled a little. "What a silly thing to say. If Grant had known this maniac would come for Mom, he would have stopped him for sure. Because he is a real hero."

"I like Grant," said Hely. "He's very handsome."

Eloy had to smile at this. "You're right, Hely. He is very handsome."

"But so are you, Eloy," said Hely. "You should be in the movies."

They all laughed, and it was nice to see the strain lifted to some extent.

CHAPTER 28

$\mathcal{T}$he investigation was in full swing, and Odelia felt she needed to step outside for a moment to get some fresh air. They had talked to most of the servants who had been in the vicinity of the breakfast room that morning and might have seen something. Unfortunately, none of them had. They had confirmed the alibis of Prince Urpo and Princess Kami, as well as the princesses Ainikki and Hely, who had indeed been in the breakfast room around the time of Princess Impi's murder, along with Grant Chubb and his mother Jo, who had also enjoyed breakfast with the rest of the family. However, any one of them could have stepped out at some point to murder the princess, so those alibis weren't really worth a lot.

The only alibi that stood up was that of Prince Dane, who had indeed been in conversation with Prime Minister Saffman. And of course King Thad, who had been in bed at the time, according to Odelia's own dad. Though he couldn't confirm that the king might be a lot less ill than everyone thought.

All in all, a lot of people had an excellent motive for

murdering Princess Impi, and their alibis weren't at all watertight.

She walked along to the lake, which had quickly become one of her favorite spots on the royal domain, and looked across the expanse of water to the other side, where the royal stables were located and also the enclosures where the horses were trained for competitions and the like. It was also where Princess Ainikki liked to ride her horse, and where her sister liked to ride her pony.

Contrary to the day before, the sky was leaden, and she had the impression snow might soon start fluttering down, covering the world in a carpet of white.

And as she stood there, thinking about the case, she suddenly became aware that she was no longer alone. When she looked over, she saw that she had been joined by Grant Chubb, with the actor giving her one of his trademark grins.

"You again," she said and didn't know what to think of the actor's flirtatious ways.

"Yeah, me again," he confirmed. "So what's all this I hear about Princess Impi being murdered this morning? Should I be afraid for my safety?"

"I'm not sure," she admitted. "As far as we can tell, there was no security breach." They had talked to the head of security, and he had confirmed that no one had breached the castle perimeter at any point during the night or early morning, so Princess Impi's killer was definitely on the premises.

"If I had known that people were going to start being murdered, I would have brought along my personal security detail," he said. "But since I know security at the castle is pretty tight, I figured that wasn't necessary. Also, my team likes to bring their own hardware, and unfortunately, there are laws in place that strictly forbid such a policy."

"And a good thing, too," said Odelia. "Imagine if every

tourist brings a small arsenal of weaponry into the country, this place would be a lot less safe than it is."

"Just for the record, I know you're interviewing people, and I would like to state that I had a brief fling with Impi. Nothing serious, mind you. Just one of those things."

This wasn't news to her, since Chase had already heard the same thing from the majordomo, who had found the love letters the actor had exchanged with both princesses, but she decided to act surprised. "You and Princess Impi had an affair?"

"I wouldn't call it an affair. We spent a couple of beautiful moments together, but at the end of the day, she said she loved her husband and her daughters, and that was that. No hard feelings. Two ships passing in the night. The whole thing was very natural and beautiful. Just thought you'd want to know—for your investigation. I know you people like to be thorough. And going through her phone, you might stumble upon the few messages we exchanged around the time of the affair."

"I thought you said it wasn't an affair?"

"It wasn't. And as far as my alibi is concerned, I was with my mother all morning." He smiled. "Speaking of affairs, if you want to hook up, my door is always open—you know that, Odelia."

"I'm not interested," she said emphatically.

He shrugged. "You don't have to be so adamant about it. Hurts my ego, you know. And as we all know, actors have very fragile egos. Me especially." He sighed. "You're a beautiful woman, Odelia, so it would be remiss of me not to suggest deepening our friendship into something more meaningful and beautiful."

"I'm a married woman, Grant. A happily married woman. And I have a daughter. So no, all right?"

"Fine," he said with a shrug. "It's one of those things I'll never understand. A happily married woman. It's such a strange phenomenon."

"What's so strange about it?"

"To tie yourself down like that. To dedicate yourself to one man. It just feels... wrong. Old-fashioned. And such a waste of a life."

"I'm sorry if you feel like that. I think that you're the one who's wasting your life, Grant. By jumping from one bed to another."

"Ouch," he said with a grin. "Is that how you see me?"

"I think that's how most of the world sees you."

He touched his hand to his chest. "Can I help it that I have so much love to give? Too much for one woman? It's a blessing and a curse, but one I'd like to share with you, if you will only let me."

"You're really something else," she said with a shake of the head. "And besides, aren't I too old for you? Your girlfriends are usually under twenty-five, right?"

"Well..."

"And Impi? Wasn't she outside of your age range?"

"A little too old maybe," he admitted. "But still worth it."

"Oh, God."

"Forgive me for being so blunt, but you asked the question!"

Just then, Princess Impi's daughter Ainikki walked up, accompanied by Tiia's son Eloy.

Grant's face lit up with a killer smile. "Well, hello there," he said as he welcomed the princess by pressing a kiss on her cheek. "First off, my sincerest condolences, Princess Ainikki. I can't say how sorry I am for your loss. Your mother was a dear friend, and I adored her."

"Thanks, Grant," said Ainikki, a little shyly. "That means a lot to me."

"Want to go for a walk?" Grant suggested.

"Oh, of course," said Ainikki, and glanced back at Eloy, who stood glowering at the duo.

Grant threaded his arm through the princess's and took her for a stroll around the lake. When Eloy made to follow, Ainikki emphatically said, "See you later, Eloy."

The boy stood frozen at the spot for a moment, then turned abruptly around and stalked off.

Grant grinned. "Back to his horsies."

"That's right," said the princess, and then they were off, leaving Odelia to contemplate the actor's behavior. Could he be involved in Princess Impi's murder? But what would his motive be? Unhappy that she had broken off their affair? He wasn't the kind of man who would be upset about that. On the contrary. He was probably glad the fling had ended when it did, so he was free to pursue other women. Afraid the fling would leak to the press? Considering his reputation as a serial womanizer, the media were the least of his concerns. If Prince Dane had found out, he could have put pressure on his mother not to invite Grant to Liechtenburg anymore, but that didn't feel like a motive for murder, especially when he had so many other places he could visit.

No, as far as she could tell, Grant had no motive.

CHAPTER 29

*I*t was a little hard to keep track of all the different principals in our investigation. We had lost Odelia since she wanted to go for a walk, and Chase had also disappeared, taking a call from Uncle Alec, who should have been enjoying a fun time at the beach but still found it necessary to check in with his subordinate. The police detective in charge of the case needed to answer nature's call and was also out of commission.

And so we decided to go for a little walk ourselves and stretch our legs. That's when we happened to wander past the king's chambers and saw how Prince Dane and Prince Urpo entered, wanting to have a word with their dear old dad.

"I would love to be a fly on the wall during that conversation," said Brutus, which gave me an idea.

"So why don't we use the trick Ariana has taught us?" I suggested. "By entering these passageways and listening in?"

The problem was that we had no idea how to get to the king's bedroom, but before long, Ariana herself came tripping up, clearly eager to expand her horizons beyond her human's sitting room, and gave us a helping paw.

"It's very easy," she said after we had explained our predicament. "You simply enter any room, look for a wall panel that gives access to the hidden maze behind the walls, and walk in!"

And to show us how it was done, she entered a room whose door was ajar, tripped up to the nearest wall, and pointed to the little flowers at the bottom. "Press them," she told me.

"Who, me?" I asked.

"Who else, Max? Just do it, don't be scared."

"It's not a matter of being scared," I said. "Just that I'm not sure what we will find behind this particular panel."

"You're not scared, are you? There's nothing in those walls that you need to be scared of."

"Just your average ghost," Brutus pointed out.

"No ghosts," Ariana assured us.

"What about mice?" asked Harriet eagerly. She was still considering her bid to become the official royal mouser.

"No mice. Okay, so maybe there might be mice in there," the Shih Tzu allowed. "But at least no rats."

"Rats!" said Dooley.

"I said: no rats," Ariana clarified.

"Just press that flower already, Max," said Brutus. "If we wait any longer, the conversation will be over."

And so I pressed that flower. The panel clicked open, and before long, we were inside those walls, following Ariana, who seemed to know her way in there pretty well.

It didn't take her long to lead us straight into the king's bedroom, where we hunkered down and listened in—just like a fly on the wall—or a couple of pets inside the wall!

"We need you to tell us once and for all," said Prince Dane, "who is going to be the next king, Dad."

"Yeah, Dad," said Prince Urpo. "You owe it to us to give us clarity. You can't go around inviting old girlfriends with their bastard sons and implying they have more rights than we do."

"Listen carefully, boys," said the king. "There is only one person who will be the next king."

"Who?" said Dane eagerly.

"Me, of course!" He laughed heartily. "You should see your faces!"

"Naturally, we want you to live as long as possible," said Urpo. "And we want you to be healthy and happy. But we have to face facts, Dad. You're not well, and you haven't been well for a while. So you need to think about the future of Liechtenburg."

"I am thinking about the future. And I'm telling you right now that I'm going to be the new king. The old king and the new one. The past *and* the future."

"But Dad!" said Dane.

"I have decided that I'm going to live forever, boys, and my new doctor is going to help me with that. He's American, you see, and so he's got all this new technology, and he's assured me that I'm not as sick as I think I am. It's all in the mind, see. And my mind is fine—perfect! Never been better. So I'm going to go on living for years and years and years, and I will always be king. Forever and ever!"

"He's nuts," was Brutus's professional opinion.

"Yeah, he doesn't sound very balanced," I agreed.

"Dad, you're not behaving rationally!" said Prince Dane now.

"No, *you're* not behaving rationally," said the king. "I am king and I will be king for as long as I damn well please. And if you don't like it, you're both free to leave. And take those dreadful wives of yours along with you! Is that clear? And now get out!"

"My wife died this morning," Dane pointed out.

"And good riddance. Whoever killed her did us all a favor. Now get lost. Out!"

And out they both shuffled, if the slamming of the door was any indication. And we'd just made up our minds to leave when the door opened again, and a new set of visitors shuffled in for an audience with Liechtenburg's supreme ruler.

"Ah, Buffy," said the King. "So wonderful to see you!"

"My dear, dear Thaddy," said Buffy, for it was, of course, her.

"Daddy," said Miko.

"My dear boy!" said the king, and sounded a lot less belligerent than he had done with his other two sons. "So nice of you to come and pay me a visit."

"Of course," said Miko. "I have to say I was surprised, though."

"Why surprised? Can't I invite my son to come and see me?"

"Well... you haven't always been so welcoming in the past."

"No, you did ask us not to talk to the press," Buffy reminded him.

"That was then, this is now. I want the whole world to know how much I've always loved you, Buffy. If I'd had any sense, I would have divorced that dreadful wife of mine and married you. But then I didn't have the guts. And also, petty politicians told me I shouldn't. Bad for my reputation. Bad for Liechtenburg. Well, to hell with Liechtenburg and to hell with politicians! I'm here to tell you that from now on things are going to change. You're officially my son, my boy."

"That's so great to hear," said Miko. "Does that mean I'm the crown prince from now on?"

"Of course! I can see many great things in your future, my

son. Many wonderful things. And Buffy—you look radiant! Beautiful as ever!"

"Thanks, Thaddy," said Buffy warmly. "But isn't your wife going to be terribly upset? She fainted last night when we arrived. And she hasn't spoken to us—refuses to meet, even."

"Well, you know Serena. A real drama queen. She'll get over it. Now let me look at you. You haven't changed a bit, Buffy. Absolutely stunning."

"Oh, Thaddy. You look… pretty good yourself."

"Give us a kiss."

The sound of kissing reached our ears, and Dooley listened intently. "Not sure if they're kissing French style," he said after a moment. "But it's definitely Hong Kong style."

In only a few short hours, he had become an expert on kissing. And since we were starting to feel a little awkward, we decided to take our leave. After all, what people do in the privacy of their own bedroom is probably none of our concern.

The odd thing is that as we made our way back, we came upon the maid whose acquaintance we had made the day before. She was listening just as intently to the conversation being conducted inside the King's private quarters as we had, and if her expression was anything to go by, she did not look happy at all.

CHAPTER 30

When Heljä Lovelass happened to see Prince Urpo enter his father's rooms, she couldn't help but listen in on the conversation. She had a feeling it was going to be one of those seminal moments in a person's life, and she hadn't been mistaken. Careful not to be seen, she had snuck into the passageway that passed by the king's bedroom and settled in for the duration. And she wasn't disappointed. Clearly, the king had no intention whatsoever to abdicate, even though he was sick, and on top of that, had behaved in a very hurtful way toward his two sons.

And just when she thought the conversation was over and she made to leave, in walked that horrible Buffy with her own son, and Heljä's world crashed down around her. Not only was the king going to divorce his wife and marry Buffy, but he was also going to make sure that his illegitimate son Miko was the next king!

With tears of rage flowing down her cheeks, she hurried out of the passageway and back to safety. If the king knew she had overheard his evil plans, he would fire her for sure.

She hurried along the corridor, swiping at her face and

trying to compose herself. Once she was in her own little room in the servants' quarters of the castle, she threw herself down on her bed and gave herself up to a good cry.

In all the years she had been at Vaasu Castle, she had been desperately in love with Prince Urpo. They were the same age, but of course didn't belong to the same class. She often wondered if he even knew she existed. Oh, he thanked her when she cleaned his rooms or when they met in the hallway, but she didn't think he actually knew her name, or even remembered her face from one day to the next.

She now bounced up from the bed and opened her wardrobe. On the inside of the door, she had pasted all the pictures of Urpo she had collected over the years, and there were many. Dozens of them, from his school days to his college years and more recent ones, too. The only pictures she hadn't put up were the ones from his wedding, which had been the darkest day of her life. She hadn't even been able to watch the live broadcast on television, along with the rest of the staff. She simply couldn't watch as he linked his lot to a woman who wasn't her.

That horrible Kami. She had ruined not only Heljä's life but also Urpo's. To seduce a boy under your tutelage. To take advantage of your position to make him fall in love with you, and then force him to make you his wife. It was a crime, pure and simple, and over the years she had tried to make people see the light, and many of them had. Only on Urpo himself it had no effect whatsoever.

Cook once told her that it was because of the Stockholm Syndrome the prince was suffering from. Kami had such a powerful hold over him he couldn't see her for what she really was: a manipulative monster. And of course, Prince Dane's wife was the same way. Impi, too, had taken advantage of a vulnerable young man and seduced him, but whereas Kami had used her mind and intellect, Impi had used her body, which was an even greater sin when you thought about it.

She studied one of her beloved Urpo's pictures closely, then placed a kiss on it and rubbed her cheek against his.

She now took a seat at her little desk, opened one of her desk drawers and took out one of the pictures of Kami she had tucked in there. She had cut out the woman's eyes with a pair of scissors and scribbled angry red lines across her face. It was the face of the devil, she just knew it was. Evil had entered the castle walls when Kami and Impi had moved in—pure evil in its most pernicious form.

And as she stared at her mortal enemy—the woman who had ensnared the man she loved in her evil web, she suddenly crumpled up the picture into a ball and threw it against the wall. Then she rose from her chair and stomped over to the piece of paper and jumped on top of it a few times, flattening it while she howled with rage. How dare she? How dare she take Urpo from her!

A sudden sound made her look up. It seemed to come from somewhere nearby. But when she glanced over, she didn't see anything out of the ordinary. She relaxed. If people knew how much she hated both Kami and Impi...

She picked a knife from her desk and skewered the paper ball, then deposited it into her wastepaper basket. Then, thinking better of it, she carried it over into her little bathroom, and flushed it down the toilet. And as she watched Kami's likeness circle the bowl, she expressed a fervent wish that one day the woman would meet the same fate. Flushed down the toilet like the turd that she was.

* * *

UNBEKNOWNST TO HELJÄ, five pairs of eyes had followed her every move. Hidden inside the wall of her little room, we had all seen and heard the entire sickening scene. It was a hunch that made us decide to go in pursuit of the maid after we had seen her flee the passageway, tears streaming down her face.

Clearly, there were deeper waters to plumb. And so we followed her all the way to the servants' quarters, and hid inside the wall of her own private space to see what she was up to.

Lucky for us, the walls had tiny holes in them, since the wallpaper was cracked in places. So, we not only heard the object of our surveillance activity but also saw how she had a collection of photos dedicated to Prince Urpo. It was cause for concern, but not overly so. Many servants probably have a crush on the people they work for and collect their pictures to hang them up in their wardrobe. And kiss them. And cuddle them. Okay, so maybe that was a little weird—or a lot!

But it was only when she took out a picture of Urpo's wife Kami and started subjecting it to a particularly awful treatment that our jaws dropped, and we hoped we would make it out of there alive.

CHAPTER 31

$\mathcal{A}$t our instigation, Chase and Odelia decided to have a little talk with the maid. Police officers had searched her room and found her 'wall of fame' dedicated to the likeness of Prince Urpo. They had taken Heljä Lovelass into an adjacent servants' room that sat empty, and the maid immediately made a full confession.

"Yes, I love him!" she cried. "I have always loved him!"

"We are talking about Prince Urpo, correct?" asked Detective Storrs.

"Urpo," she murmured as she pressed a tissue to her nose. "The loveliest sound in the universe. Urpo, Urpo, Urpo. If only he would see me... hear me... love me! But of course, it could never be. I'm just a maid, and he's a prince. I must have watched *Maid in Manhattan* a thousand times and dreamed of the day that I would catch Urpo's eye. I've thought about setting up a similar scheme, you know, sir." She swept her gaze up to the detective.

"What scheme would that be?" he asked kindly, for he was essentially a kind-hearted man, and who could remain indifferent to the heart's cry of a simple maid who had fallen head over heels in love with a prince?

"To pretend I'm a lady. To dress up in Urpo's wife's clothes and pretend that I am her. And then he would see me for who I really am, you know. And fall in love with me. But I didn't have the nerve. Although one time I did try on her new hat. But instead of the prince, it was Kami herself who walked in on me and flew into a righteous rage. So I lost the courage to go through with the plan. Besides, I'm not Jennifer Lopez, sir, so I'm not sure if it would have worked out like it did in the movie. But that hasn't stopped me from dreaming about such a scenario."

"We found several pictures of Prince Urpo's wife with their eyes cut out," said the detective now. "And also a few of Princess Impi having been subjected to the same treatment. You didn't like Princess Impi very much, did you, Heljä?"

"Oh no, sir. I hated her. I have hated her since the moment she walked in here and started throwing her weight around. She's a stripper, you know, not an actual princess. And still she puts on all of these airs. As if the sun is shining out of her... well, you know what I mean. And the same goes for Kami. She's a teacher, for crying out loud, but pretends she's God's gift to mankind. They're both from the same rung of the social ladder as me, so why do they get to marry a prince, and I have to spend my days cleaning up after them? It's not fair, sir. It's just not fair."

"And so you decided to get something of your own back, didn't you, Heljä? You decided to put Princess Impi down a peg or two."

"I'm sure I don't know what you mean, sir," said the maid, giving the detective a wide-eyed look of such innocence I thought she would have made a wonderful actress. In fact, she could have given Jennifer Lopez a run for her money.

"Come, come," said the detective in fatherly tones. "You

know exactly what I mean. You hated Princess Impi so much that you decided to get rid of her once and for all. To wipe her from the face of the earth. So you went into the kitchen, grabbed a meat tenderizer, and killed the princess. And if we hadn't caught you, you probably would have done the same thing to Princess Kami."

"But I didn't, sir," she said. "I swear I didn't."

"But you admit that you hate both princesses for coming in here and acting like the grande dames while you were forced to clean up after them."

"Well, that's true enough," she said, her face coloring when she thought of the way the princesses had treated her over the years. "But that doesn't mean I would murder them, sir. I couldn't. I simply couldn't. Ask Cook. I can't even kill a mouse, let alone a human being."

The detective now held up a diary that had been found at the bottom of the maid's desk drawer. "Is this yours, Heljä?"

"Well, yes, it is, sir," she said. "But you're not going to read it, are you? That is my private diary."

"I'm afraid I have to, Heljä. As uncomfortable as it may be for you, it's my duty to get to the bottom of this murder." He opened the diary and read a little snippet. "'Sometimes I just want to take a big hammer and smash Princess Kami's skull right open. Crack it like a nut. I have a feeling I will find there's nothing inside. No brain, no nothing. Just a vast emptiness.'" He looked up at the girl. "Did you write that, Heljä?"

"Well, yes, sir, I did. But it doesn't mean anything. It's just idle fantasies."

"Do you harbor such violent fantasies often?"

"Every single day, sir," she admitted. "But I wouldn't act on them. I hate that woman, that's true, but I could never hurt her. Or Princess Impi. I mean, what about the girls, sir? What about Ainikki and Hely? They're going to miss their mother something terrible. I could never do that to them, sir. I love those girls—they're wonderful. Impi may have been a horrible person, but she did one good thing when she gave her husband those two lovely girls."

"And what about Princess Kami? She doesn't have children."

"No, but she will soon. I'm sure of it. She has to, if she wants to stay married. All women who marry a royal know this to be true. It's part of the deal. And if Cook isn't mistaken, she will probably give Urpo a son, which is what he's been hoping for. So I couldn't do anything to harm that woman, sir, no matter how horrible she truly is."

The detective gave the girl a paternal smile. "So if you didn't kill Princess Impi, then who did?"

"I'm sure I don't know, sir. I'm not a police detective. But Cook says it must be an outsider. Someone who walked in here, due to our lax security, and took a hammer to the princess. She reckons it's probably someone who's escaped from a mental institution. They do get these hormonal rages, as Cook calls them."

"I think she means homicidal."

"Oh, no, sir. It's to do with their hormones, Cook says. They're not balanced properly, and they get these terrible rages, and then they go on a killing spree. It happens all the time, Cook says."

"I think Cook has been watching too many movies," said the detective.

"I'm not sure about movies, sir, but she does read a lot of books."

"One final question, Heljä," said the detective. "Where were you this morning between nine-thirty and ten?"

A crease appeared between her brows as she gave this question every consideration. "Well... I can't say for sure, but I was probably doing Prince Urpo's rooms at that time. You see, I have a very strict schedule. I always start with the king's rooms, then the queen's, and then I start on the princes. But with the king being laid up as he is, the queen has asked us not to do his rooms for a couple of days, so as not to disturb him, sir. So I did Queen Serena's rooms first and then I started on Prince Urpo's rooms." She nodded to herself. "Yes, that's where I must have been. Urpo's private quarters." She heaved a little sigh of bliss. "I feel ever so close to him when I'm doing his rooms, you see. Sometimes I even lay down on his bed and smell his pillow. He has such a wonderful smell. Not his wife, though. She smells like the latrine that she is."

The detective shared a look of concern with Chase, then got up from his seat. "Heljä Lovelass, I'm placing you under arrest on suspicion of the murder of Impi Skingle."

"But, sir!"

CHAPTER 32

*W*hen Cook heard the news about the arrest of her good friend and colleague, Heljä, she was beside herself with rage.

"How dare they!" she fumed to anyone who would listen. "Those rotten royals! They just made the biggest mistake of their lives!"

Several of the kitchen staff shrugged their shoulders. They were used to the cook's outbursts and her occasional rants against the royal family, so they didn't particularly pay her any attention now. That wasn't to say that they weren't all greatly upset that Heljä had been arrested, for the royal staff was like a close-knit family. Many of them had been with the royal family for years, sometimes even decades of service, and the turnover was minimal, in spite of the fact that King Thad wasn't the easiest person to work for. But then most of them only dealt with Queen Serena, and contrary to her husband, Serena was loved by all for her sweet-natured temper and her calm demeanor.

The cook had grabbed her phone and was furiously typing a fresh post on her social media, as was her habit. Her colleagues might not be all that interested in her rants, but her thousands of followers were. And when she denounced the royals as an evil cult, intent on persecuting innocent members of their staff, it didn't take more than half an hour for the likes and shares to start pouring in.

* * *

Now that this whole murder business had been dealt with to everyone's satisfaction—except perhaps Heljä, but then that was a murderer's fate—Harriet figured it was time to launch her own little project. When she saw how pampered Julie and Anne were, and how they even had their own Instagram with millions of followers, she knew she had to make a go of it herself. If only the Pooles would decide to stay on at the castle and become part of the royal household, she had a clear shot at becoming the third royal mouser, and then she would have her own Instagram and her own army of followers who would adore her, love her, and idolize her. In other words: she would become a star! An overnight success!

And all she had to do was catch a mouse.

Of course, therein lay the rub. She didn't like mice. In fact, she pretty much despised them. But that didn't mean she was prepared to kill them. As a strict felinitarian, she felt it was beneath her to take the life of another living creature, even if that creature was an annoying little mouse.

So she had to find some other way to go about this. And as luck would have it, the opportunity came when they were returning from the servants' quarters and she happened to spot just one of those murine creatures sticking its nose from a little hole in the wall.

So she decided to hang back and engage the creature in conversation. At first, the mouse didn't appear eager to talk to her, which was probably not surprising, considering the fact that Anne and Julie had made it their mission in life to rid Vaasu Castle of every last mouse. But when she told the mouse that she had an offer it couldn't refuse, the mouse stuck its little pointy nose out of the hole and squeaked, "I don't trust you, cat."

"Oh, but I totally understand," she said. "If I were in your shoes—well, if you wore shoes, that is—I wouldn't trust me either. But just hear me out, will you? My name is Harriet, by the way. What's yours?"

"Jiminy Mouse," said the mouse. When Harriet gave him an odd look, he added, "Hey, I didn't choose the name. It's the name my pop gave me. He's big on Disney."

"Okay, Jiminy Mouse," said Harriet, glancing up and down the corridor to make sure they weren't being over-heard. "See, the thing is that I want to become a royal mouser. But to do that, I have to catch a mouse and be seen while catching a mouse, and preferably even be photographed while catching a mouse."

"Okay. But why do you want to become a royal mouser? Mousers are vicious killers, you know. They almost caught my aunt once, many moons ago, and she only barely made it out alive. Lost a piece of her tail in the process. So if I were you, I would look for a different purpose in life than being a contract killer."

"Oh, but I don't want to kill anyone," Harriet was quick to assure the mouse. "I just want to be seen with a mouse between my teeth, not actually harm any of you. And then once I'm established as the royal mouser, I'll be on velvet. The best food, the best place to snooze, and of course, world-wide fame. As royal mouser, I'll have my own Instagram with millions of adoring fans."

"Is that so? Well, I think you're nuts, but that's just my personal opinion."

Knowing that a simple mouse would never be able to

grasp the importance of her most fervent wish and ambition, Harriet moved on. "Okay, so I want you to be that mouse."

"What mouse? What are you talking about?"

"I want to set up a little stage play. I pretend to catch you and dangle you from my jaws, making sure the royals have seen me—and most importantly, Prince Asko, since he seems to be the one who goes over this royal mouser business, and then once our performance is done, I'll move into the wings and let you go."

"Nah, too dangerous," said the mouse. "How do I know you won't actually bite down and swallow me whole? I'm taking a pretty big risk here, cat."

"Harriet," she said. "And there is no risk involved whatsoever. It's just theater, you see. Nothing about this will be real."

"Your teeth will be real," said the mouse with a shiver.

"Well, I guess that's a risk you'll have to take." She couldn't very well get rid of her teeth, could she? She was ambitious, but she wasn't that ambitious!

The mouse thought for a moment. "You're lucky I'm known in my family as something of a daredevil," he said. "But first, I need to know what's in it for me."

"Lifelong protection from the other royal mousers," said Harriet immediately. She had thought long and hard about this, and it seemed like the right thing to do. As a pacifist, she didn't believe in violence, and she thought this whole concept of royal mouser was a cruel and outdated tradition that should be abolished. And what better way to do that than to become a royal mouser herself and start working for the other team? Attack the enemy from within and all of that.

"You're going to protect me from your fellow cats?"

"That's correct. I'll make sure that no mice will be killed at Vaasu Castle from now on. And you have my word on that. But first, you need to help me become a royal mouser.

And not just once, but multiple times. And when Prince Asko sees I'm a feline who gets results, he will appoint me as royal mouser."

"And you will put a stop to this dreadful business."

"I will become your royal protector," she said.

"It all sounds a little fishy to me," he said, eyeing her closely for any sign of possible subterfuge.

"There's nothing fishy about it. I want to become an official royal mouser, you want protection for your family, so let's make a deal and we both get what we want."

"A deal with the devil is what my pop would call it," the mouse grumbled.

"Call it what you will. But there is no downside, is there?"

"The downside is that you will eat me," the mouse pointed out. But he did seem to see the possible merits in the deal. Finally, he said, "Okay, fine. I guess I like to live dangerously. And you do look like a cat that can be trusted, unlike these other creeps. So when do you want to do this?"

"Tonight, during dinner," she said, her eyes glittering as she pictured the scene. "In front of the whole room. That way, there will be no mistake: the only real royal mouser at Vaasu Castle is me!"

CHAPTER 33

*A*fter their audience with their father, the princes Dane and Urpo decided that the time had come for a one-on-one conversation about the future of the kingdom and the monarchy. And since they knew from experience that the walls at the castle had ears, they took a walk around the lake.

"Isn't that your daughter?" asked Urpo, pointing to Ainikki standing near the horse's enclosure with Grant Chubb.

Dane's face darkened. "If that guy tries anything funny..."

"Mother should never have invited him here," said Urpo. "He can't meet a single woman without trying it on with her. I even caught him flirting with one of the maids this morning. Probably trying to talk her into bed."

"Mother seems to like him," said Dane. "Anyway, let's not get distracted. We need to fix this, brother. If we don't, Miko will be the next king, and I don't think either of us wants that, correct?"

"No, that's the last thing I want," Urpo agreed. He might not like his older brother all that much, but this whole episode that their father had suddenly sprung on them reminded him of that old standby of two dogs fighting for a bone and a third dog taking off with it. So it was important that Dane and he settle their differences and fight this wicked intruder and his scheming mother.

"If only we had known about it," said Dane. "We could easily have prevented Buffy from entering the country."

"Yeah, Dad really played us a nasty trick," Urpo agreed. He had known about Buffy, of course. By now, probably the whole world knew, and it was one of those things that had soured the relationship between the two princes and their father. "Somehow we have to get rid of that woman. Once she's gone, her evil spawn will follow, and the spawn's wife."

"But how do we get rid of Buffy? Now that she's here, and on Dad's invitation, no less, it will take a bulldozer to dislodge her."

"Isn't there something Mother can do? She is still the queen."

"Mother is badly shaken by this whole business. Dad humiliated her in front of the whole family by inviting his ex-mistress."

It was a difficult situation, and a very delicate one to resolve, that was for sure. "How are you holding up?" he asked.

"Oh, as best as I can," said Dane, dragging a hand through his hair. "Impi and I hadn't been getting along all that well, but it's still a great shock. Especially to the girls, of course."

"If they need a shoulder to cry on, Kami has already offered to take care of them for a while."

"That's very kind of her," said Dane. "Oddly enough this woman, this Marge Poole, has been staying with them all morning. She seems like a very nice person, and both Ainikki and Hely have taken to her in a big way. Maybe we should ask her to stay on longer."

"Yeah, they seem to have made a big splash. Doctor Poole taking care of Dad, and Poole's daughter assisting in the investigation." He thought for a moment. "Isn't there some way we can enlist them in getting rid of Buffy?"

"I don't see how. And besides, this is family business, Urpo. I wouldn't like to ask a bunch of outsiders to interfere."

"No, I guess you're right."

They glanced in the direction of the horse enclosure and saw how Grant Chubb had placed an arm around Ainikki's shoulder. "Oh, for crying out loud!" said Dane and stalked off in the direction of the actor and his daughter.

Urpo shook his head. Having kids was great, but it certainly came with a lot of problems. And then he hurried after his brother, hoping he wouldn't challenge the frisky Hollywood actor to a fight.

When he arrived there, Dane was relying on his impeccable upbringing to settle the matter in as diplomatic a way as possible, by telling his daughter that she was wanted at the castle by her grandmother, and then telling the actor in no uncertain terms that Ainikki was underage and that if he ever caught him with her again, he would have to take measures.

The actor gave them one of his trademark smirks. "I was just trying to do what any decent person would do," he said. "The girl has just lost her mother this morning, and she's clearly suffering."

"Be that as it may, please stay away from my daughter," said Dane.

The actor shrugged, then walked off. "Have it your way," he said as he left, shoving his hands into his pockets.

"I hate that guy," said Dane as they watched him return to the house. "There's something utterly revolting about him."

"Depravity," said Urpo. "That's the word I mostly associate with Grant Chubb."

Dane smiled. "It's been a while since we were on the same page about something, little brother."

"Nothing but a good tragedy to bring people closer together."

Dane sighed. "That's true enough. At least they caught my wife's killer. And in record time, no less."

"Yeah, who would have thought that sweet little Heljä would be desperately in love with me and hate our wives to such an extent."

"The detective in charge told me she was probably going to kill Kami next," said Dane. "We've been nurturing a viper to our bosom, and we didn't even know it."

At least they could sleep easy again, knowing that Impi's killer was safely behind bars where she could do no harm. Now if only they could get rid of Buffy, things might finally start looking up.

CHAPTER 34

*D*innertime had arrived, and once again the whole family and added guests were gathered in the main dining room, with the four of us on the sidelines as before. Though when I say four, I actually mean three, for of Harriet there was not a single trace.

"Where is Harriet?" I asked.

"No idea," Brutus confessed. "I kinda lost her after the maid was arrested and haven't seen her since."

"What do you mean, you lost her?" I asked.

"It's a big castle, Max, if you hadn't noticed. One moment she was there, and the next she was gone. I've looked all over, but so far I haven't been able to find her."

"Maybe we should organize a search party," Dooley suggested. "We could ask Odelia, and then she could tell the queen, and we could all look for her." He gave us a look of concern. "I mean, she could be stuck somewhere, or fallen down a ravine or something."

"What ravine?" asked Brutus. "There are no ravines here, Dooley."

"Well, there are probably secret nooks and crannies that

we haven't explored yet, so Harriet could have fallen into one of those. Some of them might even lead all the way down to the hidden depths underneath the castle—like crevasses in a glacier!"

"Oh, Dooley," said Brutus with a shake of the head. "You're such an alarmist sometimes."

"What's an alarmist?" asked our friend immediately.

But before Brutus could explain, suddenly there was a sort of commotion at the entrance to the dining room, and when we looked up, we saw that Harriet had arrived... and she was clutching a mouse between her teeth!

"Now will you look at that?" I said.

"What is she doing?" asked Brutus.

"She's holding a mouse between her teeth," Dooley supplied helpfully.

"I can see that, Dooley," said Brutus. "But why!"

"Because... she's hungry?" Dooley suggested.

Harriet now cleared her throat, but if she had thought that someone would notice either her or the mouse, she was sadly mistaken. People were so busy eating and talking that they didn't pay her any attention at all. Even when she started mewling, they still ignored her, since the volume of the conversation was so loud it drowned out all other sounds.

The only ones who had noticed, in fact, were two more additions to our merry band of four: Anne and Julie had appeared behind Harriet and sat eyeing her askance.

"Uh-oh," said Brutus. "There's trouble ahead!"

He was right. Clearly, the two official royal mousers didn't take kindly to Harriet stepping on their domain. They probably figured that they had some kind of monopoly on the catching of mice at the castle, and from the way they were staring at the back of Harriet's head, I could sense they were about to pounce.

"Harriet, watch out!" I yelled, therefore.

"Behind you!" Brutus added for good measure.

Just in time, Harriet turned, and when she saw the two felines giving her nasty looks, she uttered a sort of yelp and hurried off in the opposite direction, that mouse still stuck between her teeth. Anne and Julie immediately raced after her in pursuit, and they might have caught her if Brutus and I hadn't decided to intervene. We sprang forward and obstructed the two cats' maneuver by running interference for our friend.

"What are you doing?" asked Dooley. But then he saw what was going on. "Never mind," he said, and joined to assist us in our endeavor.

"Get lost, Max!" Anne growled when I wouldn't let her pass.

"Would you care for a dance?" I said, for it very much felt as if we were dancing.

"Whose side are you on anyway!" she snarled.

"Isn't it obvious?" said Julie. "Their side, of course!"

And since we were three and they were two, they finally decided to leave us be.

"This isn't over!" Anne said as they left. "Not by a long shot!"

The danger had been averted, but now we still had to find Harriet, who was nowhere to be seen. But after we had gone in pursuit of the white Persian, we finally found her at the foot of the stairs, panting a little, and having deposited the mouse on the bottom step.

"Gee, that wasn't what we agreed on!" said the mouse.

"Max, Dooley, Brutus," said Harriet, looking a little discombobulated. "Meet Jiminy Mouse. Jiminy Mouse, meet my friends."

"Jiminy Mouse?" I asked with a laugh. "Are you sure?"

The mouse gave me a dirty look, and I realized my faux

pas. When you've just stared death in the face, it's not a good time to crack jokes about your name.

"I didn't know they were going to be there, did I?" said Harriet.

"You should have known. Those two are everywhere. They act like they're in charge of the castle, which probably they are," said the mouse.

"At least they didn't hurt you," said Harriet. She gulped. "Or me!"

"So what's going on?" asked Brutus. "You disappeared on me, sweet puff. You had me worried there for a moment."

"Brutus was going to organize a search party," said Dooley.

"You were?" said Harriet. "Oh, that's so sweet of you."

"She wants to become the new royal mouser," Jiminy explained. "But she doesn't want to hurt any mice in the process. Which is a little hard, as you can imagine. Especially when nobody pays attention to the show!" he added with an angry look at Harriet.

"I thought they would see me," said Harriet, looking crestfallen.

"I could have told you," said Jiminy. "Humans are the most self-absorbed species on the planet. All they can think about is themselves. Next time you should probably jump on the table. Make sure they can't ignore you."

Harriet's face lit up. "That's it! We'll jump right on top of the table and stomp all over their dishes!"

"Don't stomp on their food!" said the mouse. "You'll only antagonize them. Humans love their food. They love it more than their children. So jump on the table, but make sure you don't get into their food, otherwise they'll be hunting us both!"

"Gotcha," said Harriet. She sighed. "I'm learning so much from you, Jiminy."

"Yeah, well, I just wish you had thought this thing through a little more before rushing into it. But I guess we're both still alive—barely."

"Let's do this again tomorrow morning," Harriet suggested. "During breakfast. Plenty of people around."

"Let's not," said the mouse as he started to walk away.

"Hey, where are you going? We had a deal!"

"Deal's off! You almost got me killed!"

"But you didn't get killed, did you?"

But the mouse wasn't amenable to reason, and before our eyes, he disappeared into a tiny hole in the wall at the bottom of the stairs.

Harriet sagged to her tush. "Now I'll never be a royal mouser."

"Yeah, probably tough to be a royal mouser without any mice," Dooley commented as he started licking his paws.

"Maybe we can find a toy mouse?" Brutus suggested. "Humans will never know the difference."

But Harriet wasn't having it. "It's not the same thing, sweet cakes. And I'll bet Prince Asko will be able to spot the difference. And since he's the one who decides who gets to be royal mouser, I guess I'm screwed."

I could have told her that our main mission wasn't to catch mice but to catch a jewel thief, but Harriet was beyond reason. And so I decided to return to the living room and hope that some tasty morsels of food would fall from the dinner table. Somehow this whole episode had given me quite an appetite.

CHAPTER 35

I have to admit we had almost forgotten that the reason we were staying at the castle was to catch a thief. What with the murder business and the acrimonious relationships within the royal family, it was easy to neglect this part of the arrangement. And so we had gone to bed fully negligent of the possibility that the thief might strike again. It was only when the door that connected our room to Marge and Tex's squeaked open in the middle of the night, and Brutus hissed, "I think there's someone in our room! Come quick!" that we jumped to attention.

And so we hurried to follow our friend into the next room, and sure enough: a dark hooded figure was searching the cabinet where Tex and Marge had placed their valuables.

This time we were not going to be defeated so easily, since we knew how the thief came and went, and so we quickly devised a plan of action: Harriet and Brutus would cut off his means of escape by positioning themselves in front of the wall panel that led into the hidden passageway, and Dooley and I would guard the connecting door so he couldn't escape that way. And to make sure he would be caught this time, we started making as much noise as we could to wake up our humans!

Unfortunately for us, both Marge and Tex must have been exhausted, for they didn't even stir!

Who did stir was our thief. He glanced over at Brutus and Harriet, then at me and Dooley, then seemed to decide that his best chance was via the window and made his way thither. To open the window was but the work of a moment, and then he was gone—escaped into the great outdoors!

We hurried to the window to see if we couldn't catch him, but when we arrived, he had already reached the corner of this section of the building by traveling across a ledge that ran along the length of the building.

"I don't want to go out there," Harriet intimated.

"I think we probably should," I said, even though I wasn't all that eager myself, to be honest. I may be something of a sleuth, but that doesn't mean I'm Spider-Man and like to scale buildings and put my life in jeopardy! And besides, even Spider-Man needs CGI and wires to do the stunts that he does.

But since we had sworn an oath that we would catch this thief, we still ventured out onto that ledge, in hot pursuit of the masked nocturnal intruder, hoping to catch him and put an end to his reign of terror once and for all.

I would like to say that we hurried after him—streaking along—but we didn't. Instead, we moved in a very deliberate fashion and quite a slow pace, making sure we didn't topple over the edge and into the abyss. Okay, so according to legend, cats have nine lives, but I, for one, don't believe all of that nonsense, do you? And even though I was eager to catch the thief, I wasn't willing to risk my life doing it.

And so, by the time we reached the corner and peeked behind it, our thief was long gone, presumably having climbed into another window and having secured his escape that way.

"You gotta hand it to him," said Brutus. "He's very clever."

"Not to mention very brave," said Dooley as he glanced down, then up again. "Maybe we can go back now? I don't like it out here!"

"You're right," said Harriet. "We lost him, so we might just as well go back."

By the time we entered the bedroom again, Marge and Tex were up, and so were Odelia and Chase. Even Gran had decided to join us and was part of the welcoming committee.

"And? Did you catch him?" asked Odelia.

But we had to admit defeat by shaking our heads and jumping down from the windowsill with hanging paws.

"He got away," I said somberly.

"He's very quick," Harriet added.

"Fast as lightning," said Brutus.

"He smelled familiar, though," said Dooley.

"He did? What did he smell like?" asked Odelia.

Dooley wrinkled up his nose. "I'm not sure, but I think I've smelled him before."

"So he's part of the castle inhabitants?" asked Gran.

"I think so," said Dooley. "Though I could be mistaken."

It was all very disappointing, and I could see that our humans weren't happy. But at least we had prevented the thief from taking any of our stuff. Or had we?

"He took my phone!" Tex cried as he checked the cabinet.

"And he took my watch!" Marge added. "And my bracelet!"

"Darn it," said Gran, which summed things up well.

"Your phone," said Odelia with a frown, "and your watch and your bracelet, Mom. They're not Tiffany's, are they?"

"Of course not. Do you really think I can afford Tiffany's

on my salary?" said Marge, looking unhappy that her personal items had been taken.

"So... I thought this guy only took Tiffany's stuff?"

"Looks like he's changing his MO," Chase said.

"So what do we call him from now on?" asked Harriet. "Just 'the thief?'"

"Sounds like a good idea," said Gran, yawning. "And now can we go back to bed? It's been a long day and I need my beauty sleep."

And since there wasn't anything we could do, we all returned to our respective rooms to continue our nocturnal activities—or lack of activities—to the best of our abilities. Though I have to say I found it hard to go back to sleep, the look of disappointment on Odelia's face searing my soul and instilling in me a powerful desire to catch this thief—whatever his moniker was—once and for all.

CHAPTER 36

*T*he next morning, the royals had a little surprise in store for their guests. Instead of enjoying a normal breakfast in the breakfast room as usual, Serena had decided to organize a picnic. It was a sort of brunch affair, a combination of breakfast and lunch, and would take us to a nearby beauty spot that was popular with the locals but also with the royal family, who had spent many happy moments there.

"Good thing it isn't snowing," said Serena as she oversaw the proceedings. We had arrived at the spot with a small fleet of Range Rovers, which seemed to be the royals' favorite mode of travel, and when we got out of our vehicles, we discovered the queen hadn't lied. The location was indeed a small sampling of paradise, located halfway up a mountain, and surrounded by meadows filled with flowers, the air so pure I thought I had never breathed in such grade-A oxygen, and I thought if I looked really closely, I might even be able to spot a mountain goat, of which there were rumored to be many tucked away high up in these mountains. Over the course of the past day or so, temperatures had risen and all the snow had melted, which suited me just fine, even if our humans didn't like it.

"I guess we won't have a white Christmas this year," said Tiia, who was helping her friend with brunch arrangements, "but at least we can have one of our traditional picnics instead, which is always nice."

After the events of the previous day, with Princess Impi's murder and the effect it had on her granddaughters, the queen thought it would be good for all of us to get out of the castle and away from it all.

At first Ainikki had refused to come along on this family outing, but in the end, she had agreed to come. She felt that it was disrespectful so soon after her mother had died, but when she was told that Grant Chubb would be joining us, she quickly changed her mind. Even though she was in mourning over the death of her mother, that didn't stop her from also pursuing the famous actor, even though she was clearly too young for him and he was much too old for her.

Her father definitely seemed to think so, for he had insisted that his daughter sit next to him, and judging from the way he kept darting angry glances at the actor, he wasn't happy with this state of affairs.

"Now that poor Impi's killer has been caught," said Serena as she sat down on the blankets that had been placed on the grass, "I think we can all breathe a little easier. Even though it will always be a shock to us that one of our own could have done such a terrible thing."

"Here, here," said Tiia, and raised a glass of champagne to the queen's good health and that of the rest of the company.

Prince Urpo was there, of course, along with Princess Kami, and also Prince Dane and his two daughters, Grant Chubb and his mother, and the Pooles, cats included. Even Prince Asko had decided to come out and enjoy this pleasant picnic.

Who weren't there were King Thad, who was still in bed, and Prince Asko's cats, which was a great relief for the four of us, since we wouldn't have been able to be at ease in our minds if Anne and Julie had been staring at us from across the blanket.

Who also were there, unfortunately, were Buffy, her son Miko, and Miko's wife Rena. Clearly, the queen had decided to try and bury the hatchet with her old rival and try to get along from now on. In other words, let bygones be bygones.

And I have to say that the picnic proceeded along lines of general cordiality and good-humored sentiment. The kitchen staff had outdone themselves by giving their best, and if the smiles on people's faces were anything to go by, the food was excellent. The four of us had our own picnic made specially for us, consisting of veal and pork country pâté, and my mood was greatly enhanced when I surveyed our personal domain and tucked in with some relish.

Odelia had told Serena about last night's theft, and our host was clearly upset about this, urging our human to give the matter her highest priority. Now that Impi's murderer had been caught, catching this thief was our number-one task.

"This is some really great nosh," Buffy said as she held up one of the tiny cucumber sandwiches.

"It is delicious, isn't it?" said Serena politely as she daintily wiped her lips with a monogrammed silk handkerchief. "I think today should mark the beginning of a new era. A time where we do our best to put the past behind us and get along."

"I salute the sentiment," said Buffy wholeheartedly. "And I think you couldn't have picked a better occasion." She, too, seemed convinced that to bury the hatchet was the best way forward.

"The weather is really unseasonable, isn't it?" said

Princess Kami conversationally. "It's suddenly warm for the time of year."

"We don't get the same winters we used to get," said Marge. "Even in Hampton Cove, we barely ever get snow anymore."

"That's too bad," said Tiia. "I like a nice snowy winter season. And especially for our skiing stations it's bad news. Did you know that they actually have to create fake snow to open their ski pistes?"

"You don't say," said Serena as she popped a cherry tomato into her mouth. "Fake snow? And can they manage?"

"They can," Dane confirmed. "It's a lot of work and a serious investment, but they all tell me it's worth it if the tourists keep showing up."

"And do they?" asked Serena as she glanced along the collected company to make sure they were all happy and enjoying themselves.

"They do," Dane assured his mother. "Liechtenburg is still one of the number-one skiing destinations, and let's hope it will stay that way."

"That's so nice," his mother murmured. She sighed happily. "I'm so glad that finally things are returning to normal, aren't you?"

Dane smiled. "I think we all are, Mother."

"How is your husband?" asked Jo Chubb. "Is he feeling better already?"

"Doctor Poole tells me there is a slight improvement," said Serena. "Isn't that right, Doctor Poole?"

"The king appeared to be in a good mood this morning," Tex confirmed. "He said he was looking forward to the Christmas ball and said he hoped he would be able to attend."

"With your kind assistance, he should be able to make it," said Serena. "And I thank you for that, Doctor Poole."

The small talk continued unabated, and when everyone

had eaten their fill, several of those present got up to stretch their legs and explore their surroundings. The four of us decided to stay put since I wasn't eager to run into a mountain goat, as you never know if they might look upon us as trespassers and give us a kick.

And we had just closed our eyes for a nice siesta when all of a sudden a loud scream sounded. It galvanized everyone, and as we went in search of the source of the scream, we discovered that it was actually Rena Kurikka who had uttered the blood-curdling sound.

We found her looking down at an inert figure, half obscured by some bushes. It was hard to know who the figure was, for she had been battered to death in quite a similar fashion to Princess Impi the day before. But then Prince Urpo cried, "It's Kami! It's my wife!"

CHAPTER 37

I experienced a powerful sense of deja-vu when the police arrived at the scene and started their investigation into the death of Princess Kami. Once again, Detective Storrs requested that Odelia and Chase act as his assistants in this most grave and tragic matter: a second murder being committed, and once again, a prominent member of the House of Skingle was the victim of a brutal attack.

As it soon transpired, Princess Kami had gone off for a smoke when she must have come upon her murderer, and the main question everyone was asking themselves was that, since the murderer was in prison, how was it possible that another murder had been committed?

It could only mean one thing: the maid was innocent.

It didn't take long for the detective to reach his conclusion, and so he vowed to release the maid and this time find the real killer.

The interviews took place right then and there, and due to the nature of the circumstances and the peculiarity of our surroundings, they happened in a more haphazard fashion.

The first person they spoke to was Queen Serena, who confirmed that she hadn't always seen eye to eye with her daughter-in-law but would definitely never have wanted to see her dead.

"Do we really have to go over this again?" she asked, looking very tired all of a sudden, which was only to be understood.

"Can't we do this later?" Tiia insisted. "Serena has already answered all of your questions, and she really needs to rest now."

"It's quite a coincidence, though, isn't it, Your Majesty?" said the detective. "That you have never hidden the fact that you thought that your sons made very ill-advised matches, and now all of a sudden both women are dead."

"Look, if you're going to accuse me of murder, have the decency to do it right," said Serena, who clearly had enough of this nonsense, "and arrest me."

Detective Storrs seemed taken aback by her vehemence. "Well…"

"I mean, frankly I've had enough of the insinuations," she said. "If you really think that I murdered my sons' wives, then go ahead and lock me up."

"I don't think…"

"That's what I thought," she said and turned on her heel. "I'm going home now," she announced. "Come, Tiia. Let's go."

And before our very eyes, they left.

"Aren't you going to stop her?" asked Chase.

"How can I? She's my queen," said the detective helplessly.

"She might be your queen, but she could very well be a killer."

The detective turned to his American colleague. "Do you really think that's likely? That Queen Serena would murder her own daughters-in-law?"

"Unlikely as it may be, she is still one of our prime suspects," Chase insisted.

"Look, it's not as if she's going to escape," Odelia said. "And even if she was, she won't get far. So let's focus on the other interviews, shall we?"

All in all, I think it's safe to say that the atmosphere was a little chaotic, but then that was to be expected. People were scared and confused, and when we talked to Prince Urpo, it was obvious that he was also very sad.

"A lot of vile gossip!" he cried when confronted with the notion that he and his wife hadn't been getting along all that well. "I loved her, and she loved me."

He was visibly distraught, and I didn't think he was acting. Clearly, the man had cared deeply about his wife.

"Who could do such a thing! What kind of animal are we dealing with here!"

"Calm down, Your Highness," said the detective.

"Calm down? How can I be calm when my wife is being butchered!"

"Poor prince," said Dooley. "He must have loved her very much."

"He did," I said.

"Is it true that she used to be his teacher?" asked Harriet.

"Yes, she was. But they only got together when Prince Urpo was in college. But according to local lore, he fell in love with her when she was his teacher, that's true."

"So who could have done this?" asked Brutus.

Unfortunately, nobody seemed to have an idea.

In short order, the investigative team talked to the rest of the company, but none of them had seen anything.

"Look, I shouldn't be saying this," said Prince Dane. "But you'll probably hear it from the others." He took a deep breath. "My brother often felt patronized by his wife. She was a few years older than he was, and in many respects more mature and also more intelligent. And even though it pains me to say this, the thing is that Urpo is a little... dumb."

"Your brother is dumb?" asked the detective, visibly surprised.

Dane nodded. "I know it's unusual to hear this from the man's own brother, but we all want this killer caught, and I think you should take a closer look at Urpo."

"You... think your brother killed his own wife?"

"Not just his own wife but my wife as well," said Dane, clearly having no qualms about throwing his brother under the bus.

"But why would your brother kill your wife, Your Highness?"

"I think we all know why. Because he wanted to become king. And with me being a widower, the rules governing the royal succession preclude me from being my father's heir."

"But now that Princess Kami is dead, your brother is also a widower. So he can't be the new king."

"Like I said, my brother is a little dumb. I'm sure he didn't think things through," said Dane with a grimace. "She probably bossed him around again, as she often did, and he got fed up and decided enough was enough and bashed her head in." He shrugged. "Case closed."

The next person the team spoke to was Miko, though we probably should be calling him Prince Miko, since his dad had earmarked him as his successor. "What can I say? This family is a nest of vipers. As soon as I entered the scene, they all started murdering each other so they could snatch the throne." He had languidly parked his gaze across the horizon, and it remained there throughout the interview. "Look, it's very simple. Serena murdered her two daughters-in-law, since she's always hated them. She couldn't do it before, since that would scupper her sons' chances of becoming king, but when I arrived, the real heir to the throne, she realized that nothing stood in the way of her getting rid of the two princesses. These people are monsters, detective. And when I'm crowned the new king, I'll make sure they're all kicked out of the kingdom, never to return. A new broom sweeps clean, and that's what I intend to do."

Prince Asko, the King's brother, didn't seem all that interested in the murder. But he did have one very important thing that he wanted to get off his chest.

"There's a lot of talk about this new kid becoming king," he said. "But that's all stuff and nonsense. There's only one rightful heir to the throne, and that's me."

"But... you're not married, Your Highness," the detective pointed out. "Don't you have to be married to become king?"

"Oh, but I intend to remedy that," Prince Asko assured us. "I'm going to marry my sweethearts, you see. I'm already in communication with the archbishop, and have been for some time, and he promised me he'll look into the matter posthaste. And if he doesn't agree, I'll go all the way to the Vatican to get permission."

"So... who is the happy lady, Your Highness?"

The prince gave him a scathing look. "Don't talk nonsense, man. I'm going to marry my cats, of course. Anne and Julie. They'll be my brides, and when I'm king, they'll be my queens."

The detective swallowed. "So... what can you tell us about the murder?"

"Murder? What murder?"

We also talked to the Chubbs, but they couldn't tell us a whole lot either. At least the actor wasn't eager to marry his cat. "I'm afraid I can't be of much assistance, detective," said Grant. "But you can rest assured I'm filing it all away."

"Filing it away, sir?"

Grant tapped his noggin. "Up here. I'm going to turn this into a movie, you see. There's enough material to create a drama of epic proportion. Or I could pitch it to HBO. Could be a ten-episode series."

"So... Princess Kami, sir? What can you tell us about her?"

He frowned. "Nice girl. Really great. I liked her. Liked her a lot."

Odelia rolled her eyes. "You had an affair with her."

"I wouldn't call it an affair," he said. "More like a fling."

"Oh, for crying out loud!"

"Can I help it that these women all throw themselves at me? I'm only human, Odelia. Even though the will is strong, the flesh is weak. And you gotta admit she was a real looker."

"Outside of your age range, though—like Impi?"

"Maybe," he said. "But I like to experiment."

His mother now spoke up. "Have you considered the possibility that this is all part of a conspiracy?"

Detective Storrs looked at her blankly. "Conspiracy, Mrs. Chubb?"

"Absolutely. A ploy to discredit the royal family. Mark my words, it's the republicans that are behind this. They want to get rid of the monarchy and install a republic."

"And who are these republicans, Mrs. Chubb?"

"How should I know? You're the detective, not me. I'm not even from these parts. But ask around, man. Just ask around. I'm sure this place is teeming with republicans. Or maybe it's the anarchists. Or the communists. Look what they did to that poor Anastasia. Poor girl never saw it coming."

"What is she talking about, Max?" asked Dooley.

"Anastasia was the youngest daughter of Tsar Nicholas the Second of the Russian Empire, and was killed along with the rest of her family by the Bolsheviks, thereby ending imperial rule in Russia and establishing a republic."

Dooley became animated. "Then that's it! Mrs. Chubb is right! Dark forces are threatening the monarchy, and they won't stop until every last member of the House of Skingle is dead!"

"It's possible," I agreed.

"I think I'll play Thad," said Grant Chubb now. "Or Dane. Or Urpo."

"Why don't you play all of them?" his mother suggested. "The father and his three sons. A real tour de force. It could probably win you an Oscar. And if you turn it into a musical, you might bag a Tony as well."

Grant's face lit up like a Christmas tree as he saw the possibilities. "Now wouldn't that be something?"

CHAPTER 38

The next part of the detective's task was to officially inform the king that his daughter-in-law had died. And since King Thad's health was still in a precarious way, the detective had asked for Tex to be present when the news was delivered.

I think we all expected him to be devastated by the news, but the old ruler seemed to bear up well.

"Kami is dead?" he said. "Well, hurray! Let's have a party!"

The detective shared a look of surprise with Tex, who shook his head, indicating the king's state of mind was such that anything could be expected to roll from the man's tongue at this juncture.

"You can't possibly be serious, Your Majesty," said Odelia, who decided to throw protocol to the wind and provide some pushback.

"Of course I'm serious. I'm always serious. As you well know, I've always been strongly opposed to this marriage, and now finally Urpo is free again, and so are we. So whoopie! This is the best news I've had in weeks—apart from Impi's death, of course."

And it had to be said he looked absolutely bucked up. A couple more murders and the old goat might be dancing and singing in the street.

"Can you think of anyone who would wish your daughter-in-law harm, Your Majesty?" asked the detective.

"Efrain, of course."

"Efrain?" asked Chase.

"The groveling weasel."

"Efrain Saffman," the detective clarified. "Our prime minister."

"I've always known that man was a closet republican," said Thad.

"Oh, so you think he's doing this to damage the monarchy?"

"Absolutely. He wants to get rid of us. But I won't let him! The moment Doctor Tex gets me up and about again, which is only a matter of time, I'll make him pay for this. Personally, I might rejoice in the news that those two wenches are dead, but that doesn't mean as the ruler of this domain I approve." A fierce look had stolen over his face, and I could see that Tex was worried. "I'll have his head!" the King now screamed, getting more and more worked up. "On a stick! And then I'll scoop out his brains and eat them for breakfast!"

"Maybe we can cut this interview short," Tex suggested.

"He picked on the wrong man, that horrible little mussel."

And since the King's face had gone from pink to puce, it was decided that it was probably best to leave him for now, lest we wanted another royal death on our hands. The prime minister might be glad—if the king's words were to be believed—but others wouldn't.

And so we left the room, even as the king kept hollering dark threats aimed at the 'leader of the republican rats.'

"Rats?" said Dooley as we left the royal quarters. "I thought he said he was a mussel."

"Rats, mussels—same difference," said Brutus. "It's clear that the king has taken leave of his senses and is now acting out his most base instincts."

"He does seem a little… brusque," I agreed.

"Brusque? The man is an animal!" said Brutus.

"So is he a mussel or a rat?" asked Dooley.

Unfortunately, we might never really know.

THE THREE DETECTIVES decided to convene in one of the downstairs meeting rooms to discuss the case and decide how to proceed.

"It's a tough case," said Eric Storrs, and his mustache drooped as he said it, indicating he was at a loss right now.

"Let's go over our list of suspects," Chase suggested. "All the people who were present at the picnic. We've got Serena, who never made a secret of being unhappy about her sons' choice of bride."

"But who was with us when Impi was murdered," Odelia reminded him. "So she couldn't have murdered her."

"But she could have murdered Kami," Chase interjected.

"Unlikely," Storrs said. "I think we need to work from the premise that both women were killed by the same person."

"Agreed," said Odelia. "Same MO. Same murder weapon."

"Okay, so then we have Dane," said Chase, going down the list. "He didn't get along with his wife and had a big fight with her the night before the murder, as his father claimed and as Dane admitted."

"But why would he target his sister-in-law?" asked Odelia. "That makes no sense."

"To make sure his brother doesn't become king?" Detective Storrs suggested. "He could have killed his wife in a fit of rage and only later realized that he had destroyed his chance of becoming king and handing the crown to his younger brother on a silver platter. So now he kills Princess Kami so Urpo won't be king."

"But doesn't that play into Buffy's hand?" asked Odelia. "Now that both Urpo and Dane are single, the only son who is married is Miko. And I can't imagine Dane wants him to be the new king."

Chase sighed. "This case is doing my head in, it really is. So who else is there?"

"Buffy," said Odelia. "She wants her son to be the new king, and by getting rid of the wives of his rivals, she increases Miko's chances."

"Or it could have been Rena," Storrs suggested. "If Miko becomes king, she will be his queen, and what woman doesn't want that? And she's the one who 'found' the body. But what if she killed her first?"

"We didn't find a murder weapon," Odelia reminded the detective. "If Rena killed her rival for the queenship, we would have found the weapon on her."

"Unless she killed her, got rid of the weapon, and then started screaming," Chase said. "Which is what I would have done."

"What about the Chubbs?" asked Odelia.

"What about them?"

"Grant Chubb is going to turn this drama into a movie. And with all the publicity these murders will receive, his movie just might be a big hit."

Chase smiled. "No actor is going to start murdering people just so he can make a hit movie, babe. I know you don't like Grant, and it's true that he is a very distasteful human being, but that doesn't make him a killer."

"No, I guess not," said Odelia reluctantly.

"It's a pity our most likely suspect has the perfect alibi," said Storrs.

"Who?" asked Chase.

"Why, King Thad, of course. He hated Impi, he despised Kami, and he's happy that they're both dead. Are you sure that he couldn't have snuck out of his room to do the deed?" He cast a hopeful look at Odelia, who shook her head.

"If my dad says he couldn't have done it, he couldn't have done it. It's that simple."

Storrs's shoulders sagged, and he threw up his hands. "Then I don't know. I really don't know!"

And judging from the looks on Chase and Odelia's faces, they were both stumped as well.

"Will you look into this accusation about the prime minister?" asked Chase.

"I will," said Storrs. "But I can't imagine a man as decent and upstanding as Efrain Saffman would go around murdering people just so he can get rid of the monarchy. As far as I know, he's all for the royals. Has been their staunchest supporter for years."

"Yeah, I guess that scenario is a little too far-fetched."

By the time the meeting was concluded, it was safe to say we hadn't really gotten anywhere. But the trio vowed to keep looking, and at the end of the day, that's all a detective can do: not give up. Keep keeping on until he hits on that one telling clue.

CHAPTER 39

"So what do you think happened, Max?" asked Dooley as we set paw for the kitchen. Castle or no castle, a well-equipped kitchen will always have a special place in my heart. After all, it is the hub of any home, with its many attractive features, such as there are: food, food and, well, not to put too fine a point to it, food!

"I have absolutely no idea, Dooley," I admitted. As it was, I was experiencing a slight rumble in my tummy, and since extensive scientific research has determined that the activities of the digestive system and that of the brain are closely connected, I wasn't prepared to engage in idle conjecture as long as I hadn't indulged my inner trencher-cat.

"There are a lot of suspects," Harriet ventured. "So who do you think did it, Max?"

"I have no idea, Harriet," I confessed, that persistent rumble becoming more pronounced with every passing minute.

"It must the queen, surely," said Brutus. "She hated her sons' wives and couldn't wait to get rid of them. And it wouldn't surprise me if her friend, Tiia, is in on it."

We soon arrived in the kitchen and went in search of something to eat. The food bowls the kitchen staff had placed there for our benefit were gone, and so we started looking around for the person responsible for this gross oversight. As it was, the only person present was the cook, and she was too busy on her phone to bother with a couple of hungry cats.

Mewling piteously didn't help, and neither did pawing her leg. She was so engrossed in whatever it was she was looking at that she was fully oblivious to her surroundings.

Finally, we saw no other recourse but to jump on top of the kitchen table, and since it was so high and so difficult an undertaking, we discussed amongst ourselves who should be our official emissary to undertake this potentially dangerous mission. For as we all know, kitchens are full of instruments of death and destruction, such as there are: knives, killing machines like blenders and ovens and stoves, and of course the meat tenderizer, which is a formidable weapon of destruction, as had recently been amply demonstrated.

In the end, Harriet volunteered for the job and took the high jump without a hitch, graceful and athletic to the last movement. But if we thought that this would get the cook's attention, we were badly mistaken.

"She's typing something on Facebook, you guys," Harriet reported from her high perch.

"Must be very important," said Dooley, "if she's prepared to neglect her duties to do so."

"Wait, I'll read some of it for you," said Harriet. "'The monarchy is an obsolete institution and should be demolished, and all of its principles destroyed. I'll see the blood of the aristocracy coloring our streets red if it's the last thing I do. The French revolutionaries had the right idea, and we should follow their lead. Let's bring out those old guillotines and get them working again. I want to see blood. I want to see heads rolling. The working classes will have their vengeance!'" Harriet was silent for a moment, as we all were. "This is some pretty heady stuff. I didn't know Cook was such a violent person."

"That's what you get from chopping the heads of chickens and turkeys all day long, not to mention chopping up fish and assorted fowl," said Dooley. "It brings out the bloodlust in a person."

"It certainly brings the bloodlust out in her," said Harriet. "She just posted a meme of King Thad with his head being taken clean off by a very large sword. Looks like something from *Game of Thrones*, with the King's head inserted—before it comes off, that is."

We all gulped a little, and then Dooley said, in an urgent fashion, "Get down from there, Harriet. She's likely to strike out at you next!"

Harriet uttered a squeal of fear and immediately jumped down from the sturdy wooden table. "Let's go and tell Odelia that we have found our killer," she said. "Clearly, she's the one who's taking out the aristocracy one princess at a time!"

And so we hurried from the kitchen and back to safety. We might not be royals, but there was no telling where the bloodlust of this murderous cook would end. As we all know, once a person gets a taste for blood, it's very hard to stop. That's how serial killers are made. They kill one person, just out of idle curiosity, and before they know it, they simply can't stop. They get in their second kill, their third, and unless they're stopped, they'll just keep going until there's no one left!

We found Odelia on the terrace with Queen Serena and Tiia. Serena was talking animatedly about a theory she had developed that the two murders had been committed by the Tiffany Thief. Having gotten bored with stealing diamonds and pearls, he had decided to venture out and spread his wings—and his tenderizer.

Without waiting for the queen to finish her speech, we quickly poured our story of the Killer Cook into our human's ear—along with a lament from Dooley that she had failed to provide us with sustenance—a minor point but still worth mentioning.

Odelia's reaction didn't disappoint. She glanced down at her phone, pretended that an urgent message from her husband had materialized there, and jumped up, an expression of shock on her face. "Oh, no!" she said.

"What is it?" asked Serena, much alarmed.

"I think we found our killer." She paused for effect. "It's the cook!"

The queen's look of dismay at learning this news was unmistakable. And so was her first reaction. "Dammit! And with our Christmas banquet coming up! Now I'll have to find a caterer!"

CHAPTER 40

*T*illy Möttönen grinned as she read one of the responses to her latest post.

'Who needs a guillotine when you can use a combine harvester!'

A meme about a dozen royals being cut down by the massive farming implement spoke volumes, and she laughed loudly. But when suddenly a small army of police officers descended upon her kitchen, the smile died on her cherubic face, and she frowned. For a moment, she fully expected the queen to have sent these boys and girls in blue down to the kitchen to be fed, and she was already thinking foul thoughts about Serena for not giving her any advance warning.

But when the leader of the pack, that annoying little detective answering to the unlikely name of Stork or Stor or something, slapped a pair of handcuffs on her wrists and told her she was under arrest for the murders of Impi Skingle and Kami Skingle, and subsequently confiscated her phone, she wondered what she had done wrong.

Moments later, that American odd couple also strode in: Case Pimpley and his wife Amelia. The buff detective stood wide-legged in front of her, clearly intent on intimidating her into a confession, with his wife hanging back and looking all bushy-tailed and bright-eyed as usual.

"I didn't do it," she said, tilting up her chin in a gesture of defiance. "And if you think I did, prove it!" There. That should give them food for thought.

But then Stork held up her phone and read, "'The aristocracy should be wiped from the face of the earth, but not before answering for the many crimes it has committed over the course of history. We need to set up new Nuremberg trials, and when convicted, hang them all from the highest tree!'" He gave the cook a serious look. "You're not a big fan of the aristocracy, are you, Mrs. Möttönen?" He held up the phone for the benefit of his associates. "There's a lot more just like it, just as you suspected, Mrs. Kingsley."

In spite of herself, Tilly blanched, and she suddenly felt very weak. Looked like the gig was finally up! She fought the aristocracy and the aristocracy won.

* * *

THE COOK HAD BEEN TAKEN to one of the small meeting rooms on the ground floor to be interrogated by the team of detectives, and this time she was more alert than she had been when we had tried to induce her to part with some good grub. Her hair was askew, her face pale as a sheet, and her cheekbones flushed like twin red lights. All in all, she didn't look all that happy for having been earmarked as a serial killer.

"I didn't do it, I'm telling you!" she cried.

"They all say that, don't they, Max?" said Dooley.

"Yeah, it is something we've heard before," I agreed.

"I just hope they'll get this over with quickly," said Harriet. "I'm starving."

"Without a cook in the kitchen, I'm afraid we're sunk, sweet pea," said Brutus sadly.

Harriet frowned. "We should have waited before turning her in. At least until she had fed us. Now what are we going to do?"

These considerations would have to be put on hold, though, for the cook clearly wasn't ready yet to start singing like a canary.

"These messages," Detective Storrs said, waving the cook's phone, "tell a very different message, Mrs. Möttönen. These messages, written as 'Royalslayer69,' tell the story of a woman intent on slaughtering as many members of the aristocracy as possible. Spraying them with machine guns. Cutting them down with machetes. Flattening them with boulders. On and on and on. There's no limit to the cruelty and terror you were prepared to unleash on these people—your own employers!"

"It's just talk," said the cook, desperately wringing her hands as big tears trickled down her cheeks. "Just idle talk. I would never actually hurt anyone."

"And yet you did. Yesterday morning you took a meat tenderizer from your kitchen and finally lived out your fantasy by murdering Princess Impi in cold blood. An innocent mother of two children! A woman held in high regard amongst the populace because she was one of their own. A commoner. And yet that didn't stop you from cutting her down in the most gruesome fashion possible!"

"No! I didn't do that!"

"And you liked it. Oh, you were giddy with the sheer excitement of finally seeing 'blood flowing in the streets like water,' as you have so often fantasized about and shared with your many followers. So you decided to do it again this morning, by taking another innocent life. This time Princess Kami, a former teacher, who was so happy to start a family with the husband she loved. But that was before you lay in wait for her and struck her down with your heinous murderous instinct and hatred for the aristocracy. What do you have to say for yourself?"

"That I didn't do any of it! I don't like the aristocrats, that's true, but I would never murder them! They're my employers. Where would I be if they all died? I wouldn't have a job!"

"You won't have a job now. Disgrace will follow you wherever you go, but first you will serve a long sentence in a high-security prison. And while you await trial, you can think about the justice system in this country, which is a lot more humane than you are."

The cook shed bitter tears. "Now who's going to cook for the banquet!" she wept. "Serena will be absolutely livid!"

CHAPTER 41

*V*esta was finally starting to enjoy herself in the strange surroundings where fate had placed her. Even though she still felt a little homesick, she was beginning to see the benefits of spending Christmas at Vaasu Castle. A huge Christmas tree had been erected in the main hallway, and it looked absolutely gorgeous. It reached all the way up to the roof and was a marvel of lights and sparkling delight. A second tree had been put in the main dining room downstairs, and presents had suddenly appeared out of nowhere, with Hely especially already eager to unwrap them and find out their contents.

And not only that, but small trees had been distributed amongst the different rooms in the castle, with one even having found its home in Vesta's own room, a gesture she appreciated very much.

To top it all off, Odelia had just announced that the murderer of the two princesses had been arrested. Much to everyone's surprise, it was the cook! Turned out that she was some kind of rabid anti-royalist who had been plotting to take the aristocracy down a peg or two by taking them out one by one. Before long, she no doubt would have murdered the rest of the family, so it was much to Odelia and Chase's credit that they had stopped the woman from carrying out her bloodthirsty intent.

Though, as Odelia had revealed to her, it was, in fact, her cats who had discovered the evil plot when they had tried to persuade the cook to fill their bowls. That's what you got when you forgot to feed your cats: they turned on you and turned you in!

So, with a pep in her step, Vesta now stepped out onto the terrace and glanced around. There was a definite nip in the air, and according to some weather reports, there might be snow at some point over the course of the next few days. Which would be just in time for Christmas. So, all in all, things were definitely looking up!

Scarlett had sent her a message with a picture of her own Christmas tree. This was before Clarice had climbed said tree and had managed to tear it down. So Vesta had to record a message that Scarlett could play each time Clarice threatened to jump into her tree again. The message told the formerly feral cat in no uncertain terms that under no circumstances was she to go anywhere near Scarlett's precious tree with the intent of compromising its structural integrity. And lo and behold: Clarice actually listened!

The extra-delicious treats Scarlett had promised if she behaved had probably helped.

Vesta wandered along the grounds and wondered where her feet would take her today. To the lake again? Or in the direction of the mountains? Or to look in on the horses? That was one of the benefits of owning an actual castle: you had so many opportunities to explore that you didn't get when you lived in a relatively small house in the city. If in Hampton Cove she wanted to stretch her legs, the park or the beach were pretty much the only destinations available.

Oh, and the woods, of course, but for some reason, she wasn't a big fan of the woods. Too creepy for her taste! Give her the great outdoors any time.

And she was just going where her feet took her when she happened upon Prince Asko again. She had to admit she liked the old bird. He was nuts, yes, but he was also a lot of fun to talk to. You never knew what he was going to say next!

"Hey, prince," she said, therefore.

He looked up and gave her a radiant smile. "Vesta! Always a delight. What are you up to this time?"

"Oh, I don't know. I thought I'd go for a walk but didn't know where to go."

"This morning's murder not enough excitement for you, eh?"

She shivered when she thought back to that horrid scene. "Oh, that was terrible. Poor Kami. She didn't deserve that."

"No, she certainly did not," the prince agreed. They fell into step, and for a moment, a companionable silence persisted. Then he said, "Is it true that they arrested the cook?"

"Yes, they did. Turns out she was the leader of an anti-royalist hate group on the internet and was planning to wipe out the entire aristocracy."

"Imagine that," said the Prince, clearly shaken. "She could have murdered us all in our beds if she wanted to, which begs the question: why didn't she?"

"What do you mean?"

"She was the cook. She could easily have slipped some cyanide into our food or some arsenic and killed us all. So why didn't she do it?"

"Well, she probably didn't want to get caught. When people die because their food has been poisoned, I can imagine the cook is the first person the police would be looking at. So she decided to take a different approach and bludgeon her victims to death instead."

"But she selected a tenderizer as her murder weapon. Wouldn't that have put the police on her trail as well? Cook? Tenderizer? It is an instrument of their trade."

"Yeah, I guess," said Vesta. Truth be told, she wasn't all that interested in this particular murder case. She had come to Liechtenburg to relax, not to get involved in the same stuff she got involved in back home. And besides, somehow she felt a little lost without her good friend Scarlett to act as her sounding board. Like Bert without Ernie. Or Laurel without Hardy. "So you think the cook didn't do it?"

"Oh, I'm not a police detective," said the prince, "so I wouldn't pretend to know anything. But it simply strikes me as odd that Tilly would be the one who murdered Impi and Kami, that's all."

"So who do you think did it?"

He smiled. "My brother, of course. As we all know by now, the man has lost his marbles and is a danger to himself and others. Instead of keeping him up there in his room, he should be admitted to a psychiatric hospital where he will be locked away."

"But... my son-in-law confirmed that he's bedridden."

"Stuff and nonsense. My brother is perfectly capable of getting out of his bed whenever he chooses to. I'm sure he's simply pretending to be bedridden to fool us all. In fact, it wouldn't surprise me if he's not also the famous Tiffany Thief everyone is in such a tizzy over. The man is crazy! And I should know since I've known him all his life."

"Okay," said Vesta. This certainly had given her food for thought, and she vowed to transmit the information to her granddaughter without delay. Though now that the cook had been arrested, the investigation was probably closed. Once the police got their guy—or gal in this case—they more or less lost interest.

They had reached the lake, and the prince took out a small paper bag and started feeding the ducks, even though a sign planted next to the lake clearly stated, 'Don't feed the ducks!'

They took a seat on the bench that offered a magnificent view of the lake, with the mountain range in the distance as the perfect backdrop.

"So why aren't you married, Asko?" she asked, deciding to broach a topic she had been thinking about a lot. Even though it had taken her a while to get used to the place, she now thought it wouldn't be a bad life to be queen of an entire country. And even though the idea was only a vague outline in her mind, the thought had occurred to her that if King Thad abdicated, and his sons weren't eligible to be his successors since they were both without a wife now, and the third son wasn't eligible because of his pedigree, Asko had every chance of becoming the next ruler of Liechtenburg.

And if that happened, whoever married the man would be queen. And since she and Asko got along pretty great...

"Like I told you before, I have every intention of getting married," said Asko.

She smiled. "Oh, that. You were kidding, though, right? Riling up your family? Giving them something to think about?"

He gave her a stern-faced look. "I wasn't kidding. I talked to the archbishop this morning, and he informed me that he has placed the matter to His Holiness the Pope. Once word comes back from Rome that they approve of the match, I will marry Anne and Julie in Vaasu's grand cathedral in a splendid service." He smiled a beatific smile. "The brides will dress in white, of course, and as soon as the marriage has been consecrated, I will be the happiest man in the world.

And God willing, I will be the new king, and they will be my queens."

Okay, so obviously it wasn't just the king who was a fruit loop but his brother as well. She sighed deeply as she saw her roseate dreams of becoming queen of Liechtenburg pop like a soap bubble.

In the distance, she saw that two-bit actor Grant Chubb harass that poor Princess Ainikki again, and wondered if she shouldn't go over there and put the guy across her knee and spank his behind.

CHAPTER 42

$\mathcal{M}$arge, who had also gone out for a stroll, once again encountered a sight she did not like: Grant Chubb in the company of Princess Ainikki. She had no clear plan as to how to proceed once she got there, but she still set out in their direction, intent on doing something about what she felt was a most undesirable match. Especially considering that Odelia had told her about Grant's numerous attempts at flirtation and also his admission that he had engaged in affairs both with Princess Kami and Princess Impi—Ainikki's own mother!

Did this man have no shame? The answer was obvious.

Her arrival coincided with that of Eloy Linnanen, and the boy was clearly as unhappy with the state of affairs as Marge herself. But when she was within earshot of the couple, she discovered to her surprise that things were quite different than the interpretation she had put upon the facts from a distance.

Ainikki was crying, and for a moment, she thought that the actor had assaulted her in some way. But then the actor turned to her and said, "I told her that there's no way I'm getting involved with her. Can you please make her understand that she's too young for me?"

"You're cruel!" said Ainikki with typical childish exaggeration. "The cruelest man in the universe!"

Grant smiled a sad smile. "You're just a child, Ainikki. And I may have something of an amoral streak running through my personality, but I'm not that amoral that I would ever cross that line. Maybe when you're a little older and you're grown up. Though by that time you'll probably realize there are other, more suitable men out there for you." He cast a meaningful look at Eloy when he spoke these words.

But Eloy clearly misunderstood the message. For he instantly held up his hands in a pugilistic stance and said, "I'll fight you, Chubb! I'll fight you for her!"

The actor gave him a curious look. "You really like her, don't you?"

"A duel!" Eloy yelled. "I challenge you to a duel. Pick your weapon, and I'll meet you tomorrow morning at dawn!"

The actor yawned. "Let's not. I don't get up before ten o'clock if I can help it. Unless Scorsese calls, of course."

The kid had taken off his jacket and was dancing like an experienced boxer, darting jabs in the actor's direction.

"This has been fun," said Grant now. "But I'm afraid I must leave you. Places to go, people to see, things to do," he added vaguely, and he walked off, holding up his hand and twiddling his fingers in a gesture of goodbye.

Eloy stared after him. "Where is he going?" he asked.

Ainikki shot him a fiery look. "This is all your fault!" she screamed. "You ruined my life!!!"

"What?" asked the kid uncertainly.

"If it wasn't for you, he would have kissed me for sure!" And then it was her turn to walk off angrily, muttering strange oaths under her breath about evil stalkers who wouldn't leave her alone.

The kid looked a little punch-drunk, even though he and Grant hadn't actually exchanged any punches. Then again, sometimes words can have an effect more deleterious than a punch, and clearly Ainikki's words had hit the young man hard.

"She hates me," he said brokenly. "I love her, but she hates me!"

"She doesn't hate you," Marge assured him. "She's just infatuated with Grant right now. A schoolgirl crush on a famous celebrity." Only when ordinary folks develop such a crush, all they can do is admire the idol from afar and possibly hang up a poster of them in their bedroom. But with Ainikki, it was a little more tricky since the object of her affection was right there, seemingly available, willing, and able to reciprocate her youthful feelings.

"What am I going to do!" cried Eloy, burying his face in his hands. Just like Ainikki, his emotions ran very close to the surface and were on the dramatic side.

"She'll settle down," Marge said. This, she knew from experience. Once upon a time, Odelia had been madly in love with a local singer who had all the hallmarks of being something of a loser. But of course, at fifteen, Odelia had been blind to the man's defects and had idolized him to no end, even going so far as to interview the man for the school paper and handing him a love letter she had written.

Finally, Marge had sat her daughter down and told her in no uncertain terms what kind of a man this singer really was. At first, Odelia hadn't believed her, of course, but then a scandal had erupted involving the singer, a cocaine dealer, and the dealer's wife. The singer had engaged in an affair with the wife, at which point the dealer had chopped off a few of the singer's digits. The upshot was that the singer's career had tanked, and soon he had joined the land of has-beens, of which there are plenty in showbiz.

Somehow she had a feeling Grant Chubb's star would soon wane if he kept up the kind of behavior he was displaying.

She gave the kid a good rub across the back and a hug.

"Thank you, Mrs. Poole," he said brokenly. "But I don't think it will make any difference. She hates me so much, I can feel it."

She smiled and said with the confidence of one who had been through quite a few storms herself, "Everything will be fine, Eloy. Just you wait and see."

GRANT WAS SERIOUSLY THINKING that maybe the time had come to leave the party before it was over. Within the space of the last couple of days, there had been two murders, and now this business with the girl. Even though he had come for the Christmas banquet and the ball, which Vaasu Castle was rightly famous for, he was starting to consider that he was better off someplace else for Christmas. His mother wouldn't agree, of course, since she loved the banquet.

He arrived back at his room after his run-in with that crazy impetuous kid and opened the door to be greeted by an unusual sight: that majordomo was going through his stuff!

"Hey, what do you think you're doing?" he said as he left the door open, just in case the man turned violent.

"I was merely ascertaining that our cleaning crew did their job to our usual standards, sir," said the majordomo stiffly.

"Your hands are literally rifling through my underwear."

The majordomo glanced down as if to ascertain the veracity of this statement, and when he saw that his hands were indeed rifling through the actor's undergarments, immediately retracted them as if stung. "I like to be thorough, sir," he said, but his words lacked the ring of true conviction.

"You're spying on me, aren't you?" he said, closing the door now. He didn't think the guy presented an actual danger. "You think I'm this Tiffany Thief, and you're going through my stuff to see if I stole any of that jewelry."

After a pause, the majordomo confessed, "The thought had crossed my mind."

"Well, I can tell you with my hand on my heart that I'm innocent. If you'll remember, my mother was one of the victims. Now would I steal from my own mother?"

"It has been known to happen, simply to throw the police off the scent," the majordomo pointed out. He seemed nervous, Grant thought, and he shouldn't wonder. His employment was probably hanging by a thread if word got out that he was subjecting his employers' guests to this kind of treatment.

"Did you find anything? Watches, rings, bracelets?"

"No, I did not," the man admitted.

"That's because you're barking up the wrong tree, my good man. I don't know who this thief is, but it's not me." Then he studied the guy a little closer. He had an amazingly fascinating face. Kind of elongated and completely devoid of emotion. And his posture was amazing as well: stiff as a board. As if he was half robot, half human. Or maybe more like 100 percent robot. "You know, I think you're an amazing character," he told the guy. "Have you considered an acting career?"

The man seemed surprised by this suggestion. "Well... no."

"Trust me, you should. In fact, I could offer you a part in my next movie right now. It's a thriller, you see. A spy thriller. I play a retired secret agent, and I get in bad with my former employer who decides to hunt me down and kill me. My opponent is this killing machine who will stop at nothing until I'm dead in the ground." He pointed to the majordomo. "I think you should be that guy."

A flicker of emotion seemed to shimmer across the man's face. "I'm extremely honored, sir. But are you sure? I have no acting experience."

"You don't need any! You've got the chops, man. A raw talent in the making. With some guidance from yours truly, you could be big. Huge! The next Arnie."

"I do like the occasional spy thriller, sir," the majordomo confessed. "I like to read them before retiring to bed. They seem to exact a certain soporific effect."

"Nothing like reading a good thriller before bedtime, huh? I'm with you, buddy. I'm the same way. So let me talk to my agent and let me get back to you, all right? And then let's make a movie!"

CHAPTER 43

ight had come, and Dooley and I were sound asleep at the foot of Odelia and Chase's bed when all of a sudden, a loud hiss sounded nearby. When I opened my eyes, I saw that the hiss emanated from Brutus, who was at the connecting door, trying to draw our attention.

"It's happening again!" he loud-whispered.

"What is happening again, Brutus?" asked Dooley.

"The thief! He's in Gran's room this time, going through her things!"

"He must be desperate," I said with a yawn. "Gran didn't even bring any of her jewelry."

"Maybe he'll steal her hairnet," Dooley said. "Gran won't like that, Max. She's very fond of that hairnet. It keeps her hair looking nice and tidy."

"He can't steal her hairnet since she wears it in her sleep," I pointed out.

"He can if he's very skilled. And this guy is very skilled. He's already managed to escape us twice."

"Well, he's not going to escape a third time," I said and jumped down from the bed.

We hurried after Brutus as he crossed Marge and Tex's room, and soon we found ourselves passing another connecting door and came upon Harriet, who was keeping an eye on the masked intruder. The man was rifling through Gran's things, and if his frantic movements were anything to go by, he was becoming more and more frustrated when he discovered that she didn't have anything purchased from Tiffany's. Gran doesn't believe in being a big spender. Also, she doesn't have a lot of money to spend, so there's that, of course.

"So how are we doing this?" I asked.

"We have to cover all the exits this time," said Harriet. "That means the window, the doors, the walls... You take the window, Max, and you, Dooley, make sure he doesn't escape through the door. Brutus, you watch that wall over there, the one with the movable panel."

"And you?" asked Brutus. "Where will you be?"

A mischievous look had appeared in Harriet's eye. "I'll go and give him a little nudge. Persuade him to make a break for it."

We all gulped. Making a break for it meant that he would try to pass by us—or through us if he was that desperate.

"What if he has a knife?" I said in a small voice.

"Or a gun!" said Brutus.

"Or a can of mace!" said Dooley.

"We'll just have to take our chances," said Harriet with a shrug.

"Or we could wake up our humans," I suggested.

"By the time they wake up, he'll be long gone. You know what they're like. Takes them about twenty minutes to wake up—at least."

That was true enough. Even in the morning, Odelia needs

gallons of coffee before her mind boots up and her body follows suit. It seems to be one of the drawbacks of being human: they're extremely slow starters!

And so we decided to follow Harriet's plan of campaign. I took up position near the window, Dooley covered the door, and Brutus stood sentry near the wall.

We watched as Harriet tiptoed to the thief, who was still going through Gran's personal belongings in blatant disregard of the laws that govern personal property, and when she had reached him, produced a soft meow.

The thief stopped his loathsome activities and looked down at the kitty-cat who had taken up position at his feet. He then bent down and spoke that tired old standby, "Here, kitty, kitty."

As he reached for her, she drew her claws and gave him a scratch across the hand.

"Ouch!" he said. "What did you do that for?"

"That's for stealing!" she said viciously. And proceeded to dig her claws into the man's leg. "And that's for making us chase you!"

The man yowled in agony, and then, as Harriet had foreseen, legged it. For a moment, we were in anxious anticipation as to where he would go, but then, as I watched on, he made a beeline for the window!

"You guys, he's going to escape through the window!" I said.

"Stop him, Max!" Harriet cried.

"But how! He's very big!"

"Just scratch him! Jump on top of him and act crazy!"

I'd seen all of the YouTube clips, of course, of cats going completely berserk and scratching, clawing, and biting, jumping all over the place and generally making quite the spectacle of themselves. It's just that I'd never engaged in that type of behavior myself, figuring it was undignified and an unnecessary expenditure of energy. But when I saw that guy running at me, and with Harriet egging me on, I guess something snapped, and I decided to go for it.

And so I screamed and yowled and jumped around and scratched and clawed and bit and showed the guy every corner of the room. When the dust settled, and I finally settled down again, I saw that no fewer than six humans were staring at me with fear written all over their features: Gran, Odelia, Chase, Marge, Tex… and the unfortunate Tiffany Thief, who was on the ground and cowering to some extent.

Even Brutus, Harriet, and Dooley sat staring at me, in awe.

"I guess maybe I overdid it a little?" I said, a slight blush mantling my cheeks.

"Oh, no, Max," said Harriet. "You were amazing!"

"I didn't know you had it in you, buddy," said Brutus.

"Are you feeling all right, Max?" asked Dooley with a touch of concern.

"I'm fine," I said. "Just… a little hyped up, you know. Must be all that adrenaline."

"Please, no more," said the thief. "Save me from that monster!"

"So you thought you could break into my room, huh?" said Gran. "Well, serves you right!" And with this, she pulled the mask from the man's face to reveal… Prince Urpo!

CHAPTER 44

"*D*o you know how boring it is to be the spare?" asked Urpo as he watched Marge dress his wounds. I felt a little embarrassed, but as Marge said, "It looks worse than it is. Like acupuncture, you know? It's probably even good for you."

They had set the prince down in the armchair, and the man looked thoroughly unsettled by the recent events.

"My whole life I've been told to play second fiddle, with Dane always getting preferential treatment since he was the crown prince. He got the best food, the best private tutors, the best education. Heck, he even had a better seat at the dinner table. And then later it turned out I couldn't even get a job, since that wouldn't be proper. So when I asked my dad what I was supposed to do with my life, he said I should support my brother. So basically, he condemned me to a life of serfdom to my big brother."

"And so you decided to become a thief," said Chase, who stood eyeing the man with a distinct lack of sympathy, arms folded across his chest and a forbidding frown on his face.

"Just to pass the time, you know," said Prince Urpo with a

shrug. "And to bring some excitement into my life. At least now people suddenly talked about me. They noticed me—or at least my work. And it's not as if they couldn't afford to miss the items I stole. All of the people I robbed belong to the upper crust."

"I'm honored that you would think I belong to the upper crust," said Marge. "But I'm afraid I don't."

"I didn't steal anything of value, did I? A phone, some worthless baubles."

Marge fumed a little. "That phone was mine, and so were those baubles."

"I was just curious to see what made you people tick. It's so rare my mother's guests aren't famous actors or singers or members of other royal houses. So I was interested to see what your family was about."

"Cats," said Gran acerbically. "We're all about cats, as you can probably tell," she added, pointing to a nasty scratch across the man's cheek.

"Yeah, I can tell that you really like cats," said Urpo as he darted a nervous look in my direction.

"I'm normally not like this," I explained. "I just felt cornered, so I lashed out."

"No need to apologize, Max," said Brutus. "You did good."

I sighed. "I don't know about that."

"We caught him, didn't we?" said Harriet. "That's what counts."

"The end justifies the means," said Dooley blithely. "Isn't that what Adolf Hitler said?"

I groaned. "Dooley, please. I feel bad enough as it is."

"Oh, I'm sorry, Max. I thought you'd like to hear a few choice quotes from history."

"Not now, Dooley," said Harriet sternly.

"So what are we supposed to do with you, huh?" said Chase.

"Well, call the police, of course," said Tex. "He may be a prince, but he's also a thief. So let the police deal with him."

"Please don't tell the police," the prince begged. "It's going to be a huge scandal, and my life will effectively be over."

"Have a heart," said Odelia. "The man's wife just died."

"What if we tell the queen?" Chase suggested.

"No, not my mother!" Urpo said. "I prefer the police!"

"Okay, so maybe you decide," said Marge, turning to her daughter. "You have a pretty good moral compass for this stuff."

Odelia hesitated. "I'm not sure. On the one hand, what he did is morally reprehensible. But on the other hand... I do feel touched by his story."

The prince winced as Marge dressed his final wound. He would have to go through life with some scratches and bruises for a couple of days, but that couldn't be helped. At least he would live.

"Oh, please," said Gran. "I mean, give me a break. The guy has led a life of privilege. Private education, private jets, fancy cars, lives in an actual castle, never had to pay for anything, never had to work for a living. So he doesn't get to be the king. Big deal! I don't get to be queen. Do you hear me complaining how life has been so tough on me I have to start robbing people? It's just a lot of hooey."

"Let's call the cops," said Tex, taking out his phone.

"Wait," said Odelia, and turned to the prince. "You can't do this again, all right? Ever. If we catch you breaking into people's rooms again and stealing their personal stuff, it's game over, you understand?"

He nodded fervently. "Absolutely. You have my word that I will never do this again. The Tiffany Thief is retiring—forever."

"Babe, you're entirely too nice for your own good," said Chase.

"I believe him," said Odelia. "He had a big scare, and I believe he has learned his lesson."

"I have," said the prince. "I have learned my lesson, and I will never do it again—I promise."

"Oh, for crying out loud," said Gran, who clearly didn't believe a word the prince was saying. But then Gran is something of a cynic.

"Thank you so much for believing in me," said the prince when it dawned on him that his secret was safe with us. "You're the most incredible woman I've ever met." And he pressed a kiss to Odelia's hand.

"Hey, watch it, fellow!" said Chase.

But Odelia smiled.

Maybe she was right. Sometimes you have to give people a second chance. And something told me that Urpo would take this chance and make something of his life now. A life that didn't revolve around his brother and the royal dynasty.

And if not, he could always ask me for another tango.

CHAPTER 45

a week had passed since the disconcerting events that had shocked us all, and things had finally settled down a little. The Tiffany Thief had been caught, and also the murderer, and preparations for the big Christmas banquet and ball were in full swing.

Odelia had told Queen Serena that the Tiffany Thief was, in fact, her youngest son, and even though the queen was surprised, she understood why Odelia had decided not to turn him in. She also understood her son's reasoning to some extent, even though she certainly couldn't attach her seal of approval to the crazy stunt he had pulled. But she had promised not to punish Prince Urpo and maybe see if she couldn't find a way to offering him a role that was more meaningful.

Even though our job was done, and we were free to return home, the Pooles decided to stick around and enjoy the queen's hospitality until after Christmas. Now that we had come this far, Queen Serena insisted we shouldn't miss the ball.

A new cook had been engaged, and this one didn't appear to harbor any homicidal grudge against the aristocracy. What was even better was that she didn't forget to feed us, like the old cook had. Heljä Lovelass, the maid who initially had been accused of murder, had returned to her station, even though she had been asked, in a discreet interview with Serena, to remove all the pictures dedicated to Urpo and not to be so hung up on the prince.

Harriet was still determined to become the one and only royal mouser and earn her spot in the limelight, and each time she passed Anne and Julie in the many hallways and corridors of the castle, she was subjected to their ire and their nasty glances. But she didn't let that affect her too much, since she knew that in the end, her perseverance would prevail.

After all, it was her plan that had been instrumental in catching the thief, and that had given her self-confidence quite a boost. To the extent that she felt that we would stay on at the castle forever, and that she would rule the roost, so to speak.

I wasn't entirely sure what a banquet was, exactly, except that it involved food in large quantities, and also alcohol, which some humans seem to enjoy and others less so. As a rule, cats don't drink alcohol, so that part of the banquet would be of less interest to us. But the food part definitely held our attention, and it was with some measure of anticipation that we looked forward to the feast.

"I think they'll have wild boar," said Dooley. "Princess Hely was reading this comic book called Asterix, about a tribe of Gaulish warriors who lived in Roman times, that apparently is very popular in these parts, and at the end of the story, they always have boar. Lots and lots of them."

"I very much doubt whether there are still a lot of wild

boars around," I told him, dashing his hopes to some extent. "And also, it's just a comic, Dooley, not real life."

"Are you sure? Because it looks very delicious. And Hely told her sister that the banquet will be just like in those comics."

"Hely is ten," I pointed out. "So I'll bet it's just wishful thinking." Next, she would be reading Harry Potter and telling everyone who would listen that the banquet would be like the feasts at Hogwarts. That wasn't to say it wouldn't be epic, of course, and I was certainly amongst those who looked forward to the bash.

Florists had been coming and going, and catering vans were littering the drive, along with the people in charge of the entertainment, and of course the haute couture dressers who had been hired to make sure the queen was the belle of the ball. Not only the castle was a hive of activity, but also the kitchen, where all the food would have to be prepared or at the very least stored before the big feast.

The only uncertainty was whether King Thad would put in an appearance. News from the ruler's bedroom was speculative, with Tex blowing hot and cold. One day he would declare the king fit for duty, while the next he would call into question any news that the king might join the banquet or even the ball. All in all, it was up in the air whether Thad would attend the feast thrown in his honor.

A light dusting of snow had covered the ground the day after we had caught Urpo breaking into Gran's room, and that dusting had gradually increased in intensity, until two days ago nature had finally made up its mind and now the ground was once again covered with a thick carpet of the frosty white stuff.

As I think I've stated before in these chronicles, I'm not a big fan of snow. I can take it or leave it alone, so guess you could say I'm agnostic about the phenomenon. I mean, it's cold, it's wet, it wreaks havoc on one's paws. But then I saw Princess Ainikki pulling a sleigh with her sister Hely perched on said sleigh, and I figured here was a fine way to adapt to these unpleasant circumstances. And then I saw Eloy pulling the same sleigh, only this time with Princess Ainikki occupying the instrument, and they seemed to be having a grand old time.

In other words: what's bad for some may be pleasant or even beneficial to others. In that sense, it's a good idea always to keep an open mind.

The day of the ball had finally arrived, and when I opened my eyes, I could tell that the weather gods had finally decided that enough was enough and had closed the tap on that big snow cannon in the sky. A glorious sun was out and turning the world into a wonderland of sparkling diamonds and glittering ice and snow.

"Oh, wow!" said Grace as she watched from our bedroom window. "Look at that! It's almost like a fairy tale!"

And I had to admit it had something. I wasn't sure what, but something. At least now the snow would start melting again, and the world would return to its old snowless form.

Okay, so maybe I'm not the best person to write a Christmas story!

Chase picked up his daughter, and when Odelia joined us, the trio stood gazing out of the window with happy smiles on their faces.

"What's going on, Max?" asked Dooley, who had just woken up.

"It stopped snowing, and everybody is happy," I summed up the state of affairs.

"Oh, good. Then maybe we can finally go for a walk again."

The only one who hadn't been adversely affected by all this snow business was Ariana, who had kept up her daily habit of going for walks. She had admitted to us that she loved doing her business in a little pile of snow, since it was so soft and your doodoo simply disappeared straight into the pile. And since she had extolled the virtues of this procedure to such an extent, the four of us had taken turns doing our business in the snow, just as she had said. I mean, it wasn't bad, but I still prefer my usual litter. Much easier on the paws, if you know what I mean.

Marge and Tex now also joined us, and Gran, and before long, they had all arranged to go for a pre-breakfast walk through the grounds. And since that left us out, we decided to go down and have a look at the big Christmas tree.

Arriving there, we found that all of Prince Asko's cats had the same idea, and also Ariana. For a moment, a certain sense of enmity reigned, until Ariana felt that enough was enough and decided to put an end to this cold war once and for all.

"Okay, you're going to apologize to Harriet at once," she told Anne.

"No, I will not!" the Persian said stubbornly. "She's a trespasser who's been trying to steal our mice and I will not apologize!"

"She is not a trespasser," Ariana pointed out with infinite patience, which endeared her to me even more, if that was possible. I didn't know how she put up with these intolerably rude cats. "She is an honored guest, as are her friends, and if you can't be nice to Queen Serena's guests, you don't deserve to be part of this menagerie. Now apologize, and be quick about it! Chop chop!"

Julie and Anne shared a look and finally seemed to decide that maybe the best course of action was to do as the royal Shih Tzu said.

"Okay, fine," said Anne. "But let it be shown in the record that I'm doing this under duress."

"Duly noted," said Ariana with an amused smile.

"Harriet, I apologize if I've treated you with less than kindness," said Anne.

"What she said," said Julie.

"Do it properly!" said Ariana.

"Okay, okay! Harriet, I apologize," said Julie. "It wasn't nice of us to chase you around the castle and try to scratch you." She darted a look at me that I couldn't quite interpret. Was it fear? Was it admiration? A little bit of both. "We heard all about what you did to Prince Urpo, Max. That must have been quite a spectacle."

"Yeah, you're a real warrior, Max," Anne added.

"Oh, well," I said modestly. "All in a day's work."

"Max did that on my instructions," Harriet pointed out.

"He did?" asked Anne, her eyes going wide. "You told him to go to town on the prince like that?"

"It was the only way to stop him," said Harriet. "He would have escaped, you know, just like he had escaped many times before."

"We knew it was him, of course," said Julie. "But we don't have the benefit of having our human's ear, like you do. So there was no way for us to communicate what we had discovered."

"You could have told me," said Ariana.

"We figured you didn't like us very much," said Anne with a touch of uncertainty.

"Not like you! We're all in the same boat here, you guys. We have to support each other, not be in competition all the time."

"I guess so," said Julie. "It's just that... with the royals being at loggerheads all the time—prince against prince, queen against king and vice versa—I guess we figured that was the way to go about things. But now I can see how wrong we were."

"Put it there, pal!" said Brutus, caught by a sudden mood

of exuberance at this thawing of the relations between cats and dog. He held out his paw, and when both Julie and Anne stared at it, not comprehending, he added, "Give me five! Give me some skin!"

It took some explaining, but in the end we all exchanged cordial greetings. Perhaps not as cordial as Brutus would have liked, but it was still a major improvement over how things had been since we had arrived at the castle. And so soon we were all chatting pleasantly. Turns out the cats weren't au courant of Prince Asko's plans to marry them, and when we explained what he was up to, they confessed their unease with this plan.

"Marry that guy? Never!" said Anne.

"God, no," said Julie. "Can you imagine us dressed in white, striding down the aisle in front of thousands of people like a bunch of freaks? We'd be the laughingstock of the whole world." She turned to her friend. "Let's elope. Deal?"

"Deal," said Anne. "Marry that fool? He must be nuts."

Clearly, the excitement of the upcoming marriage of Prince Asko and his cats was entirely one-sided. I just hoped it wouldn't turn into one of those forced marriages you always hear about.

But then if that happened, wiser councils would surely prevail.

One thing we learned from Prince Asko's collected cats, and also Ariana, was that rumor had it that the king had decided to put in an appearance at the banquet to announce that he would appoint his illegitimate son his rightful heir.

"The queen is very upset about it," said Ariana. "As you can probably imagine. And she vows to put a stop to it."

"But how can she?" asked Anne. "The king is still... well, the king. He can do as he pleases."

"Oh, she will stop him," said Ariana. "Thad might be the king, but Serena is no pushover either. She'll find a way to get rid of Buffy and that son of hers, if it's the last thing she does. At least that's what she told Tiia. And I believe her."

I shared a look with my friends. Things were hotting up again, and not just outside, where the sun was giving of its best, but inside the castle as well.

CHAPTER 46

*J*iminy Mouse wasn't entirely sure this whole business with the theatrics was a good idea. Mrs. Jiminy Mouse had told him he was crazy, and perhaps she was right. His kids had all expressed a fervent wish for him to "Stop this foolishness now, Pop!" and he couldn't deny they might have a point. After all, who in their right mind would voluntarily go and sit in the gaping maw of the most dangerous creature known to mouse-kind? But then Jiminy had always been a special mouse. Not long ago were the days he used to race through the castle on one of Princess Ainikki's roller skates, just for the heck of it. He and his buddies, a motley crew of no-good punks who liked to call themselves the 'Riot Rodents,' had been the bane of their parents' existence, with their crazy stunts and their dare-devilry.

Now settled down and a paterfamilias himself, he fully understood the terrible ordeal he'd put his parents through back in the day. Karma had blessed him with a son who liked to get up to similar stunts, calling himself Murine Menace and occasionally sneaking into the kitchen to steal all kinds of treats and challenge the servants. At least he had the good sense never to fall into the trap of being caught in a mouse-trap. Jiminy had raised his kids better than that.

And now this business with Harriet. A stranger, as his wife had pointed out, whose antecedents they knew nothing about, except that she lived far away, so when things turned bad, she could always go home while they had to live at Vaasu Castle and suffer the fallout if their crazy stunt backfired.

And then of course it had backfired to some extent, with no one paying even the least bit of attention to them, except those horrible cats belonging to Prince Asko, who had almost caught them.

So when Harriet showed up on the eve of the big annual Christmas banquet and asked him to give this idea of hers another shot, at first, he'd been inclined to shoot it down. But then it got him thinking. A lot of people would be present at the banquet, and amongst them probably plenty of folks who worked for the media, since this type of bash always drew a lot of attention from the press. So what if this time they managed to make a go of it? What if they managed to land their picture on the front page of the *Liechtenburg Times* or one of the lesser rags?

And so even though he had told his wife and kids that he was quitting Harriet's scheme, he decided to give it one more try. And if this time things didn't work, that was it: he quit!

The evening of the banquet had finally arrived, and the castle was buzzing with activity. Catering vans were driving up and down the drive, unloading trays and crates filled with all kinds of delicacies to be enjoyed by the king and queen's hundreds of guests. Since the bash was invitation-only, it would be a select company who were privileged to attend. Plenty of royals, of course, and the movers and shakers of the kingdom, but also surprisingly many so-called commoners, who had received an invitation—a golden ticket, as many called it—to attend this once-in-a-lifetime opportunity to rub shoulders with the upper crust, perhaps even venture out onto the dance floor and swing with the queen.

The sound system had been tested, the DJ was ready to party deep into the night, servers had been hired, and all had been instructed as to their specific tasks, and generally the mood was frantic, electric, jazzed, but also one of great expectation. And so when Harriet came to collect him at the entrance to his cozy little home, he made sure not to alert his wife of his departure, lest she put her paw down and forbid him to join the Persian on her quest, and together they set off in the direction of the great ballroom, where the feast was already in full swing.

Harriet's friends had decided to make themselves scarce and monitor the whole thing from a safe distance. Hundreds of people gathered in the same space, plied with great food and plenty of alcohol, made for a very dangerous combination for your smaller pet. Lest you wanted to be trampled underfoot, it was best to stay away. Which made what they were about to do all the riskier.

"Are you sure you want to go through with this?" asked Harriet, a touch of concern lacing her voice. "It could all backfire terribly."

"I know," he said. "And I'm willing to take the risk if you are."

She took a deep breath. "I hope it works out, Jiminy. And I hope I'll be able to keep you safe. We made peace with the other cats this morning, you know, but that doesn't mean they might not be on the lookout for you. They are the royal mousers, after all, so they have a reputation to uphold."

"You will make sure we are protected from now on, right?"

"I give you my solemn word as cat choir's leading soprano."

He had no idea what she had just said, but it sounded good enough. And so he also took a deep breath and said, "Let's do this."

And so Harriet gently took him between her teeth, making sure not to bite down, and tiptoed into the ballroom. The noise was something terrifying, with the sound of clinking cutlery and chinking glasses and loud conversations on all sides. Servers hurrying to and fro to make sure those dishes kept coming and those glasses were topped up, and generally a good time was clearly had by all.

The main table consisted of the royal family—minus the king, of course, since he had overdone it on his previous fifty banquets and was now laid up with terminal indigestion, or so he had been told—and the rest of the tables were all occupied by Serena's guests. He could see Harriet's humans off to one side, looking cheerful and happy, since according to Harriet they had caught not one but two evildoers over the course of the past few days. As Harriet strode to the fore and took up position in the center of the ballroom, for a moment nothing happened.

Conversations continued unabated, jaws chewed large slabs of meat and other delicious morsels, wine was being chugged down eager gullets, and Jiminy started to get that sinking feeling you get when the best-laid scheme of mice and men goes awry. Though in this case, it was the best-laid scheme of mouse and cat.

And then suddenly, a miracle happened. Someone pointed in their direction and said, "Look! That pretty kitty over there caught a mouse!"

More eyes turned to regard them with interest, and before long, conversations halted, knives and forks were put down, and phones came out. Soon everyone seemed to be chattering excitedly as they took pictures and videos of 'the kitty with the mouse' and they were the talk of the ballroom! Even the queen deigned to take out her phone and snap a few shots, possibly to add to the official royal Instagram, and as an impromptu applause broke out, Harriet took a bow, and then, quite regally, strode from the room, stage left, their mission accomplished.

In this case, stage left consisted of the terrace outside, and once they were in the garden, safely hidden behind a convenient fir, Harriet ever so carefully deposited Jiminy on a bed of greenery. He could see that her eyes were shining with excitement, and he had to admit his own heart was also going pitter-patter.

"That was the bravest thing anyone has ever done!" said Harriet, giving praise where she felt praise was due. "Jiminy Mouse, you are something else."

"And so are you," he said. He didn't want to say it out loud, but it takes a lot of self-restraint for a cat not to gobble up a tasty treat when it voluntarily takes up residence between its teeth!

"I think we did it," said Harriet. "I think we can call this a resounding success. If they don't make me an official royal mouser now..."

"They won't!" suddenly a loud voice sounded nearby. And when Jiminy looked up, he found himself gazing into the unforgiving and cold eyes of... Anne and Julie!

CHAPTER 47

*E*ven though Harriet had half expected the encounter to take place at some point—you don't go out in front of an entire group of human inmates of a royal castle without attracting attention from its feline counterparts— she was still taken aback by the suddenness of the meeting, and the forcefulness with which Anne expressed herself. It was obvious that if nothing was done, the life of Jiminy Mouse would soon come to an inglorious end, and his family would be without a provider.

And since she couldn't let that happen, she stepped in front of the small rodent and said, with all the power of her being: "You shall not pass!" It was a neat little saying, though where she had picked it up, she couldn't quite remember. Possibly from the back of a pack of cereal.

For a moment, tension whipped through the air, and the atmosphere felt electric. She knew from experience that things could go either way, and prepared herself for a cat fight of epic proportions.

But then both Anne and Julie seemed to relax. "You think

you did a great thing tonight, Harriet," said Anne. "But you're wrong. And if you thought that you were going to be a royal mouser from now on, you're sadly mistaken."

"Oh, and why not, pray tell?" she said.

Anne shrugged. "Because there are no royal mousers, that's why."

For a moment, she stared at her fellow Persian, then laughed a light laugh—or at least what she thought was an utterance of careless jollity. "You're very funny, Anne. Of course, there's are royal mousers. You're a royal mouser, and so is Julie."

"No, we're not," said Julie, in much softer tones than her friend. "I don't know where you got that information, Harriet, but there is no such thing as a royal mouser."

"But…"

"Julie is right," said Anne. "You were fed some bad intel. There has never been a royal mouser, and there never will be, for the simple reason that we made a pact with the mice population living at the castle a long time ago. The deal is that they make sure not to be too conspicuous, and in return, we won't try to kill them."

Harriet turned to Jiminy, who was hiding behind her back. "Is this true?"

"First thing I've heard of it," the tiny mouse confessed.

"That's because the deal was negotiated on the highest level," said Anne, darting a look of utter disdain at the mouse. "And since a deal like this is obviously of a very sensitive nature, it was agreed that things would be kept on a need-to-know basis."

"And you, Jiminy Mouse," said Julie finely, "do not need to know."

"Well, I never," said Jiminy, scratching his little head. "So all of this was for nothing?"

"I wouldn't say it was for nothing," said Anne. "It did

bring home to us the obvious need to control the narrative in a more democratic way."

Harriet stared at the cat. "Meaning?"

Anne rolled her eyes. "We probably went a little overboard with our insistence on secrecy. And so from now on, we might be forced to disseminate the historic truce that was made between cats and mice living at Vaasu Castle a little more widely."

"Huh?" said Jiminy.

"Oh, for crying out loud," said Anne. "Because of your little stunt, we'll have no choice but to tell everyone!"

"So why didn't you?" asked Harriet, the obvious question.

"Well, duh," said Anne, rolling her expressive eyes once more. The cat truly was absolutely insufferable, and for a brief moment, Harriet wondered if she was the same way. Then she discarded the notion. Of course she wasn't. She was the loveliest creature in all of Hampton Cove, and by extension, the rest of the world. "If we told every mouse living at the castle, they would simply take advantage of the opportunity and start stepping high, wide, and plentiful. In other words: they'd take over the castle and run rings around us."

"The upshot," Julie continued, "would be that our humans would become very upset when they saw a colony of mice turning the corridors into a racing circuit, sleeping in their beds, and having parties in the pantry, and come down hard on us to do something about it. And then we'd be forced to start hunting you all down for real—or be punished with exile ourselves, with more cruel methods to dispense with mice brought in."

"What could possibly be more cruel than being eaten?" said Jiminy, and Harriet thought he made a pretty good point.

"Where do I begin?" said Anne. "Mousetraps, poison, glue traps…"

"Glue traps!" said Jiminy, gulping a little. "But that's…"

"Cruel," said Julie with a look of concern. "Yeah, we know. Which is why we have to avoid it at all costs. Which means it's very important that both parties stick to the deal."

"Only now that you made it clear that there are still mice at Vaasu Castle," said Anne, with a scathing look at Harriet, "the humans will be extra vigilant and will be on the lookout. So you singlehandedly scuppered a deal that was years in the making and has stood the test of time for generations!"

Harriet blinked. "Well, I guess if you had been a little nicer to me and had told me about this deal of yours, I wouldn't have felt compelled to pull my stunt."

For a moment, both Persians faced off, then Julie decided to interfere. "Guys, we're all friends here. Let's not fight, all right?"

"Fine," said Anne between gritted teeth.

"Fine!" Harriet shot back.

For a moment, no one spoke, then Jiminy cleared his throat. "So what if I tell my people not to take advantage of this deal that you made, and you tell your people to uphold your end? That way, we can still make sure we get the happy ending. How does that sound?"

Anne gave him a slightly contemptuous look. "And how will you be able to control the rest of the colony? Last time I looked, you weren't in charge or anything."

"Oh, I'll get them to behave, all right," said Jiminy. "You just make sure you don't start coming down hard on us."

Anne and Julie shared a look, then Julie shrugged. "I guess it's worth a shot."

"Okay, Jiminy Mouse," said Anne, extending her paw. "Looks like you've got yourself a deal. But if you overstep your boundaries again, we'll have no other choice but to intervene. Do I make myself clear?"

"Crystal," said Jiminy, and bumped his little fist against the fearsome Persian's paw.

CHAPTER 48

*I*t took us a little while to learn about Harriet's stunt with the mouse, and also her subsequent run-in with Anne and Julie. The three of us had been wondering what to do during the banquet and the evening ball that followed on its heels. Odelia had suggested we stay in the room upstairs and wait things out, since it was probably a lot safer that way, while Gran had figured we might be offered an official table behind theirs: a sort of cat's table.

But when it came time to ask the queen, wiser counsels had prevailed. Marge argued that Serena had enough on her plate to bother with a table designed for cats, and people would simply think the Poole family was a bunch of weirdos for insisting they keep their cats nearby. And so in the end, the consensus was that we would stay in our rooms while our humans partied the night away.

It seemed a little harsh, but then since it was for our own safety, it was probably the best thing to do. But then, of course, Harriet decided that she wanted to repeat her stunt with Jiminy Mouse, and since being locked up in those rooms wasn't the most fun prospect, we figured we might as well go explore a little. Especially when we got a visit from an unexpected guest in the form of Ariana.

Harriet had just left when a soft tap sounded in the room. The three of us were lying on the bed, wondering what to do, and Brutus was the first to hear the strange noise.

"What's that tapping sound?" he asked.

It seemed to come from the wall, and then I had it: the hidden passageways! And when the panel slid open and Ariana appeared, a big smile on her face, it was clear she had been undergoing the same fate as we had, and it hadn't sat well with her either.

"I'm bored," she announced. "Why don't we go explore a little, you guys?"

"Exactly what we were thinking!" said Brutus.

And so we followed the little doggie back into the passageway, and before long, had traipsed behind her and into the downstairs area, where the noise of the party indicated that people were enjoying themselves. And since everyone knows that walls have eyes—and ears, too, of course—we experienced a thrill of excitement when Ariana showed us the best vantage point where we could look into the ballroom and see what was going on—without the risk of being trampled by a pair of clumsy feet.

"There's Odelia!" said Dooley. "She's feeding Grace!"

Unlike us, Grace had been welcome to attend the banquet.

"It's Harriet!" Brutus cried. "Look—she's doing it!"

The 'it' Brutus was referring to was the stunt he had told us she was going to engage in, and to her credit, she pulled it off to perfection. And when a massive applause followed, she was beaming like a minor superstar at all of the attention and a job well done.

"We have to go and congratulate her," said Ariana.

"Yeah, let's go find her," Brutus agreed.

And so Ariana led us out of the passageway and into one of the nearby rooms, which was used by the caterers and the waitstaff as a staging area for the banquet, and from there we quickly made our way outside. Several people stood smoking on the terrace, looking up at the stars and the mountains glittering in the distance, lit up by a full moon, and as we searched around for a trace of our friend, it was the sound of raised voices that finally gave us a clue where she could be.

We arrived at the tail end of an obviously heated conversation between Harriet and the castle cats that had just concluded, and witnessed a very peculiar truce being arranged between Jiminy Mouse and Anne, in her guise as the official spokesperson of the royal cats.

"There is no royal mouser, you guys," said Harriet with a touch of disappointment.

"There never has been a royal mouser, and there never will be," said Anne in measured tones. "But there is a truce, which is quite unique in the animal kingdom, I might add, and of which you are all witnesses tonight."

"It's not that unique," said Dooley. "Where we live, there's also a truce. We even helped an entire mouse colony move house not so long ago."

Anne stared at him. "You are by far the weirdest cats I have ever come across."

"Thanks," said Dooley cheerfully. "That's very kind of you to say."

"It wasn't a compliment."

"Oh, look, it's the king," said Julie suddenly.

And when we looked where she was pointing, we saw that the king had opened the windows of his royal bedroom and was sucking in the bracing fresh air with visible relish.

"Why is he dressed up like that?" asked Harriet.

She was right: the king was fully dressed and wearing his full royal regalia. He was wearing a red tunic with gold epaulets and had an abundance of medals pinned to his lapel. His hair was nicely combed, his beard perfectly coiffed, and generally, he looked as much like his official portrait as he could.

"I think he's going in," said Anne.

"Going in?" asked Brutus.

"He's going to attend the banquet," said Julie with a touch of excitement lacing her voice.

"But… I thought he was too sick?" I said.

"Not anymore he's not!" said Anne, and hurried away from us, clearly with a view not to miss the spectacle that was about to unfold.

"I wonder if Tex has given his approval," said Dooley. "Without his doctor's approval, the king shouldn't be up and about like that."

"He's the king," said Julie. "And a king never needs approval to do anything. That's the fun part about being a royal ruler: you can pretty much do whatever you like and no one can stop you!"

And since it was clear that something was about to go down, we decided to throw caution to the wind and attend the banquet. Quite possibly at this point, people were so intoxicated they might not be able to move and wouldn't mind sidestepping a brace of cats.

I think Dooley said it best, though: "It's not really happening unless we're there!"

No idea what he meant by that, but it sure sounded good.

CHAPTER 49

*K*ing Thad had to confess that he had never felt so excited in his life. Okay, so maybe at the time of his coronation, which had been a great day. And that time he got married, though in hindsight that may have been a mistake. But apart from that, he felt invigorated to such a degree that it was almost as if he'd gotten a new lease on life. And the person he had to thank for it was Doc Tex, that wonderful American doctor who had traveled across the ocean to come to his assistance.

"I feel great, Doc!" he announced as he got dressed. "Absolutely amazing!"

"I wouldn't recommend you going down, Your Majesty," said the doctor. "You haven't left your room—or your bed—for weeks. You should probably take it easy, and to join the banquet—"

"Is going to do me a world of good!" He clapped the man on the back. "I can't thank you enough, Doc. If it hadn't been for you, I might be dead right now!"

"Well…" said Tex with customary modesty.

"And to think that other quack tried to poison me," he said darkly.

"We can't say for sure that—"

"Let's go!" he boomed, feeling all of his old strength returning. It was almost like a miracle. For weeks, he had felt sapped of life. As if a great weight was bearing down on him and keeping him under its thumb. And now that the weight had finally been lifted, he could have danced—he could have sung—he could have yelled out to the world how great he felt. And he was going to do just that!

"I'm not sure…"

"Oh, I am sure. I'm absolutely sure. And you're coming with me, Doc. You should be with your family on a night like this, not looking after an old buffer like me. So have some fun, all right? Make love to your wife, hug your daughter, dandle that amazing granddaughter of yours on your knee, and have a ball!"

And so without further delay, he stepped out of the room that had been his home and his tomb for the past couple of weeks and swung the door wide.

"I'm back, baby!" he yelled at the top of his voice, startling one of the servants who was just passing by with a stack of clothes in her arms, causing her to drop them to the floor.

He would have slid down the balustrade of the main staircase, but since he was still the king and a certain royal decorum was in order, he regally strode down the marble steps instead, the good doctor in his wake.

And then: *le moment supreme*. The moment he walked into the ballroom and greeted his loyal subjects gathered there.

He wasn't disappointed by the reception he was awarded. Startled utterances of surprise sounded on all sides, one person screamed so loud he thought she must have suffered a heart attack, and one person even fainted when they laid eyes on their liege lord.

NIC SAINT

He spread his arms to encompass the entire room. "Your king has returned from the grave! And finally, all is well again!"

The only person who didn't seem pleased to see him was, of course, his queen. But then Serena never seemed pleased to see him, even before he had fallen ill.

He strode up to the table where his family was seated—on a dais where they could oversee the room, as was customary —and took the seat that a servant hurriedly placed at the center of the table, shifting over Serena and putting her in her rightful place: at his right side. His two sons were to his left, exactly as they should.

"My dear loyal subjects!" he said as he addressed the crowd. "I have a very important announcement to make, so listen carefully! I know there has been a lot of speculation about my health, and about the state of the House of Skingle. Some reporters polished off my obituary and certain people, who shall not be named, conspired to organize my succession. Well, I'm here to tell you there will be no succession. I'm still the rightful ruler of this realm and I will remain king for as long as I live, which I now know will be forever. Thanks to that man over there!"

He pointed to Tex Poole, who had just been on the verge of taking a seat next to his lovely wife Marge, and who now looked caught, like a deer in the headlights, as all attention shifted to him. He blinked and then plastered a weak smile onto his face and gave those gathered a tentative wave.

"Doctor Tex has saved my life. I know it sounds bombastic and you may be inclined to think I'm exaggerating, but it's the truth. If it hadn't been for Doctor Tex Poole, I might not be here right now. I may have succumbed to the illness that held me in its grip for all of these long weeks."

Even though no official communiqué had been sent out, he knew that the whole kingdom had been abuzz with speculation about his health, and that by now, everyone knew what was going on with him, so there was no reason to deny the obvious. Still, to hear it from his own lips was different than having to read it on social media or in the usual tabloids.

"But rest assured I'm fully healed and ready to take on my official duties once more." He turned to his wife. "Serena, I know these past couple of weeks have been particularly challenging, and I want to thank you from the bottom of my heart for your never-ending support. You brought Doctor Tex to me, and in doing so, you have saved my life."

Serena looked a little flustered at this. Obviously, she wasn't used to her husband being so magnanimous and kind-hearted. But praise where praise was due: if it hadn't been for Serena, he probably would be dead right now.

He now raised a glass. "To Doctor Tex! My savior!"

And as everyone raised their glasses, and loud cries of 'Doctor Tex' echoed through the room, the doc blushed. Clearly, he wasn't used to all of this attention.

He then sat down, and said, "And now I want to eat. I'm starving!"

And as waiters started hovering and fussing around him, Serena leaned in to him and whispered, "What did Doctor Poole do to revive you?"

He nodded. "It's a long story, and if you don't mind I'll tell you in private." He glanced at his two sons, who sat looking before them with stoic looks on their faces. "But prepare to be shocked, my dove."

She looked intrigued. "Can't you tell me something now?"

He hesitated. "I'd better not." After all, it was Christmas. A time to be merry and to celebrate with family and friends. The last thing he wanted was to spoil Christmas for Serena, the only one who had stood by him throughout this long ordeal. He gave her a reassuring smile. "Let's just have a good time, shall we?"

She gave him a searching look but finally nodded.

But before he could dig in, suddenly Asko rose to his feet and tapped his glass with his knife, causing it to break.

"Your attention, please!" he yelled in an effort to raise his voice above the noise. When finally the hubbub had died down, he said, "I also have an announcement to make. After long consideration, I have decided to finally get married."

Thad stared at his brother, then at his wife, who shrugged.

"And not just to one but two happy girls!" said Asko.

People turned in their seats and looked stunned by this announcement, as was Thad himself.

"The lucky girls are named Anne and Julie," said Asko.

"But... aren't his cats named Anne and Julie?" asked Thad.

"They are," Serena confirmed.

"You don't think..."

"Yes!" said Asko triumphantly. "I've just received confirmation from the archbishop that he will sanction the marriage. And so you're all invited as I'm about to cross the rubican and marry Anne and Julie—my two lovely—"

"Don't say it," Thad murmured. "Please don't say it."

"—cats!"

CHAPTER 50

*I*t certainly couldn't be said that the evening so far was boring. As Marge took stock, she could see several good things and a few lesser aspects of the proceedings. On the plus side was the fact that her husband had been promised an actual medal of some kind. King Thad had called it an Order of the Liechtenburg Empire or OLE, and it supposedly was the highest honor that a person could receive for important contributions to the arts and sciences, charitable organizations, and services to the public. In Tex's case, he was being feted for saving the king's life and in the process earning the man's everlasting gratitude, which was always a good thing to have.

Then, of course, there was the announcement that Prince Asko was getting married to his cats, which had elicited a grunt of annoyance from Marge's mom, who apparently had harbored certain designs on the prince's affections at some point before he was revealed as 'the crackpot to end all crackpots,' as she described it.

On a more positive note, Harriet's stunt with the mouse was one of the highlights of the evening, with the Persian earning herself plenty of pictures and videos posted on social media. However, the nomination of 'royal mouser' would forever prove out of reach, since apparently such a position didn't even exist.

But the best part of the evening, in Marge's personal view, was the ball. And more specifically when Eloy walked up to Princess Ainikki, who had been quietly sulking on the sidelines, and asked her for a dance. After a moment's hesitation, the princess had graciously agreed, and the two youngsters had been dancing up a storm ever since, clearly having a great time. Ainikki had managed to exorcise her infatuation with Grant Chubb from her system and had moved on. It was such a joy to see the two kids looking so happy and carefree again—even though it would probably take time for the princess to get over the loss of her mother. But with Eloy there as her good friend, Marge was sure that in time she would recover.

"You did great, honey," she told her husband as they watched the dance floor nicely filling up. Even Serena and Thad were treading the measure, and of their former coolness, there was no trace, which was probably a good thing for the country they were supposed to be running as a tightly knit unit. "How did you manage to cure the king?"

"Apparently, that's a state secret now," said Tex, much to her surprise, "as is everything that's connected to the health of the King, but I can tell you—if you promise not to tell anyone else."

Her husband's sudden sense of secrecy surprised and intrigued her. "Of course I won't tell. What was wrong with the man?"

"He was right all along. Turns out he was being poisoned."

"What? But I thought you said he was just an old crank?"

"He may or may not be an old crank, but he was definitely right about one thing: when I finally took a blood sample and shipped it off to an independent lab in Luxenstein, as Thad asked me to, since he didn't trust the local labs here in Liechtenburg, they found elevated traces of benzodiazepines in his blood."

"But isn't that…"

"Anti-anxiety medication. When ingested in large quantities, they can lead to memory loss, sleepiness, confusion, low blood pressure, and in some cases, aggression, rage, anxiety, delusions, depression, hallucinations, psychosis, restlessness, even personality changes. In other words, a whole range of problems might occur. And as it happens, Thad suffered from all of those problems."

"But who was feeding him this stuff, and why?"

"Doctor Storrar," said Tex, keeping his voice down so they wouldn't be overheard. "And he was giving them to the king in large quantities, pretty much mainlining the stuff."

"But why?"

"That's what Thad needs to find out. He thinks his sons may be behind it, trying to get their dad to abdicate the throne. He's going to order a full-scale investigation into the doctor, and hopefully that will tell us what's going on. But until then, he's asked me to stay quiet as he doesn't want to jeopardize the investigation. As we speak, Doctor Storrar is being placed under arrest."

"I can't imagine he would be doing this on his own."

"No, I'm sure he was working on someone's behalf."

She glanced at the royal table and wondered if it was possible that Thad's own sons could be behind this terrible ploy to get rid of him. She couldn't imagine being so hated by her own child they'd want to poison her and pay a doctor to do so.

"Does that mean that we'll have to stay here?"

"Oh, no," said Tex. "Thad will hire a new personal physician, but he has asked me to stick around for another couple of days to talk to the police and give evidence. Another week or so, I'd say."

"Good," said Marge. In spite of all the hullaballoo, she had enjoyed her stay at Vaasu Castle, but the prospect of going home was starting to exact a powerful appeal. Whatever way you sliced it, she was a homebody at heart.

They both looked up when a commotion erupted near the doors that led to the terrace outside. People were shouting and running up to the royal table. And as they exchanged a few words with Thad and Serena, it was clear that something terrible must have happened, for both the king and queen immediately rose from their seats and followed the person who had brought the news.

Moments later, one of the king's personal aides hurried over to Chase and whispered something into the cop's ear. Chase jumped up, along with Odelia, and they strode off with purposeful step.

"Something happened," said Marge, stating the obvious.

"Looks like it," said Tex.

"This place," said Ma, shaking her head. "Always something going on. And here I thought we were going to spend a fairy-tale time at a fairy-tale castle, having a fairy-tale time. And what do we get? Murder, intrigue, lots of backstabbing, and some freak who wants to marry his cats. Frankly speaking, I can't wait to go home."

CHAPTER 51

*I*t had taken us a while to locate our humans, and just when we had, they hurried off again!

"Is it something we said?" asked Brutus as we watched them race off.

"I doubt it," I said, "since we didn't even get the chance to announce our presence."

"I guess this is our cue to see what's going on," said Harriet.

"Is life with the royals always this stressful?" asked Brutus.

"Not usually," said Ariana, who had decided to stick with us while Anne and Julie had gone in search of their own human—or should I say their future husband? "At least it wasn't like this before. With the murders and stuff." She gave us a curious look. "In fact, this whole business began when you guys arrived."

"Oh, don't you go and pin this on us!" said Harriet.

"By the way, where is your little mouse friend?" I asked.

"He decided to go home. And probably a good thing he did," said Harriet, "considering that all hell seems to have broken loose."

She was right. A sort of stampede was taking place, with people all moving to the doors to see what was going on outside. And for a moment, things looked a little dicey, as I didn't think we'd be able to safely pass the horde of rubber-neckers. But luckily for us, Ariana knew a shortcut and led us out of the ballroom and through a maze of rooms until we found ourselves outside and attacking the scene of interest from a nor'-nor'-eastern direction.

Police had already cordoned off the area when we got there, so we slipped through their legs, and then we found ourselves in the company of Chase, Odelia, and Detective Storrs as they stood gathered around the lifeless body of what could only be termed the victim of a heinous crime.

Like the two previous victims, someone had decided to give her features a profound makeover, to the extent that she was unrecognizable, and I got the impression that once again, the murderer had wielded that formidable tenderizer with devastating consequences.

Odelia glanced down at us and gave me a smile, then mouthed, 'Rena Kurikka.'

It took me a few moments to remember who she was, but then I got it: the wife of Miko and daughter-in-law of Buffy, she hadn't really played a prominent part in recent events, taking a backseat while her overbearing mother-in-law stole the limelight.

"Who is she, Max?" asked Dooley.

"Rena Kurikka," I said. "Buffy's daughter-in-law?"

"Oh, the future queen," said Dooley, nodding.

"She won't be queen now," said Harriet sadly.

"No one will be queen," Brutus added. "Except Serena, of course."

"There can be only one," said Ariana softly. She looked greatly impressed by the sight of the victim, so we decided to remove her from the scene, as it was no sight for innocent little doggies. It wasn't a sight for anyone, but at this point, we were a little more used to this type of thing than most. Hampton Cove may be the loveliest little hamlet on the East Coast, but it also suffers its fair share of crime.

Suddenly, there was some kind of hubbub nearby, and as we looked over, we saw that none other than Heljä Lovelass was being carted off, her hands outfitted with handcuffs, and looking frightened and confused. When Detective Storrs came hurrying over, along with Odelia and Chase, the arresting officer explained how they had found the maid loitering nearby and smoking a cigarette.

After she had been arrested on suspicion of the murder of Princess Impi, and then released when Tilly the cook had been caught spreading incendiary messages targeting the royal family, the maid had returned to the castle to take up her old position. Now it seemed as if the police once again suspected her of wrongdoing. Which was understandable, as the cook was in prison and couldn't possibly have continued her murderous spree.

As the maid was carted off, Odelia, Chase, and Detective Storrs convened for an impromptu strategy meeting.

"The maid and the cook must have been in cahoots," Storrs opined. "It's the only logical explanation."

"Or both the maid and the cook are innocent," Chase ventured. "That's also an explanation."

"But who else could have done it?" asked Storrs. A good question, I thought. But what was the answer? "As we've already established, the persons with the best motive are Queen Serena and King Thad, as they both thoroughly disliked their daughters-in-law, and Queen Serena especially despised Buffy and her son. Now that Miko's wife is dead, there's no way he'll be able to claim the throne, since the main stipulation is still that the heir has to be married."

"Serena and Thad were both in the ballroom all this time,"

said Chase. "They only left when one of the servants came to alert them of the discovery of Rena Kurikka's body. So it couldn't have been them. And it couldn't have been Dane or Urpo either, since they were seated at the royal table along with their parents."

"And it couldn't have been the cook, since she's in jail," said Storrs, who was starting to look a little desperate. "And the maid was in jail at the time of Princess Kami's murder. So it must have been the two of them working in tandem!" He sighed. "Though I have to admit that doesn't exactly seem likely. The maid may have been in love with Prince Urpo, but why would she want to murder all three of the prospective queens—Impi, Kami, and Rena?"

"Which means we've been looking in the wrong direction all this time," said Odelia, and for some reason looked in our direction as she said it.

"Max?" asked Harriet. "Who do you think did it?"

"Well…" I said, and tried to look intelligent as I said it. Frankly, I had nothing. Nothing! If the cook didn't do it, and neither did the maid, and Queen Serena and King Thad had been in the ballroom, along with the rest of the royals, then who did it? Who had murdered these three women in such brutal fashion?

CHAPTER 52

$\mathcal{A}$s is customary in these situations, the detective in charge of the case interviewed all the principals while his officers talked to everyone else, hoping to find a witness to the crime or anything that might lead to a breakthrough. So even though the maid had been arrested, it was clear from the way Storrs instructed his officers to collect witness statements that he didn't really believe that she was the person they were looking for.

One of the people of interest that Chase and Odelia talked to was their countryman, Grant Chubb, and his mother Jo. Grant had been in the ballroom at the time of the murder, along with most of the guests, and didn't have a lot of relevant information to share until he made one startling revelation.

"She was a fine young woman," he said with a touch of sadness. "Even though we were only in each other's lives briefly, I was very fond of her."

Chase and Odelia stared at the actor for a moment, then Odelia said, sounding incredulous, "Don't tell me you had an affair with Rena Kurikka?"

"I wouldn't call it an affair," said the actor. "More a physical thing. Well, you know how it goes. You meet someone and connect. And since I'm a very tactile person, I gave her a hug at the end of our meeting. I immediately felt it. Like electricity running down my spine. And I could tell that she felt the same thing. So we decided to explore things a little further. I invited her up to my room..."

"And you did some exploring," said Chase grimly.

"There's no law against two people enjoying each other's company, is there, detective?" asked the actor innocently.

"When was this... exploring?" asked Odelia.

"Um... let me think. Well, last night. Her husband had to go into town for business, and so we spent that time getting to know each other a little better. And we had a great time, I have to say. She was very... shall we say eager?"

"We don't need to know the details," said Chase, holding up his hand.

"Do you get involved with every woman you meet?" asked Odelia, and it was a valid question, I thought.

The actor gave a modest grin. "Only if they want to. And for some reason, a lot of women want to."

As the actor talked about his conquests with distinct pride, I studied his mother, wondering what she thought about her son's seemingly insatiable need to seduce every single woman he met. To my surprise, she was eyeing her son with a particularly venomous look on her face. Clearly, she wasn't a big fan of all this sleeping around.

"Do you know of any threats that had been made against Rena Kurikka recently?" asked Chase, getting the interview back on track.

"Not that I know of," said the actor. "She did tell me that Serena had threatened them with expulsion from the castle. But since they were Thad's guests, there wasn't a lot Serena could do. But Rena felt uncomfortable with the situation and didn't like to stay in a place where they weren't welcome, so she asked Miko if they couldn't go and stay at a hotel while he concluded his business with Thad. But Buffy rebuffed her. She felt they had every right to stay at the castle, and Serena was the one who should leave."

"Was she in direct contact with the princesses Impi and Kami?" asked Odelia.

"Not really. They considered her an interloper and wouldn't talk to her. In fact, she told me that I was the first friendly face she had met here. The first person who actually treated her like a human being and not like a threat. But then I had no dog in this fight."

"But I thought you were supposed to be Serena's friend?"

He spread his arms. "I'm an equal opportunity sort of person. I like everyone."

Well, that was true enough, especially if they were of the female persuasion.

"After all, you never know who will be in charge tomorrow. Could be Serena, but it might as well be Buffy. I guess you could say that I like to play the field."

"Yeah, we get the picture," Chase grunted, clearly not a big fan of the actor. But then, of course, Grant had tried to seduce Odelia.

From the corner of his eye, Grant saw the majordomo, who was being interviewed by one of Storrs's officers. "If I were you, I'd take a closer look at that fellow over there. I haven't told you this, but I caught him with his hands in my underwear drawer the other day. Claimed to be trying to catch the Tiffany Thief. Very suspicious."

"We will certainly look into it, sir," said Chase formally. "Thank you for the information."

"What happened with this thief business, by the way? Have you caught him yet?"

"The investigation is ongoing," said Chase noncommittally. "Thank you for your time. If you think of anything else—"

"I've got your number. Sure thing." He seemed a little disappointed and had clearly expected more excitement from Chase when revealing the story about the majordomo rifling through his underwear. But Chase could hardly tell the actor that Oskari was a police informant. After all, entering the private bedroom of a major Hollywood actor and searching through his personal stuff is a big no-no.

All in all, the investigation so far was proving to be a bust. And as we returned to our room to have a nap, I wondered if we were ever going to crack this case. It certainly proved to be a real head-scratcher!

CHAPTER 53

"*M*ax?"

"Mh?"

"Why does that man like to kiss all the women he meets?"

"I'm not sure he likes to kiss *all* the women, Dooley."

"He sure likes to kiss a lot of women," Brutus grunted.

"Young women, mostly," Harriet pointed out. "I haven't seen him try to kiss Serena, for instance, or Marge, or Gran."

"He doesn't seem to be kissing maids either," said Dooley. "Or cooks or cleaners or chauffeurs or any of the castle staff."

"He could be kissing maids," said Harriet, "only they probably belong to the 'kiss and don't tell' category."

"How old is he, this Grant Chubb?" asked Dooley.

"Um… fifty or something," I said.

"And he only dates women twenty-five or younger," said Harriet. "He takes great pride in that. The moment they turn twenty-five, that's it. They're gone."

"Mostly models, right?" asked Brutus with a yawn. Clearly, this whole Grant Chubb phenomenon didn't interest him all that much.

The four of us were lying on Odelia's bed, trying to put in

some nap-time, but so far not a lot of napping had been accomplished.

"Here," said Harriet as she referred to her trusty tablet. "Grant Chubb has dated no less than twenty-five women, and as he grows older, the age difference keeps getting bigger, and none of them have been over the age of twenty-five."

"Except the princesses Impi and Kami," I pointed out. "And wannabe princess Rena. They were all older than twenty-five." Somehow I had a feeling there was an important clue in there somewhere, but I couldn't really put my paw on it.

"You're right, Max," said Harriet. "Princess Impi was thirty-five, Princess Kami thirty, and Rena Kurikka was twenty-eight."

"Much too old for Mr. Chubb," said Brutus with a grin. "He's losing his touch. Or maybe he decided that since he was abroad he could lower his usual standards since the media wouldn't notice."

Just then, Harriet's tablet made its presence known by announcing that a call was coming in. "Ooh, it's Kingman!" she said and pressed the Connect button. "Hey, Kingman! How are things in Hampton Cove!"

We all gathered around the tablet and saw that our voluminous friend was grinning back at us against the backdrop of his human's living room. We could see Wilbur Vickery pottering about in the background while Kingman meowed up a storm.

"Oh, it's been pretty quiet around here," he said. "Too quiet. When are you coming back? Things haven't been the same without you. Even Shanille is complaining. Says cat choir misses its best voices—and I think she means you, Harriet."

Harriet actually beamed with pride. "I almost became the

royal mouser," she announced, "until I discovered that there is no royal mouser. But at least I made friends with a very sweet mouse and some really interesting cats. Oh, and Max has been busy trying to solve a triple murder case. Haven't you, Max?"

"So far I haven't solved anything," I confessed. "This case is a real enigma, I have to say."

"I know all about enigmas," said Kingman. "I've been dealing with one myself. Just because I have a strange spot on my nose, cats have been avoiding me, can you believe it!" He pointed to a very small red spot on his nose.

"I believe you're referring to a stigma," I told him.

"I don't know about that, but it's not a lot of fun."

"Try licking it," Harriet advised.

"What? Why?"

"The same thing happened to me once. I thought I had a spot on my nose, but then it turned out it was a piece of kibble that was stuck there. Just give it a lick, Kingman, and remove the enigma."

"Stigma," I murmured.

"Okay," said our friend, and we watched as his pink tongue stole out and he gave his nose a good lick. And lo and behold: the spot disappeared! "And?" he said.

"It's gone!" said Harriet. "You did it, buddy!"

"Oh, phew!" said Kingman. "It's not a lot of fun walking around with an enigma, I can tell you that. And of course, this is the week that Wilbur's mom decided to pay us a visit."

"I didn't even know that Wilbur had a mom," said Brutus.

"Everybody has a mother, papa bear," said Harriet. "Even Wilbur, however unlikely that may seem."

"She's a difficult woman, is she?" asked Brutus. "Tough as nails? Critical of her son and his lifestyle?"

"Oh, no, absolutely not. Ma Vickery is the sweetest woman on the planet. But she fusses, you know. Fusses over her son, fusses over me, fusses over Wilbur's brother, who is in Brazil, by the way, where he's taken over a coffee plantation and swears he's going to revolutionize the coffee industry. He's calling it Starstrucks. Says it's the greatest thing since—"

"Yeah, we get the picture, Kingman," I said. "So she's nice, is she, Ma Vickery?"

"An angel. Says I'm underfed and has been trying to get my weight up."

We shared a look of concern. Since Kingman is already the biggest cat we know, getting his weight up was probably not such a good idea. "How long is she staying?" I asked.

"As long as it takes to get her son married off to a nice woman. And knowing Wilbur, that probably means she will stick around forever! Wilbur may be a great human, but it's safe to say he's not exactly a great catch. Though Ma Vickery is convinced he will make some lucky girl a great husband. I guess she's one of those mothers who only see the good in their sons and overlook the bad."

"Very much attached to her son, is she?" asked Brutus.

"Oh, absolutely. Loves her two boys to pieces."

"What about the dad? Is he still in the picture?"

"No, he died a couple of years ago, which is probably why Ma Vickery likes to stick to her sons like glue. They're all she has left."

"She probably wants grandkids," said Harriet. "That's why she's so adamant that Wilbur find a good woman to settle down with. It's basic human instinct, Kingman."

"Oh, don't I know it! All she can talk about is why Wilbur hasn't given her any grandkids yet. And poor Wilbur just stands around looking like a shmuck. 'But Ma, I'm too old to have kids!' 'Nonsense. You're never too old to have kids! Now get me some!' Okay, so maybe she didn't say it like that, but the meaning was clear." He grinned. "It's like watching a sitcom, but without the commercial breaks." He paused, and a look of concern came over his furry face. "Max? Why are you looking so funny all of a sudden? Are you constipated?"

My friends all turned to me, and Harriet smiled. "I have a feeling that Max just had an idea. Isn't that right, Max?"

I nodded. And oddly enough, it was Kingman's account of his live sitcom that had been the impetus. It was just the tiniest embryo of an idea, but at least it was something. And as Kingman continued to give us the skinny on the goings-on in his home, I lapsed into thought and wondered if possibly my idea had merit.

CHAPTER 54

*O*delia needed a breather. After the discovery of Rena's body, they had interviewed dozens of people, trying to find a witness to the murder. Unfortunately, the killer had once again been able to hide their tracks very carefully, just like the two previous times. They hadn't even been able to find the murder weapon, even though a team of crime scene technicians had gone over the crime scene with a fine-tooth comb. They had found several tenderizers in the kitchen and had confiscated all of them, hoping to find traces of the victim's blood and possibly fingerprints of the killer, though Odelia thought that was highly unlikely, considering how cunning he or she had so far proven to be.

She ventured out into the night, deciding to go for a stroll around the lake. Snow was still covering the ground and glittered in the moonlight, offering a stunning view. Gran might think that the fairy-tale qualities of Vaasu Castle were greatly exaggerated, but she thought that it did look exactly like a fairy-tale land and fully expected Santa to zoom across the sky in his sleigh, propelled by his trusty reindeer.

For a moment, she stood regarding the surface of the

lake, which glittered like crystals, and listened to the horses quietly neighing in the distance. Apart from that, the world was quiet, and after the banquet and the ball and then the discovery of the murder, she was glad of the reprieve and the silence.

And she had been standing there for perhaps five minutes when all of a sudden a loud cry of alarm sounded behind her. As she whirled around, she was just in time to see Jo Chubb swinging what looked like a hammer at her. She ducked, and the hammer missed its mark. Moments later, Chase was upon them and grabbed the woman's arm to wrestle the weapon from her hand. It wasn't a hammer, of course, but a meat tenderizer, and in the hands of Grant's mother, it formed a formidable and highly lethal instrument of destruction.

"Let me go!" the woman yelled as she tried to fend off the burly cop, but Chase wasn't even thinking about letting go of her, and as more police officers descended upon the scene, led by Detective Eric Storrs, finally Jo realized that her struggle was in vain, and she relented.

"Jo Chubb," said Storrs sternly, "you're under arrest for the murders of Impi Skingle, Kami Skingle, and Rena Kurikka."

"Oh, for crying out loud!" said Jo. "You're hurting me, you big brute!"

In no time, she was cuffed and led away. There was no question of her guilt, for she had been caught red-handed, trying to do to Odelia what she had done to the three other women.

Chase stepped forward and enveloped her in his arms, then breathed in her hair, "I should never have gone along with your crazy scheme, babe. That woman almost killed you!"

"Well, she didn't, did she?" said Odelia with a smile. She

knew her hubby would be in time to ward off the danger. Though she had to admit it had been touch and go there for a moment. If Chase hadn't shouted out his warning, that glancing blow might have found its mark: her exposed noggin!

Back at the castle, the entire royal family awaited them. Even though it was now well past midnight, they had all stayed up when they discovered that a police operation was being set up. The only ones who hadn't known were the Chubbs, for obvious reasons. By the time Chase and Odelia arrived back at the castle, Grant Chubb was also being led away. He would have to face charges for aiding and abetting a murderer, since he had known about his mother's homicidal tendencies all along and had done nothing to stop her.

They convened in the main ballroom, which was a mess after the big ball, but that was fine, and nobody cared about anything but the story of how a murderer had been stopped.

"For a long time, we thought that the murderer was a member of either your staff," said Odelia as she told the tale, "or one of the family."

"Nonsense," said King Thad. "None of us could have done such a horrible thing." He and Serena sat side by side, and even held hands, which was probably the first time since the king had fallen ill. Their two sons sat at a little distance, clearly not at all at ease in their minds.

"Serena disliked her daughters-in-law to a great extent," Odelia pointed out, "and so did you, Your Majesty."

"Well, that may be true," the king admitted. "Since I always thought our boys could have done better for themselves. But then I guess every parent wants the best for their kids."

"We had the best, Dad," said Prince Dane moodily. "Only you couldn't see it that way."

"Be that as it may," said Odelia, "we soon discovered that

none of you could have done it, as you all had alibis for at least one of the murders. So unless you were all in cahoots, there was simply no way you could have done it. Which brought us to the staff."

"The maid and the cook," said Urpo acerbically.

"Yes, the maid and the cook," Odelia confirmed. "And the same story was repeated: either they had worked together, which seemed unlikely, or they were innocent of these crimes."

"So what finally led you to suspect Jo Chubb?" asked Buffy. She might not be officially part of the royal household, but like it or not, she was an integral part of the story of the eventful past few days.

"Well, over the course of several conversations with Grant Chubb, it soon became clear that he'd had affairs with all three of the victims."

Gasps of dismay rang through the room. "No!" said Urpo, standing up.

"Sit down, son," said Thad.

"Impossible!" said Dane.

"You mean… Rena?" asked Miko.

Odelia nodded. "Grant had what he called a close physical relationship with all three women at some point. Which in the end proved to be the link that connected the three murders. At first, we thought that Grant might be our killer, but then why would he murder the women he said he had formed such a wonderful connection with? That made no sense. And I have to admit that the truth eluded us until…" She glanced down at her four cats, who were listening intently, along with Ariana, Serena's Shih Tzu. She couldn't very well tell the royals that Max had solved the case, so instead she said, "Until we started looking at Jo Chubb."

"Grant always had a very special relationship with his mother," Chase said. "She traveled everywhere with her famous son, walked the red carpet with him, accompanied him to movie premieres, the Oscars, the Cannes Film Festival, important events. Everywhere Grant went, Jo went with him. And oddly enough, even though he's pushing fifty, Grant has never been married or even engaged to be married."

"Almost as if the relationship with his mother precludes any other relationship in his life," said Odelia. "Especially that with another woman."

"The fact of the matter is that Jo never wanted her son to marry," said Chase. "Over the years, and especially after her husband died, she developed an unhealthy relationship with her boy and couldn't bear the thought of him with another woman."

"But he was with other women all the time," said Serena.

"Yes, but those were just flings," said Odelia. "Nothing serious. As soon as things turned serious, she told him to break it off."

"And he did?" asked Miko, shocked.

"He did. There was a clear understanding between mother and son that he shouldn't get married or even develop strong feelings for any one of these women. There was to be only one woman in his life, and that was Jo. And Grant kept up his end of the bargain by leading a fairly superficial romantic life and limiting himself to meaningless flings and shallow connections with other women."

"Jo's cut-off age was twenty-five," said Chase. "The moment a woman reached that age, she was escorted to the exit."

"And why was this?" asked Tiia. "It seems so... random."

"Because Jo was twenty-five when she had Grant," said Odelia. "She felt that if Grant got together with a woman over the age of twenty-five, things might get serious, and she might win over his heart, and get pregnant and tie Grant to her."

"And she felt she would have lost him forever."

"So she couldn't have that. The problem began when Grant arrived here in Liechtenburg and started an affair, first with Impi, no doubt captured by her exceptional beauty and grace, and the fact that she was a princess, and then also Kami and later Rena. When Jo found out, she told him in no uncertain terms that he was playing with fire, and when he still wouldn't stop fooling around with the three princesses, she decided to take matters into her own hands."

"And kill them?!" asked Serena.

"My God," Thad said.

Odelia nodded. "Yes, she killed all three of the women, and she would have killed me if she had the chance."

"Why you?" asked Serena. "You weren't having an affair with him, were you?"

"No, I wasn't, but we had arranged it so that Jo thought that I was. We had enlisted a member of your staff to whisper into Jo's ear that he had caught me with her son and that things looked very serious."

"What member?" asked Thad with a frown.

"Oskari," said Chase. "Your majordomo."

Oskari had played his part to perfection, and Jo had fallen for the ruse hook, line, and sinker. When she heard about the affair of her son with a woman who posed a definite threat to her own relationship with Grant, she had immediately taken measures to put a stop to the affair once and for all.

"But where did she find the weapon?" asked Buffy.

"The kitchen," said Chase. "She and Grant had stayed at the castle many times before, and so Jo knew all about the secret passages and used her knowledge of them to sneak to and from the kitchen unseen, to take one of the meat tenderizers, and then later return it, dropping it into the sink so the traces of her crime would be washed off. Only this time we were there to watch her every step. We saw her sneak into the kitchen, and then we saw her follow Odelia and attack her."

"This is just... terrible," said Serena. "Who would have thought?"

"I saw that you arrested Grant," said Prince Dane. "Was he also part of this?"

"He knew that his mother was murdering his girlfriends, yes," said Odelia. "And he did nothing to stop her or to inform the police."

"We even suspect that these weren't Jo's first murders," said Chase. "We still have to look into the matter further, but several of Grant's girlfriends have died under suspicious circumstances, so we think she may have had her hand in that."

"And Jo's husband also died in a mysterious way," said Odelia. "He fell off a cruise ship that he and his wife had gone on, in the company of their son. Grant was ten at the time, and his father's body was never found. It's quite possible that Jo pushed him overboard when he protested the unhealthy obsession his wife had developed with their son. But for now, that's only speculation."

"This is just..." Urpo shook his head. "Such a terrible..."

"I want to thank you both," said King Thad. "You did an excellent job. And Detective Storrs, of course. I'll see to it that you're all in line for a commendation commensurate with your contributions to this case." He now turned to his sons. "There's one other matter I would like to discuss. And that's how you two have been conspiring with Doctor Storrar to have me killed!"

CHAPTER 55

ane and Urpo shared a look, then Dane said, "Look, Dad. The last thing we wanted was for you to die. But you have to admit that these last couple of years, you've made some really bad decisions."

"Decisions that have cost the House of Skingle a lot of goodwill," his brother added.

"What decisions? What are you talking about?"

"The bridge," said Dane. "Remember the Thad Bridge?"

"Built in the middle of nowhere, simply because you felt you needed a bridge named after you."

"That bridge was built to connect the ring road!" said the King.

"There will never be a ring road, Dad," said Dane with a sigh. "Every urban planner will tell you that it's expensive and unnecessary, and that bridge is an eyesore, and everybody hates it."

"We want it gone," said Urpo.

"And then there's the new cathedral."

"It's a nice cathedral," his dad sputtered.

"It's ugly, and it will swallow up ten percent of the state budget!"

"I'm sure it won't," said the King stubbornly. He raised his head. "Thad Cathedral will be beautiful. A work of art."

"It's a white elephant," said Dane.

"Nonsense."

"I talked to Efrain, and he agrees it's time for you to step down. The population wants it, we want it, Mom wants it— heck, the economy of this country needs it!"

"But... people love me!"

"They do, you're not wrong," said Urpo. "But they also want you to gracefully abdicate and become the wise old man in the background while a younger generation takes over."

"And that's why you tried to kill me?!"

"We didn't try to kill you," Dane insisted. "Just tried to slow you down a little. Make you think about your future. And the only way we could think how to accomplish that was to feed you these pills."

"You're like a freight train, Dad," said Urpo with a grin. "You just keep steaming ahead, and there's simply no stopping you."

"So we did stop you in your tracks, with the assistance of Doctor Storrar, who made sure that the dosage you received wasn't lethal but would simply put you in bed so you could be induced to—"

"Abdicate," Serena added.

Thad looked up in surprise. "You were in on this as well?"

Serena nodded. "Honey, you have to admit that you haven't been yourself these past couple of years. I don't even recognize the man I married. The sweet husband who used to come home every night to pay me compliments or give me flowers... You've turned into a boor. So when Dane and Urpo approached me with this plan of theirs to force you to take a break, I thought it might be the only way to save our marriage."

"And the county," said Dane.

"Our marriage needs to be saved?" asked Thad, a pained look in his eyes.

Serena nodded seriously. "I came this close to throwing in the towel. Tiia will confirm this."

Her friend nodded. "Many were the times when I had to console her after you had snubbed her again, Thad. Or ignored her or generally acted like a brute. So I was fully on board with the plan."

"Call it an intervention, Dad," said Dane.

"Because that's what it was," said Urpo. "A family intervention."

"This family is even crazier than I thought," Buffy remarked.

"Tell me about it," said Miko.

"Take them, for instance," said Serena, gesturing to Buffy. "What man invites his old mistress to his home and parades her around in front of his own wife? Not a loving husband, that's for sure."

"That was not a nice thing to do, Dad," Urpo said.

"But... that was the drugs," Thad sputtered.

"Nonsense. The cocktail Doctor Storrar gave you was designed to make you feel weak. To sap your strength so you wouldn't charge around like a bull in a china shop as usual," said Serena. "That wasn't the drugs. That was you, Thad. And your gross disregard for our marriage—for me."

Thad hung his head at this. "You're... right," he said finally.

Serena exchanged a look with her two sons. "Can you repeat that?"

He looked up. "I said you're right. And I'm sorry."

"But you love me, don't you, Thaddy?" said Buffy,

scooting forward on her chair. "And you love dear sweet Miko here, your boy? He's going to be the next king, isn't he?"

But Thad sat shaking his head. Clearly, this had all come as a complete surprise to him and a great shock. "I need to think," he confessed. "This…" He glanced up at his wife. "I'm sorry, Serena. I guess… Well, I don't know what happened, but clearly I've wronged you, and I've wronged our boys."

And it was with a hanging head that he left the room.

"Thaddy!" said Buffy desperately. "Sweetheart!"

But 'Thaddy' was gone. Of the proud king, not much remained. What the drugs hadn't been able to do, this intervention had: to make him think about his behavior and see himself through their eyes. A boorish, rude, and obnoxious brute of a man, who treated his wife and kids with a stunning lack of respect.

"I hope he has learned his lesson," said Ariana.

"Wait, you knew about this?" I asked.

Ariana nodded. "You can't be a person's constant pet companion and not be privy to all kinds of personal information. Of course, I knew about it. But I didn't feel it was my place to tell you guys. And besides, it had no bearing whatsoever on the reason you were all here: to catch this Tiffany Thief."

She was right, of course. It was a private family matter and didn't involve us at all. Still, it would have been nice to know, especially for Tex, who seemed to think that the king's family had tried to kill him.

Buffy now rose and said, "I think we'll go now. Come, son."

"But Ma, I'm going to be the new king soon," said her son.

"Fat chance," Buffy snarled as she cast a dirty look at her main rival, Queen Serena. "I have no idea who will be king, but it sure as heck won't be you!" And then they both left, with Miko insisting, "but Ma, can't you talk to the guy? Make him see reason?"

"Good riddance," said Tiia, and I had a feeling she spoke for all of those present in the room.

It was late, and the general consensus was that it was time for bed. And so we all said our goodbyes and turned in for the night. Tomorrow was another day, and hopefully, there would be no murders, break-ins, family interventions, or old girlfriends showing up with sons who wanted to be king.

All in all, it had probably been one of our most eventful Christmases ever!

CHAPTER 56

*T*he next couple of days were a time of healing for the Skingles, and as we watched from the window, we could see the old king and his wife walk the grounds for hours, talking and trying to save their marriage. The two princes also spent a lot of their time talking, but to the prime minister, arranging for a future after King Thad had stepped down from the throne. And after Marge had had a little chat with Prince Dane, he saw the error of his ways and decided to spend more time with his own family as well.

All in all, I guess you could say that things had come to a head, and we now were experiencing the immediate aftermath. Jo and Grant Chubb had both been charged, and it looked as if the actor and his mother were facing a radical change in lifestyle, as they would go from living in castles and million-dollar mansions and private yachts to a prison cell. And instead of wearing designer clothes, they'd have to make do with ordinary prison garb.

As for us, our time in Liechtenburg had come to an end, and so we all said our goodbyes. Goodbye to Ariana, the faithful and loyal dog who had been our good friend just when we needed one. Goodbye to Anne and Julie, who might not be mousers, but were still formidable cats. And goodbye to the Skingles, a peculiar and fascinating family of individuals, who, I reckoned, would never be boring, which is one accomplishment they could be proud of.

It took us a little while and some discomfort, but we finally made it back to the States in one piece, and I have to say that when a taxi dropped us off in front of our home, I shed a tear or two of relief. They say that there's no place like home, and I guess 'they,' whoever they are, are right. When Fifi came to greet us on the street, and also Rufus, our two neighboring canines, I was so glad to see them I shed a few more tears, and as we told them all about our Liechtenburgian adventure, they were both surprised and ultimately glad that we had made it out of there in one piece.

I couldn't blame them. Stealing princes? Murdering moms? Scheming families? And a prince intent on marrying his cats? All in all, it was a miracle we hadn't been stolen/murdered/drugged/married off!

Our return coincided with Uncle Alec and Charlene's return from their honeymoon, and even though their trip had been less eventful than ours, they still couldn't wait to tell us all about it. And so as is the custom in our family, Tex fired up his grill, Marge set the table, and Gran made the potato salad, and before long, we were all gathered in Tex and Marge's cozy living room, a fire blazing in the hearth, and stories flew back and forth at dizzying speed.

Scarlett had also dropped by, and she had brought Clarice along, and so as our humans told their tall tales, we told the same tales to our friend, who, contrary to our human counterparts, wasn't the least bit impressed. "If I were Anne and Julie, I would have told this prince to take a hike," she said as she bit down on a piece of prime beef. "Marry his cats? Was the guy crazy or what?"

"In the end, he decided not to go through with it," said Harriet. "Though the fact that his brother leaned on the archbishop to call off the wedding may have had something to do with that."

"So is this king going to abdicate or not?" asked Clarice.

"He is," confirmed Brutus. "After long deliberation, he has officially announced his retirement."

"And who's going to be the new king?"

"Dane and Urpo both."

"Is that even possible?"

"It is," I confirmed. "It's called a co-regency, and it's pretty rare, but it does exist, and they're determined to make it work. They'll share the burden of the crown and make it a co-rulership."

They'd have to get past their own differences first, though. When Urpo learned that his brother had tried to pin the murder of Princess Kami on him, he wasn't happy. But then I guess it was all par for the course in the House of Skingle.

"Nuts," said Clarice, but her eyes were glowing, and her jaws were moving at a rapid pace as she tucked away all of the food.

"I had a shot at the crown, you know," said Gran. "But the guy was more interested in his cats than me, so things didn't work out."

"Good thing they didn't," said Scarlett. "Otherwise, I would have lost a friend."

"No, you wouldn't. You would have moved to Liechtenburg, and we would have had a great time there."

"I'm not so sure. I'm not into mountains, you know. I'm more of a beach girl."

"You could have both. They have beaches in Europe, and plenty of them."

"Yeah, but can you walk from your apartment to the beach in less than fifteen minutes? I don't think so."

"Yeah, I guess I would miss Hampton Cove too much. And besides, castles are pretty drafty. We'd probably catch our deaths."

"So how did you do, Dooley?" asked Clarice. "Have a good time?"

"Oh, absolutely," Dooley confirmed. "We met mice, we met cats, we met royals, we met horses. So it was great. Though sometimes they forgot to feed us, and castles are very big, so we had to travel miles and miles to go anywhere, and sometimes we even had to travel through walls, which was fun but also scary. And there was a man with a deep throat, and a woman who wanted to murder all the royals and watch their blood flow through the streets, and another woman who loved a man so much she wanted to poke his wife's eyes out. And a woman who called the king Thaddy and wanted to become the new queen, but the old queen wouldn't let her, and then in the end, the king wouldn't let her either. And then there was a famous actor whose mother killed all of his girlfriends because they gave him too many Hong Kong kisses. So it was wonderful."

Clarice shared a look with me, and I shook my head. Better not to engage, that look told her, and so she didn't. Dooley was still very much caught up in our adventure and would take a few days to settle into his old routines once more. And I guess the same applied to all of us. That's what you get when you travel: you're swept along in a tidal wave of sights and sounds and experiences, and sometimes an actual tidal wave, as in Uncle Alec's case, who had tried something called bodyboarding and had been swept off his board by a huge wave and swallowed so much water he had sworn off bodyboarding for the rest of his honeymoon.

"Is it true that Shanille missed me so much?" asked Harriet.

"No idea," Clarice confessed. "Haven't been to cat choir since you guys left." She shrugged. "Not much sense going when your friends are out of town. But now that you're back, of course I'll go."

I gave her a smile. "We love you too, Clarice."

She frowned. "Who said anything about love?" But as she placed her head on her front paws, I could tell that she was smiling.

"Maybe next time you can join us, Clarice," Brutus suggested.

"And be married off to some goofy prince? No thank you."

Pretty soon, we were all dozing pleasantly, lying in front of the hearth, our bodies warm, our tummies full, and also our hearts.

Like the poet said: the best part of going on vacation? Is coming home.

THE END

Thanks for reading! If you want to know when a new Nic Saint book comes out, sign up for Nic's mailing list: nicsaint.com/news

EXCERPT FROM PURRFECT GOLD (MAX 75)

Chapter One

Dooley wondered if he had done his ten thousand steps for the day. Ever since Chase and Odelia had gotten into this new craze with the ten thousand daily steps they needed to do, they had inadvertently transferred the bug to their pets. And now Dooley, Harriet, and Brutus had all gotten into the habit of making sure that at the end of each day they had gotten their steps in. The only one who was lagging behind in this bold ambition was Max, but then he felt that he was healthy enough as it was and didn't need any fancy gizmos telling him how many steps he had taken or should take or any of that nonsense.

"It's just a load of commercial voodoo!" Max had said when his three friends had urged him to get on board with the program and join the fun. "And if you think I'm going to allow Corporate America to control my life, you've got another thing coming."

Dooley didn't know about the American corporation Max kept referring to, but he liked this whole stepping business. Take today, for instance. It wasn't even lunchtime, and he must have already gotten half of the steps he needed. And then he still had cat choir tonight, which would also require an additional thousand potential steps. And if he took very small steps, as Harriet had advised, he would get there even faster.

Harriet had gotten into the habit of taking very small steps, more like tiptoeing through life than stepping wide and fanciful, and according to her, it was so much better for her health. She hadn't felt quite so good in ages. "And if everyone took smaller steps, the world would be a much better place," she had told Dooley. "People would be able to stop and smell the roses, you know."

Dooley didn't quite know how smelling the roses and taking small steps worked exactly, but then Harriet was very clever, so he knew she was probably on to something. And so today he had vowed to take small steps all along his morning walk and smell as many roses as he could find. Unfortunately, there weren't all that many roses in the vicinity, but there were plenty of other plants. So he had taken to smelling those, even though they often didn't smell all that nice. Then again, if it was good for his health and made the world a better place, it seemed like a small sacrifice to make.

And he had just reached the end of Harrington Street when he came upon a large canine looking at him with menace written all over his features. It was a dog of what he thought was the bulldog variety. And if the globs of saliva dripping from the corners of his mouth were an indication, this dog was very hungry indeed.

Poor creature, he thought. Clearly hadn't been fed properly. And so he approached the dog, his heart full of the right spirit, and said, "If you want, you can have a bite to eat at our place. There's plenty of kibble to be found, and I'm sure

Odelia—that's our human—won't mind that we share some of it with a hungry stranger like you, sir."

The bulldog looked at him with a strange look in his eyes. "What are you talking about, little fella?" asked the dog in a not unkindly tone.

"Food," he specified. "You seem awfully hungry, and I know what that feels like, so I figured I'd offer you some of mine."

The dog's look of menace immediately lessened to a large extent, and even the slavering seemed to diminish, as if having been turned off at the tap. "You would do that for me?" asked the bulldog. "Even though you don't even know me?"

"Of course," said Dooley. "I've always been taught to be kind to strangers, and since you're a stranger and you look very hungry, it's the right thing to do. And besides, I'm almost home again after putting in my steps for the day. I'm at five thousand already, I just know I am, and so it's time to take a break."

The bulldog looked up at his human, who was a very large man, both vertically but also horizontally, who was checking something on his phone, as all humans seemed to do lately, and gave Dooley a tentative smile, which clearly wasn't an easy feat, possibly on account of the fact that he hadn't practiced those specific muscles in quite a while. "I won't forget this, fella. What's your name?"

"Dooley," said Dooley. "What's yours?"

"Muscles," said the dog. "On account of the fact that I'm very muscular."

"Well, Muscles, are you coming?"

"I can't," Muscles admitted. "Unlike you, I'm tethered to this person with this chain, you see. So I'm not free to go anywhere without this guy's approval. If it wasn't for that, I'd be happy to accept your invitation."

"Oh, well," said Dooley cheerfully. "Maybe some other time?"

"Definitely," said Muscles with a lopsided grin and eyes that spoke of his appreciation for the kind offer. "Until we meet again, Dooley."

And so he said his goodbyes to Muscles and went on his way. Home was only a few houses away, and before long he was setting paw in his backyard and went in search of his friend Max. Max might not be fully on board with the ten thousand step phenomenon yet, but Dooley knew it was only a matter of time. When he saw how much his friends loved to put in their daily steps, he would come around to their way of thinking. And then they could all go and do their steps as a family: Odelia, Chase, and their four cats. What fun they would have!

He searched around the backyard for a sign of his friend, and when he didn't see him, passed through the pet flap and into the house proper. As he could have guessed, he found the voluminous blorange feline stretched out on the couch, putting in his ten thousand naps—possibly dreaming of ten thousand steps.

And since the last thing he wanted was to disturb his friend when he was enjoying his nap time, he toddled over to his bowls for a bite to eat and a sip of water, then joined Max on the couch and closed his eyes for a nice and well-deserved nap.

That was probably the best part about putting in those steps: your nap time was so much better. A qualitative difference that made the exertion all the more worthwhile. And he would have closed his eyes to dream of making new friends and influencing bulldogs when there was a commotion at the pet flap, and in short order, Harriet and Brutus strode in via the passageway.

"Max! Dooley!" Harriet cried, looking very much

alarmed. "Come quick! It's Odelia! Something happened to her, and we can't wake her up!"

Chapter Two

It was with some reluctance that I let sleep slip from my grip and returned to the world of full wakefulness. As it was, I had been dreaming of taking steps—lots and lots of steps! And I fully blamed Harriet for the lessening in the quality of my nap time. If she hadn't pushed me into joining the program the rest of the family had embarked upon, I would have dreamed of soft meadows filled with flowers, or broiled chickens flying into my mouth or some such felicity. But instead, I had to occupy my most precious resting time with an activity I thought of as mere folly.

Why subject the body to a lot of unnecessary torture? It seems counterintuitive and counterproductive, not to mention against my most basic instincts as a cat. Move when it's needed, not because some app commands you to. And so when I finally did throw off the veil of slumber, I felt more tired than when I had begun.

But then the message of Harriet's lament penetrated my admittedly snoozy noggin, and I frowned in her direction. "What are you talking about? Odelia is right there."

I pointed to the other couch, hidden from view from Brutus and Harriet's vantage point near the door, and where our human had been taking a nap herself. Which went a long way to proving my point: all this unnecessary moving around and frantic activity is mostly bad for one's health. Case in point: Odelia, who had never been in the habit of taking naps in the middle of the day, but ever since she had started monitoring her steps and trying to put in as many of them as she could, had done nothing else but nap, always complaining about how tired she felt.

Harriet and Brutus now joined us and regarded with consternation written all over their features the strange phenomenon of Odelia asleep on the couch.

"Well, I'll be..." Brutus said as he came this close to scratching his head in befuddlement. He turned to his mate. "Then who is the Odelia lying on the lawn?"

"What are you talking about?" I said. I had a feeling they were deliberately pulling my paw, and if there's anything I dislike, it's being made to look like a fool.

"Well, Odelia is right here," Harriet explained. "But she's also out there."

And since I could make neither heads nor tails of her statement, I decided to go and see for myself. And so it was with great regret that I deserted my favorite napping location and hopped down to inspect this second Odelia, supposedly napping on the lawn. The four of us moved to the window and looked out, and much to my surprise, they were absolutely right: a second Odelia was lying prone on the lawn, apparently asleep, and she looked so much like 'our' Odelia that for a moment, I thought my eyes must be deceiving me.

"She even smells like Odelia," Brutus said, a touch of awe in his voice at this wondrous occurrence.

"Maybe she's Odelia's sister?" Dooley ventured.

"Or a hologram?" Harriet said.

"Holograms don't smell," Brutus knew. "And they don't take up actual physical space. This Odelia is real, sugar plum. I touched her with my paw to ascertain whether she was alive or dead." He gulped a little. "And she's all too real!"

Just to make sure this wasn't some trick being played on me, I returned to the sofa and saw that Odelia was still fast asleep. Then I returned to the window and saw that Odelia II, as perhaps I will name her from now on, was also present and accounted for. So there were effectively two

Odelias, and both of them were dead to the world, so to speak.

And since I'm of the inquisitive bent, I decided to take a closer look at Odelia II, just to make sure she was, as Brutus had indicated, a real person and not some figment of our imagination. We hadn't eaten any magic mushrooms lately, but one never knows. An enterprising cat food manufacturer may have decided to put some hallucinogens in his cat food, and we could be the victims of food poisoning.

So we all ventured out through the pet flap, single file, and approached the woman lying on the lawn with some trepidation, not unlike a member of the bomb squad approaches a live grenade.

"She could be Odelia's twin," said Dooley softly as we approached the figure.

"Odelia doesn't have a twin," I pointed out. Unless Odelia's parents had been holding out on us.

"Is she alive or dead?" asked Harriet.

"Her chest is moving," said Brutus. "So I guess that means she's alive."

It is one of those litmus tests for the uninitiated that is proof positive of being amongst the living. It still didn't explain what she was doing in our backyard and why she looked so much like our own human.

Dooley now directed his gaze heavenward and gasped. "It's an alien!" he said. "She must have been brought here in an alien spaceship and dumped on our lawn." He gave us a look of excitement. "You guys—this is an alien clone!"

"Of course it is," said Brutus as he took a step closer to the mystery woman. "And I'm George Washington's secret love child."

"You are?" asked Dooley, much intrigued.

"Of course not."

He was the only one of us who had the guts to approach

the lifeless figure, and Harriet said, "Sugar britches! Don't go any closer!"

"What could possibly happen?" asked Brutus. "She's just a human who—"

"She moved!" Harriet cried. "Her arm! It twitched!"

And indeed it had. For a moment, there had been a definite twitch in that arm, as if it was reaching for Brutus and trying to make a grab for him!

But our friend wasn't deterred. "It's uncanny," he said quietly as he now studied the woman's face. "Spitting image, I'd say. Absolutely the spitting image of our very own Odelia."

And since we couldn't contain ourselves any longer—twitching arms or not—we all moved a few steps closer to study the woman's face. And I had to admit that Brutus was absolutely right. The resemblance was uncanny. If I hadn't known that the real Odelia was peacefully resting on the couch, I would have thought that this was her.

And just as we all stood gazing at her up close, suddenly her eyes sprang open!

Chapter Three

We all screamed like little girls and scrambled to get away from this strange person as fast as we possibly could. Then, once we were at a safe distance, we eyed her in abject terror. Harriet was in a nearby tree, which she had climbed in record time. Brutus was on top of the hedge. I was hiding behind a nearby bush. And Dooley? I glanced around, and when I couldn't find a trace of my friend, whispered, "Dooley? Where are you?"

"Up here, Max!" his voice came back. When I looked up, I saw that Dooley was on the roof of the house! Actually in the gutter, hunkering down and making sure this 'alien clone' couldn't get at him.

The woman didn't seem to be overly aware of the powerful effect she'd had on the four of us. She groaned and clutched at her head as she tried to sit up and failed. Her eyes sort of glazed over, and I had the impression she wasn't feeling A-okay. I had a sneaking suspicion she might have taken too many steps, but wasn't ready to voice this theory yet.

"The alien is trying to phone home, Max," my friend whispered from his location in the gutter. "We have to stop her, or otherwise millions of her kind will invade our home!"

"Dooley is right," said Brutus in a low voice. "She's one of those pod people. You can see it in her eyes."

I wasn't sure about the pod thing or the alien clone business, but one thing was for sure: this lady wasn't feeling well and was in urgent need of some medical assistance. And since Odelia's dad happens to be a doctor, I decided to throw caution to the wind and go and get help.

And so I abandoned my safe location underneath those bushes and hurried into the next backyard, hoping to find Tex and persuade him to take a look at this strange woman who had found herself in our backyard.

"Max! Where are you going?" Brutus demanded. "Max! Come back!"

"I'm going to go get help," I told him before I slipped through the opening in the hedge and started on my rescue mission.

It wasn't long before I found Gran, who was boiling an egg in the kitchen for some reason and gazing idly out of the window with a smile on her face. "Have you ever felt truly happy for no reason at all, Max?" she asked when I popped in through the pet flap. "I mean, this feeling of happiness just surprising you out of the blue?" Her face sagged. "Yeah, me neither. Now when is this egg finally going to boil!"

I could have told her that to boil an egg, first you have to turn on the gas, but since I had more important things to worry about, I decided to forego giving our human cooking lessons. "Gran, there's an unconscious woman in our backyard. Is Tex home?"

"An unconscious woman?" asked Gran, immediately alert. "What, next door?"

I nodded. "Well, she's not unconscious now, since she just woke up. But she doesn't look well, and I think she needs a doctor."

"Teeeex!" Gran immediately bellowed at the top of her voice. "We need a doctor!"

Tex came hurrying from the next room, still clutching a magazine he'd been reading. Contrary to what I would have expected, it wasn't a copy of the *New England Journal of Medicine* or *The Lancet*, but *Us Weekly*, with a picture of Brad Pitt and Tom Cruise on the cover and the burning question: 'What is the secret of their good looks?'

Clearly, even doctors wonder about this strange phenomenon. "What?" he asked, looking greatly perturbed. "Is it Marge? Where is she? What's going on?"

"Max has found a woman in his backyard, and he thinks she needs a doctor."

"And don't be surprised," I said, "but she looks like the spitting image of Odelia."

Gran frowned. "What are you talking about? How can anyone be the spitting image of Odelia? Don't you know that every human being is unique, Max? Take this egg, for instance," she said and fished the egg from the pot. "It may look like every other egg out there, but I can tell you right now that this egg is totally unique and unlike any other egg.

And the same goes for everything in nature, and that includes Odelia."

"Well, she does look like her," I insisted. "Down to the color of her eyes." Which were sea-weed green, just like Odelia's eyes.

And as Tex and Gran joined me to take a closer look at this strange phenomenon, Gran told her son-in-law about our observations. Judging from his frown, he registered concern at this, possibly professional curiosity, and a slight sense of annoyance that he'd been so rudely interrupted while trying to get to the bottom of the secret to Tom Cruise and Brad Pitt's eternal youth.

We arrived next door, and I found that the scene was pretty much as I had left it only moments before. Dooley was still hunkering down in the gutter, pretending to be part of the constellation of leaves gathered there. Brutus was on top of the hedge, which must have been very uncomfortable, since those hedges tend to sting. And Harriet was high up in her tree, watching the world below with a baleful eye.

"My God," said Tex as he crouched down next to the woman, who was awake, but barely so. "Max is right. She looks exactly like my daughter."

"Who are you?" asked the woman, in weak and croaky tones.

"I'm a doctor," Tex explained, employing his doctor's voice as he spoke these words. Soothing, reassuring and avuncular, if you know what I mean, and designed to put the patient at ease. "What happened to you, young lady?"

The woman shook her head. "I... I have no idea. Where am I?" She glanced around, then winced, as if the mere movement of her head struck her a powerful blow all afresh.

Tex did what doctors do on these occasions, and gave her a quick medical examination. He even shone a light in her eyes and touched her head and examined it, then nodded. "You've suffered quite a blow. Any headaches?"

The woman nodded. "Terrible. But who... I mean, how did I get here, wherever here is?"

"You're in my daughter's backyard," said Tex. "So you have no recollection of how you got here?"

"Nothing. And when I try to remember, my head hurts even more."

"We better get you inside," said Tex and gestured for Gran to give him a hand. Together they managed to get the woman into an upright position and then slowly walked her into the house. As it was, I was the only one who followed them in, since Dooley was stuck on the roof, Brutus was stuck on top of the hedge, and Harriet was stuck in her tree. The three of them mewled piteously for me to call for help, but as I felt my services were needed elsewhere for the moment, I told them I'd be back and hurried after Tex and Gran and the mystery woman.

The moment we walked in, Odelia woke up. And when she came face to face with the new arrival, she blinked a few times.

"Am I dreaming?" she asked.

Gran shook her head with a sort of grim-faced look. "The cats found her on the lawn. She's been hit over the head and lost her memory. Where do we put her?"

Odelia pointed to the spot where, until a few moments ago, she had been asleep herself, and very carefully Tex and Gran lowered the woman onto the couch. The moment her head hit the throw pillow, her eyes closed again and she was asleep.

"Nasty knock to the head," Tex said quietly when the trio had convened in the kitchen. "I think we better call your husband, honey. This is clearly a matter for the police."

Odelia nodded. "I'll give him a call right now. But the resemblance. Did you also notice the resemblance?"

"Are you kidding?" said Gran. "That woman could be your twin sister." She now directed a suspicious look at Tex. "You didn't secretly father a second daughter, did you?"

Tex looked shocked. "Of course not. How could you even think that?"

"Because chances are that she's Odelia's long-lost twin. And if that is the case, you've got a lot of explaining to do, Doctor Poole!"

ABOUT NIC

Nic has a background in political science and before being struck by the writing bug worked odd jobs around the world (including but not limited to massage therapist in Mexico, gardener in Italy, restaurant manager in India, and Berlitz teacher in Belgium).

When he's not writing he enjoys curling up with a good (comic) book, watching British crime dramas, French comedies or Nancy Meyers movies, sampling pastry (apple cake!), pasta and chocolate (preferably the dark variety), twisting himself into a pretzel doing morning yoga, going for a brisk walk, and spoiling his feline assistants Lily and Ricky.

He lives with his wife (and aforementioned cats) in a small village smack dab in the middle of absolutely nowhere and is probably writing his next 'Mysteries of Max' book right now.

www.nicsaint.com

Made in the USA
Middletown, DE
09 April 2024